Tiger Sky

Rachel Billington has published fourteen novels, including *A Woman's Age*, *Loving Attitudes*, *Theo & Matilda* and, most recently, *Magic and Fate*. Her highly acclaimed novel *Bodily Harm*, published in 1992, shares many of the themes of *Tiger Sky*. She is co-editor of *Inside Time*, the national newspaper for prisoners. Rachel Billington is married to the film and theatre director Kevin Billington, and has four children.

Rachel Billington

Tiger Sky

PAN BOOKS

First published 1998 by Macmillan

This edition published 1999 by Pan Books
an imprint of Macmillan Publishers Ltd
25 Eccleston Place, London SW1W 9NF
Basingstoke and Oxford
Associated companies throughout the world
www.macmillan.co.uk

ISBN 0 330 37668 3

1 3 5 7 9 8 6 4 2

A CIP catalogue record for this book is available from
the British Library.

Typeset by SetSystems Ltd, Saffron Walden, Essex
Printed and bound in Great Britain by
Mackays of Chatham plc, Chatham, Kent

To Rose

A POEM

Rachel
you gave me
one sheet of paper
a task and a pen
to
write about something
I knew nothing about
I chose hope
with alacrity
I decide
I don't want to write
about the hope of optimists
nor the hope of dreams
but the hope you want
and sometimes need
plus the hope
by which you've been deceived
I think
this is easy
it's coming along
yet
suddenly as I write this
I know it's gone wrong
looking at the page
I count the thirty-two lines
That I've already written oh
Shit! I curse
you hoped ....
I'd only use eight
which brings me to the point
I've been trying to make
that
hope is for other people

                          G.N.

'When G.N. was seventeen he murdered his girlfriend. I visited him in prison, where he served eighteen years of a life sentence.'

                          R.B.

Part One

Chapter One

Nine o'clock on a late October evening. The village was dark but not quiet. Wind rattled the dry leaves of a giant sycamore tree and, although the trunk was far too sturdy to budge, the thick branches moved uneasily. The village sat at a meeting of three lanes, a green in the middle, on which the tree was rooted firmly, bullseye in a grass target.

A small manor house, a church tucked in behind, a cottage or two slotted in between the lanes. By the gates of the manor the branches of a young tree crossed and uncrossed, like a man slapping his body for warmth. Other smaller houses were sprinkled along the roadside, becoming gradually further apart as they were further from the centre. So far out as to be hardly part of the village was a final cottage, and beyond it a shed and some ramshackle farm buildings. Lights showed there, and loud music rose above the sound of a milking-machine.

The wind, racing up the lane to this little outpost, lifted a loose section of corrugated-iron roofing then dropped it down again. A man's voice shouted, 'Damn you. Hold still, can't you?' But the words were muffled.

The music stopped and a figure appeared. The light fanned out from the open door, silhouetted the man's height, strong profile and thick, curly hair. He looked at his watch. 'Now what?' he muttered to himself.

A car came down the road and drew up beside him. 'You're early, Joe!' called a man from the window.

'Same as usual, Ken.'

'No, you're not. You're an hour early.' The driver laughed good-naturedly. 'That's what comes of seeing nobody all day. Didn't you know the clocks went on?' The car moved away again.

'Telly's on the blink, that's what.' Joe continued grumbling to himself. 'What a fool. Still, I might as well continue as not for today.' Then a new thought struck him, which made him hold his head higher and, with a purposeful air, shut and lock the door behind him.

In another cottage, on the far side of the village, a young woman lay in bed with a man. Neither of them were completely unclothed, as if they had gone upstairs hastily, fallen on top of the bed, snatched at each other's bodies. The woman had very long dark hair, and as she made love, she moaned and smiled. The man was silent, his face concentrated.

Downstairs, a little girl sat cross-legged on the floor, intently watching the television. Her hand rested on a bag, packed as if she were waiting to go on a journey.

Joe walked down the lane. The wind had become even stronger. He passed the great sycamore, rattle-clapping, creaking and grinding now, like a tree orchestra, and didn't even notice it. As he neared a cottage where the lights shone out, he walked slower, buttoned up his jacket, tried to calm himself.

Through the open curtains, Joe watched the girl still sitting unmoving in front of the television. Seeing that she was on her own and noting with some interest the bag beside her, he stood back and looked up. The bedroom curtains were closed, which did not surprise him, but he could hear a noise above the chit-chat of the television, the tide of the wind, above the scratch of a rose clawing at the window-panes. He stood completely still, listening. Only when a cry rose high above every other sound did he move stiffly into the shadowy corner of the house.

Five, ten minutes passed. The curtains moved, opened briefly and closed. Feet came downstairs. The cottage was so small that the man outside could follow every movement within.

'Come on, Amy. We should be off,' said a man's voice.

'It's not finished,' objected the little girl.

'We don't want to be too late, darling.' The man was good-humoured, persuasive.

'Oh, all right. Where's Mum?'

'She'll be down in a minute.'

A woman's light step came down the staircase. 'Now, don't leave anything behind like you did last time.'

The man and the girl came out, the man swung the bag high on his shoulder and, with his free hand, held on to the girl.

'Bye, Mum!' She sounded excited.

'Goodbye, Maria,' said the man.

'Yes. Yes. What a wild night! Drive carefully.' The woman stood at the door watching them go. She wore jeans and a sweater, her hair blowing about her face. She stayed there until she heard a car starting further along the lane, then she turned. As she was about to close the door, Joe came out of his dark place and stood behind her.

'Ah!' She screamed, turned, saw him with the light full

on his face. Tears lay on his cheeks, his mouth shaped words he could not pronounce.

'Oh, God. Come in.' She took his heavy arm and pulled him into the sitting room. The television was still on but neither of them took any notice.

Joe stood in the middle of the room, huge, silent.

'He was my husband, Joe. You know that. It was just. Just. Even though we're separated . . .' Her voice died. 'He was picking up Amy. It just happened. It didn't mean anything.' She was pleading but the look in his face made her realize it was impossible. 'Look, Joe. You won't be able to understand. Whatever I said, you wouldn't understand. You're right, too. I shouldn't have done it. It was a bad thing, I'm ashamed. No, that's not quite true. But I didn't want you . . . Oh, hell.' The woman gave up. She tried to sit in a chair. But Joe took her arm.

'You thought I was milking.'

'No. I didn't think. Yes. I suppose I did. Look. Joe. I suppose I've given you the wrong impression. I'm not such a very good woman. I'm weak. I—'

'You didn't think I'd come by so early. It's always nine when Joe comes by, that's what you thought.' His unhappy voice slurred the vowels with a West Country drawl. Her voice was clipped, light, London, educated.

'You think too much of me, Joe.'

'I think the world of you.' He paused. 'I thought the world of you.' He paused again. 'Now I don't know what to think. My mother always said—'

'Don't,' she interrupted him quickly. 'Let's sit down. Let's sit on the sofa.' He allowed her to draw him down beside her, although his face had lost none of its shocked immobility. 'Hold me. See, I'm still here for you.'

'Here for me,' repeated Joe, wonderingly.

'I told you. That was just about the past. It wasn't important. You mustn't set so much store on it.'

'But I *heard* you!' It was a cry of horror.

'Oh, God. Look, Joe, perhaps we should leave this till the morning.'

'And now you want me to sit close, hold you, touch you.'

'No. Yes. Just trust me.' But she could see he didn't hear a word she was saying. He seemed struck deaf, blind. She stood up impatiently. 'You must be sensible, Joe. We were two lonely people. Not much else in common. Two lonely people in a very lonely place. It was natural we came together. But there are things you don't understand about me, things I don't understand about you. We come from different worlds. Your mother was right to warn you.'

'Don't talk to me about my mother!'

'I'm sorry.' The woman leaned forward to the man. 'I really think we should talk in the morning.' Wanting now to get him off the sofa, she moved as if to take his hand and then lost her nerve at his expression. Resigned, she sat down beside him again.

'I thought the world of you.'

'I know. I know.' This time she summoned up courage and touched his face, but instantly regretted it as he started back.

'Don't touch me!'

'Sorry. Please.'

'I see it now.' Joe fixed his eyes on his big hands, clasped together between his knees. 'You were playing with me. Making a fool of me. Poor old Joe. Can't speak proper. Can't write proper. Poor old Joe. I don't doubt you laughed at me with your smart friends.'

7

'No, Joe.'

'Don't come near me!' There was a new sound in his voice, a dangerous anger.

'I won't. I won't.' The woman looked despairingly at the window, at the television set, still filled with chit-chat and grimace. 'I could make us tea.'

Joe let her go, didn't lift his head.

The woman stood in the kitchen, trembling. Slowly, with clumsy hands, she filled the kettle, plugged it in and then came back to the man.

He lifted his head. 'Each cow I bought. The calves I bred. The shed. The yard. Cutting down those apple trees. Working twenty hours out of the twenty-four.'

'What?' The woman was bewildered.

'It was all for you. That's what I thought.'

'You didn't know me then. We've only known each other since the summer.'

'April the ninth. It was all for you. And the little girl. I didn't worry you had a little girl.'

'But, Joe.' The woman couldn't think what to say. She only knew one sure way of making a man happy. She came closer to him, put her delicate white fingers against his cheeks, bristly from yesterday's shave, smoothed his neck, touched his forehead lightly, placed her face next to his.

He let her, as if in a dream, staring wide-eyed, yet not seeming to see or feel. 'Yes. You would,' he said eventually, but more to himself than her. 'You would. Take me up there, too. I wouldn't doubt.'

Her face touched his now, her lips soft and pink, parted slightly. Slowly, Joe brought his hands to her neck, as delicate as the stem of a flower.

In the farmyard, the cows moved gently and chewed

the silage neatly placed in iron mangers made out of old bedsteads. From the cottage nearby a dog barked, and now and again whined. A scream, abruptly cut off, made no more sound than the random cry of a night bird. The wind still made most noise, clapping the sheet of corrugated iron with the vigilance of a cymbal.

Chapter Two

Seven years later

There was a cold red sun, a flat disc suspended in a great sky. The red matched exactly the colour of a woman's coat, bent forward as she hurried along the pavement. The street was off the main roads and not busy. Only the occasional car and a few pedestrians broke the silent hum of a big city.

The ambulance was at first part of that endless sound, far away, but gradually it detached itself and came closer. When it entered the narrow street, the sirens filling the whole space with a sense of dread, the woman stopped for a moment, put her hand to her heart. The ambulance passed her, going the same way, and she followed after it, moving even faster than before.

The playground, with its tall railings, ran beside the pavement. The school was behind and beside it, a modern design, all glass, spaghetti tubing and brightly coloured panels. It seemed like something built by a child, and the shiny white ambulance, with its blue light, reflected in the glass, like a child's toy.

Already a man and a woman crouched by a small figure lying on the ground, near a climbing frame.

A distraught teacher, bulky in anorak and boots, hung over them. 'She didn't fall. She'd been climbing but she didn't fall. I'd been talking to her a moment before. I stayed behind to watch her, you see, because her mother was late. Everybody else had gone. Of course, we were all told about her heart but we weren't supposed to treat her any differently. That's what her mother wanted. She's dead, isn't she? I felt her pulse.' The teacher began to cry, big, painful tears. 'She'd just called me out to show me how high she could climb. But when I got there she was down already and she looked a bit funny. And then she sat down and then she lay down. I did realize. I did everything I'd been told to do. I breathed into—'

'Yes. Yes.' The ambulance worker looked up from the child. 'You do expect her mother, then?'

'Oh, yes! She's only a little late. Everyone always goes off so quickly. Today especially. I wish there had been someone else . . .'

The woman in the red coat had stopped her desperate rush. Instead she walked with a stiff deliberation. Her face was completely white, her dark hair hung round it with a geometric precision. She seemed to be staring at the sun, which was now suspended in the space at the end of the street.

She approached the playground and the little scene of tragedy. Everybody looked up but no one spoke. She crouched down and, unbuttoning her coat, lifted the little girl so she could press her close to her body. She wrapped the coat round her again and began a slight rocking motion.

'I heard of a girl whose heart stopped for twenty minutes,' began the teacher, wiping her eyes, 'and then they started it off again and now she's the mother of two children.'

The ambulance man shook his head.

'Was she climbing?' The mother looked up, tears sliding out of her eyes. The ambulance workers registered the American accent with a little look of surprise.

'She didn't fall. She came down quite normally first. I—'

'Was she – was she happy?' Her voice was the smallest whisper, as if she were afraid to disturb the child clasped against her breast.

'Oh, yes, Mrs Halliday. Very happy. Very pleased with herself.'

The woman took a breath. 'Not upset. Not cross with me for being late?'

'Oh, no! No. She was in high spirits. She didn't doubt you'd be here in a minute.'

The mother looked at the ambulance workers. 'There was nothing you could do?'

'Nothing. No. I'm so sorry.' The woman ambulance worker who had bent close to hear, sniffed and searched for a handkerchief. Beyond the railings, a small group of curious onlookers had gathered. At the end of the street the red disc slipped below the horizon, leaving behind only a gentle wash of pink. The light became blue-grey and even colder.

Natasha Halliday had taken off her coat, revealing a smart black suit. She stood in the corridor of the hospital holding a mobile telephone to her ear. 'Of course, he would be at the Cockerel,' she said, with tired bitterness. 'I'm sorry to have bothered you.' Once again the tears began to roll gently down her cheeks.

The pub was very crowded, smoke filling the spaces

between people. Most were wearing suits, men or women at the end of their working day. Noisy, relaxed. It was Friday.

Natasha stood at the door, apparently too frail to push her way through. She held it slightly open, as if undecided whether to retreat altogether.

'In or out before we get frostbite!' bellowed a jovial voice from a bench nearby. A man, passing from the gents' to a table in the corner, was attracted by the bellow and looked towards the door, bright eyes peering under double-folded lids.

'Tasha.' He sounded pleased, surprised, wary.

She came towards him at once, took his arm, tried to lead him outside.

'What? What are you doing?' he protested. 'I haven't got my coat.' A longing look to the snug table in the corner. 'I've ordered another drink.'

But she held on to his arm grimly and he found himself outside on the pavement, swaying and huffing at the cold.

'It's happened,' she said, adding, as if trying to catch his attention or perhaps to mollify him, his name, 'Frank.'

'What? What do you mean?'

'The thing I've been waiting for. Naomi.' She put both hands to her face and pressed her pale cheeks.

Now she had all his attention. 'What do you mean? Christ, Natasha.' He had started to shake.

'Yes. Do you want me to say it?' Her voice rose.

'Yes. I do want!'

Three young men pushed between them, a man and a woman, doubtless husband and wife, standing on the pavement having an argument.

'You can't be so drunk!' cried Natasha, hardling notic-ing the intervention.

'Oh, yes, he can,' riposted one of the passers-by, making the others laugh.

'This is unbearable, unbearable.' Natasha began to run away down the pavement. Her panting breaths left white puffs behind her. After a few steps she stopped and faced her husband, who stood, head wobbling with the grey shock of hair, eyes staring.

'She's dead. Naomi's dead. Now do you see?'

Chapter Three

Nine years later

After three days of continuous rain, London had the sodden, surprised look of someone who had swum too long underwater. Its gratings were clogged and reduced to slits, its trees and buildings seemed swollen, its colours blurred. Yet the sun shone. At last, an energetic June sun had appeared to suck out the moisture from the heavy air. At lunch-time, play had started again at Wimbledon and the covers were off at Lord's.

By evening, the streets were filled with festive workers released from their offices into this new, hopeful world. They raised their eyes to the blue sky and, can of beer in hand, thought they could see to eternity. Tourists emerged from their hooded anoraks, like snails from their shells, and children, who hadn't taken much note of the rain, suddenly felt a longing to ride as high and fast as the escaped silver balloon, hardly a speck above their heads. The noisy exhilaration on the crowded pavements competed with the din of the cars, coaches and taxis nose to tail on the road, engaged in an endless struggle which, in a few seconds, turned from torture to joke. How ridiculous to be stuck so fast. Faces craned out from windows, music trumpeted, and a police car, siren whinnying, turned jauntily and shot down a one-way street.

The crowds swarmed most densely around the entrance to the Underground station, as if no one was quite willing to probe down into the dank darkness. Amid all this energy, a tall man stood uneasily, as alone as he could make himself. Although black-haired, he was very pale as if the rain had washed all colour from his skin. He clutched two plastic bags because whenever he tried to prop them at his feet they were in danger of being swept away.

Joe had been waiting for half an hour, and if he felt he had any choice in the matter, he would have left after the first five minutes. His mind was as blank as he could make it but that did not stop an agonizing self-consciousness. He began to believe he wouldn't recognize the woman when she did arrive.

Natasha saw him standing there, and her heart lurched nervously. She had never seen him outside prison. He had been out of prison before, of course, to work in some garden or other on day-release. But she had only seen him behind a table with prison officers banked behind. She had been hurrying, late because she had forgotten how much harder it was to walk in high heels, and how crowded pavements slowed down possible progress, and how hot and stuffy the city was compared to the country. But now she hesitated, looked away and back again. He would have been a handsome man if his expression were not so hangdog.

With renewed determination, Natasha pushed her way through the crowds. 'You're made it. Congratulations!'

Joe swung round. It was a shock for him to see how glamorous Natasha looked, so much leg on view. 'I was early. I'm sorry. I've never been to London before.'

'I'm the one who should be sorry for being late.'

Natasha smiled and brushed her black hair from her face. 'So, shall we head for the party?'

Walter Harris, the newish editor of *The Cucumber*, looked out of his office window with surprise. The garden below him, previously a lugubrious mix of heavy leaves, slimy stone and treacherous grass, had now sprouted urns of gaily-coloured flowers and tables, crisp and spry with white cloths and gleaming glasses and bottles.

He walked to the other end of his office and here, too, the scene had changed, from a dismal prospect of miserable, scurrying pedestrians to a clear, clean road, with a fine view of late-afternoon sunlight and happily loitering passers-by. In less than an hour they could watch the arrival of ministers, captains of industry, editors, authors, beautiful women and powerful men, or even beautiful men and powerful women.

Sighing, Walter returned to his desk and opened a drawer where three ties lay, still in their packaging. Annabel had bought them for him a week ago, one reddish, one bluish, one greenish, and now was the time to choose. Walter ripped open the top package with unnecessary savagery, and flung the tie round his neck as a man might reach for a noose. There was a knock on the door.

'Come.'

A woman entered behind a square of card. 'I've printed it enormous.'

'*Absolutely Private. Keep Out.*' Walter read it loud. 'Spot on, Annabel.'

*

Frank looked at the clock on the wall of the Cockerel and estimated the two glasses in front of him. Were they enough to cross the desert of deprivation that lay between the pub and the party? Making up his mind, he flicked his fingers in the direction of the bar.

The sun was glinting low over the wall at the end of the garden. Its violent hues did strange things to the hair and faces of the guests already crowding across the terrace and spilling on to the grass. Walter, however, was still on welcome duty at the street door.

'So glad you could make it, sir.' Walter held out his hand to the Home Secretary, who at once produced his name: 'Walter Harris. Glad to meet you', and then gave up further conversation in favour of addressing the proprietor.

'Steven, let's have a word some time.'

The proprietor, who had personally picked Walter to be his editorial plum, gave him a wink before closing in the minister. 'More than a social word, you mean?'

'Just a bit more. Just a bit more.' A big fair man, the Home Secretary smiled, displaying teeth more usual in the mouth of a film star than a politician.

Looking beyond these two men of power Walter witnessed the arrival of Frank.

'Walter, you young blood! Flanked by the great men, I see.' Battered old drunk or not, Frank had no hesitation in interrupting a conversation that to others had seemed intimidatingly private. 'Home Secretary, I hear you're planning to stop Europe becoming the stepping-stone for any old rag, tag and bobtail that wants a UK passport? Reassure me. Hearsay and gossip is right, as always?'

Knowing that whatever hare Frank was following would find its way on to the editorial desk, Walter did not try to overhear and continued to observe his guests, arriving now in a continual flow. Many knew each other and few knew him, so the majority walked past him talking vivaciously.

'I'm Frank's wife, Natasha.' Walter, who had no idea Frank boasted an extant wife, tried not to look too astonished at this announcement by a good-looking American.

'So glad you could make it.'

'And this is Joe,' continued Natasha, in a forceful manner due to her recent fear that her guest would bolt when he saw the two policemen on duty at the door. 'He's a farmer up for the day.'

'Most people are in the garden.' Walter stared at the tall handsome man with the two plastic bags and the strange expression, while Natasha stared at this stiff not quite young man with his crinkly red hair, undertaker's black suit and garish tie.

She recalled that Frank had said, with caustic disapproval, that the new editor had been hired to inject a note of principle into the paper. Now he looked at her enquiringly. 'Poor flowers,' she said, feeling foolish.

'I'd rather be out than in.' Joe's words ran together in a quiet drawl but his pleading eyes drew back Walter's attention. Here was someone who seemed to be enjoying the party even less than he was.

'We'll go through, then,' said Natasha, moving at once. When they had fought their way to the garden she turned to him. 'I thought you'd like to see a bit of London, a bit of life.' But even she knew that wasn't it.

'Dirty, rushing place.' Joe's voice found a bit of energy. 'If a man dropped dead in the street, they'd step over him.'

'I don't know why you think that,' began Natasha, and then, as they reached the garden and she saw her husband in the middle of a chattering throng, it struck her that Frank might easily step over a man who dropped dead at his feet, that is, if he noticed. 'I'd better introduce you to my husband.'

'Tasha! This party is filled with dazzling women who got away from me.'

Natasha kissed Frank, and thought she had never seen him look worse. His eyes, always venous, seemed to have dropped down in their sockets and the sockets themselves, no longer elastic, splayed outwards to reveal a streaky red lining. His pale suit, baggy and none too clean, hung formlessly over what was obviously a skinny, unhealthy body. She had once been passionately in love with this man's body.

'This is Joe,' said Natasha.

'Joe?' Frank eyed the young man with benevolence, as if to suggest that his wife's tastes were ridiculous but her own business.

Natasha reminded him, sharply, 'I told you. I met him through the Long Boat.'

'Ah, your good works.' Disappointed, Frank turned to Joe. 'I suppose I should congratulate you on joining the wicked world.'

'It's his first day,' said Natasha.

'By God, it is! So why aren't you celebrating with wine, women and song?' Frank pawed at Joe's arm complicitly.

'He's nothing to do with you.' Natasha removed

Frank's hand and directed Joe away from him through the crowd.

The sun had now dropped out of sight so that the hellish flaming had changed to a softer swathe of puce, which turned bright lips black and pink cheeks dusky. The air was cooler, too, but its effect was hardly felt by the massed ranks whose hot bodies were pressed so close.

Joe sweated. This world he'd entered seemed even more claustrophobic than the one he'd left. He was stifled for country air. Knowing no one, he had no one to recognize and the faces, all so violently animated, blurred under his gaze.

'Can we go now?'

If Natasha heard his appeal, she made no sign. She had just noticed the large figure of the Home Secretary, thickly surrounded, and his security guard a foot or two away, peering outwards.

'Excuse me.' She pushed her path determinedly and made sure, by taking his elbow, that Joe followed her.

Walter sank into his chair at his desk. Just a momentary break, he told himself and, already feeling guilty, rose immediately to watch the party from his window. He was amused to spot Frank's wife's escort, the strangely handsome farmer, in conversation with the Home Secretary. Now they parted, the farmer swiping someone with one of his plastic bags as he turned away. Sighing, Walter took a step back to his duty.

*

21

Natasha stood under a tree which dripped yellow flowers. She had been accosted by an old friend – an old lover, in fact. He was the only man to speak to her and the man she least wanted to see in the world.

Somewhere behind her, as tall and dark as the trunk of the tree, Natasha sensed Joe's reproachful presence. It was a relief to turn her mind from the animated face in front of her. Why had she been so keen to introduce this simple murderer, this rightly convicted killer, this dangerous, pathetic woman-slayer, to Her Majesty's representative? She had told herself that it was to draw attention to the Long Boat so that the next time they applied for Home Office funds, the letter could begin, 'Dear Home Secretary, As I explained to you when we met . . .'

'Do you mean you really live in the country all the time?' enquired this old ex-lover, seven years older, still the same. 'You look far too elegant.'

Natasha reminded herself that none of it had been his fault. She tried to smile. 'Very elegant people live in the country. They just don't waste their time looking elegant when they're weeding the herbaceous border.' Once more she turned to Joe. The Home Secretary had been polite to him after her introduction. What words had she used? Something about him just having left Her Majesty's pleasure. 'Back into the arms of your family, I hope?' the Home Secretary had said, perfectly agreeably.

'No family that need concern you!' Joe's outburst had been received into silence and then swallowed into animated conversation. Natasha had led him away. At least Frank hadn't been there to laugh, to tell her she knew nothing about English politics and ask her why she had felt moved to bring a murderer to the party of the year.

All this was better than the man standing in front of her, trying politely enough, to catch her attention.

'Don't tell me you bought that suit in the country,' he persisted. He was a designer, hard-working, successful.

'I bought it in New York.' He meant nothing to her and never had.

'How's Frank?'

'Here, somewhere.'

'I see you're not very interested in talking to me,' said the designer, smiling ironically.

Natasha watched him go. He was a small, strutting man and she had not been kind.

'Can we go on now?' Joe loomed out from the shadows. 'I've had enough too.'

But such a thickness of bodies had closed between them and the exit from the garden that it needed a strong will and a strong body to break through. Joe had both. Giving up any pretence of manners, he shouldered his way through the crowds.

'For God's sake, Joe, you don't have to kill anyone!' Natasha stopped, horrified, as Joe turned briefly to her, and then continued his course even more violently. At last he was out of the house and striding, then running, down the road.

Walter, having retired once more to his office after a rather satisfactory series of compliments on the new life he was breathing into the newspaper, witnessed Frank's wife at a hectic run after her large friend. The two policemen on the door also watched curiously. Since the window was open, Walter was able to overhear one say to the other, 'Now, if he was chasing her, we'd be running too.'

The garden was dark and damp, wine no longer available at the tables and only those who had nowhere else to go stayed on. Walter's sallow cheeks were flushed, his hazel eyes bright. He stood in a circle that included his newly appointed art critic, a young would-be journalist called Sheena and a Conservative ex-minister, who couldn't get used to having time on his hands. Now Walter felt relaxed. Notoriously unsusceptible to female charms, he listened to Sheena's bright London voice and wondered if her display of obvious feminine characteristics, exposed cleavage, pouting red mouth in dusky skin, might disguise a clever mind.

'Shall I cook you spaghetti?' she was offering him now.

'We could all eat together,' suggested the art critic, jealously.

Annabel arrived in a hurry. 'The drunks have decided this is their home for the night. What we need is a good hard shower.'

During this intervention the Member of Parliament took the opportunity to caress Sheena's naked upper arm. She turned to him, and seeing the lust in his red-tinged eyes, found an answering flame in her own. She glanced at Walter and adjudicated a brief struggle in her heart between ambition and lust. 'I bet you could buy me something better than spaghetti.'

Walter watched as the two disappeared through the shadowy murk of the trees towards the house.

*

24

Joe and Natasha sat over a table in a pizza house. Joe felt his knees trembling with exhaustion. He had scarcely slept during his last few nights in prison.

'It's cold in here.' Natasha shivered.

Perhaps that was the reason for his trembling. The sweat had dried now leaving his skin with a damp stickiness. He could have done with a wash. In his cottage, he had used water piped down from the hillside. His mother would never let them be put on the mains but the water ran sparingly and they usually kept buckets filled, standing round the kitchen and bathroom.

'You must be starving.' Natasha looked at her guest despairingly.

Joe nodded. The trouble was, his mother had died. Not even sixty years old.

'Perhaps you wish you'd gone to your sister tonight? I'm sorry if I made a mistake.'

Startled, Joe raised his eyes to stare at her. His sister had only visited him a handful of times at the start of the sixteen years he was away. She had told him straight that her husband and family came first. 'She hasn't time for me.' He paused. 'Perhaps I should have stayed inside.'

'Not at all!' cried Natasha. Joe's probation officer had not been able to get his cottage open till tomorrow. And Joe had been due out today. That was the problem she'd determined to solve. Or was it that she'd wanted to show him off at the party? The smartest party for the smartest people in England where she was nobody or something worse than nobody, that rich American ex-pat, and Frank was king, king of the jokers, at least. The party where she met the one man in the world she didn't want to see. Well, it was mostly over now and all Joe had done was insult the

Home Secretary and make a fool of her as she chased him out. 'You'll like the flat anyway.' Natasha, taking courage from the arrival of the pizzas, smiled encouragingly.

Joe began to eat and, enjoying the taste of the food, dared to imagine what it would be like to walk on his own land. He pictured the grasslands dotted with his golden cows, the thin stretch of ploughed field, his hand-built farmyard and the steep hillside where the sheep grazed amid bracken and nettles. It would have changed, he knew that. That was part of the penalty. Natasha suddenly found blue eyes staring at her intensely. 'I'll be glad to see the land.'

'Of course you will,' agreed Natasha, relieved by this innocent confidence.

Joe looked down at his plate. There was no 'of course' about it, at least, not the way she said it, but he did not try to explain further.

This year's garden party was over. Walter was happy. He loved being in his office late at night. Sometimes he even slept on the sofa. He stood up, stretched and, going to the open window, began to take breaths of night air. At once a disembodied voice began to recite in lugubrious sing-song:

'Glory be to God for dappled things –
For skies of couple-colour as a brindle cow;
For rose-moles all in stipple upon trout that swim;
Fresh-fire-coal chestnut-falls; finches' wings;
Landscape plotted and pieced – fold, fallow, and plough;
And all trades, their gear and tackle and trim.'

Walter stopped inhaling and listened attentively. He had last heard that poem read out loud in a seminary in Maynooth. Later he had decided poetry was the pornography of religion, an artificial whipping-up of religious fervour as pornography stirs sexual desire. But that had been when he was mad.

Walter spoke with his head out of the window:

> *'All things counter, original, spare, strange;*
> *Whatever is fickle, freckled (who knows how?)*
> *With swift, slow; sweet, sour, a-dazzle, dim;*
> *He fathers-forth whose beauty is past change;*
> *Praise him.'*

'Alleluia!' bellowed Frank from below.

Walter wandered down the stairs.

'It's time we did another piece on old Ireland.' Frank was unsurprised to see his boss. After a million or so bottles down the hatch, he had lost the art of being surprised. It made him a comfortable companion.

Walter sat down beside him. 'You're a loose cannon, Frank.'

'My boy, that had a patronizing ring.' Frank laid his hand on Walter's knee. 'Time I went home. My balls would chill a martini.'

'I'll ring for a taxi.'

Frank half stood then collapsed. 'On second thoughts, don't hurry it. We have a murderer in the home.'

'A murderer.'

'My wife's house guest. She's keen on that sort of thing. Doesn't like me, though. Hasn't for years. Can't blame her. Don't like myself.' Frank looked dismally at his hands. Empty of a glass, they had a curiously incomplete look. 'Worst thing I ever did, driving her off.'

'I'm sorry.'

'She's a great woman. A rich woman. A fucking rich American. But even that didn't fuck her up. What a fuck.'

Walter had never found swear words easy to listen to and, although darkness and Frank's drunkenness were mitigating circumstances, three fucks in a row and one of them transitive, were more than he could take. 'I'll get that taxi.'

Joe lay in the narrow bed that had once belonged to Natasha and Frank's child, although he didn't know that. He didn't even know that Natasha had once had a daughter because she had never told him. He was glad that the room was small, precise and neat, not unlike a cell. Since he had no pyjamas, he had only partially undressed and felt more protected by it. His mother, an old-fashioned woman, had taught him that nakedness was never necessary. One of the lesser agonies of prison had been dealing with this modesty. His fellow inmates had soon picked up on it and, although his size and strength had protected him from serious assault, he had still been taunted and mocked.

As he lay, stiff and straight in this child's bed, Joe was once again trying to come to terms with the idea that he had been let out to live the rest of his life 'on licence'. This idea that he was 'licensed' to be out, like a television, seemed against nature. A life for a life, he could understand that. But the idea that he could be walking up a hill, hammering in a fence post, ploughing a furrow with a kite's tail of birds, or just sitting, doing nothing, but still 'on licence', still liable to be tossed back into prison if he put a foot wrong, he just couldn't get his head round it. That was what a life sentence meant, they'd told him often enough, but it didn't seem right, as if he wasn't properly free. Best thing not to think about it.

He needed to go to the bathroom. Very quietly, so that he should not disturb Natasha, Joe slid his legs out of the bed and stood up.

Frank approached the door with his key as a short-sighted person brings the thread to the eye of a needle. The keyhole was small, perhaps smaller than usual. But it was just a question of perseverance, a calm stalking technique, gently, gently, and *voilà*! the key would be in the lock and he would be in his flat.

'Shit. Fuck. Sod.' As, yet again, the key jammed into the wood and fell to the floor, Frank's patience gave way and he aimed a series of vengeful, if feeble, kicks at the door.

Joe had no difficulty in recognizing the tones of his host and, as he happened to be passing the door, opened it speedily. Frank, who was slumped against it, fell in after it and, before Joe could grab him, crashed on to the floor where he lay senseless.

'I'm so sorry.' Natasha, wrapped in a dressing-gown, peered from her bedroom door. She came closer. 'He'll sleep it off now.'

'Do you want me to move him?'

'Please. Put him on the sofa in the living room.'

Joe carried him easily, fireman style. Laid him out with respect. He was pleased to be of service.

Chapter Four

Frank's flat stood in an avenue in Chelsea, one of a row of red Edwardian houses, converted for modern times. At about six in the morning the emerging sun became swathed in clouds banking up from the horizon. They rose upwards until the whole city was enclosed in a streaky grey and purple dome. Then it began to rain. All the hot cleanliness of the previous day was undone in an hour or two. Hideous rain – hideous in June, at least – weighted the leaves, floated rubbish in the gutters, dragged at rose petals until they became soft and speckled, like an old woman's cheek.

The flat was on two floors, a living room with balcony, kitchen and bedroom at the top and two bedrooms and a bathroom below. Natasha slept downstairs but a gutter ran close to her window so that her dreams became accompanied by the continuous sound of water, hard and cross, battering against the old iron pipe. Finally, it woke her and, she got out of bed and went upstairs to make herself a cup of tea. She had not yet thrown off the sound of the water clattering in the pipe, and as, still half asleep, she entered the living room, it seemed to increase in volume.

'Frank!' Why should she gasp at her husband's silhouette as he sat typing at a table by the glass doors to the balcony? He had always claimed that he wrote best with a hangover. Behind him, the long glass doors ran with water, turning the view outside – the not-very-interesting pots of unhealthy plants, the wall, railing and houses beyond – into a blurred image of an abstract world.

'Caught you staring!' Frank stopped suddenly and tore paper from typewriter in traditional triumphalist way. 'Coffee?' He jumped from his chair, although Natasha now saw that his hands shook and his face trickled with sweat.

'I'll make it.'

Frank followed her into the kitchen. Still energetic, he insisted on filling the kettle and ground the coffee, his idea of cooking. 'So where's your murderer?'

'Please don't.'

'OK, OK. Some things are beyond humour. Discuss. Not that humour was ever your strong suit, a failing you have in common with many of your compatriots. Your strengths are theirs also. Directness, honesty, an even temper, a sweet naïveté . . .'

'Frank!' Natasha sat down, exhausted.

'I just wrote an excellent piece on the colonization of Ireland. Want me to read it to you?'

'No.'

'Let's hope the new editor of The Cucumber doesn't feel the same. I present myself as the heart of the news-paper. As Samuel Johnson said, "A cucumber should be well sliced and dressed with pepper and vinegar, and then . . ."'

'"Thrown out as good for nothing."' Natasha completed the quotation.

'You remember.'

'It's printed on the front of the paper.'

'I'm glad you still read it. That's what you did to me. Sliced me, peppered me and threw me out.'

To her surprise, Natasha found herself laughing at the sentimental look on Frank's face. 'You *are* a fraud! You know you were well peppered before you met me, and I did not throw you, I just walked away while I still had the strength.'

'I do not deny your walking away. You might say it was a characteristic of my wives. And you graciously left me this lovely home. Shall I pour coffee?'

Natasha watched Frank pour and thought that she must not be taken in by this early-morning, post-column charm. 'I spoke briefly to your new editor. He seemed a serious sort of man.'

'Seriously serious. At his heart, in the space left over from me, stands a crucifix. Between midnight and dawn, he is writing a life of Christ.'

'How unlike *The Cucumber*.'

'We will see. Our move to the left may hasten or decline. Walter's religious beliefs do battle with his ambition. He has far greater confidence in political situations than I do.' Frank pushed away his cup with a dejected air.

'Time you went to bed,' said Natasha.

'Yes.' He looked up at her. 'Beautiful, almost beautiful, your nose is a mite too short. I suppose you and your murdering friend will be gone when I awake?'

'I expect so.'

Frank slumped lower and lower over the table as if he might sleep there. His thick white hair grew in tufts like a boy's, a duck's tail down his bony back. 'Tasha . . . Do you ever think of Naomi?' His voice was low, without his habitual tone of mockery.

'Of course I do!' Natasha cried out angrily. 'Every day. Every minute. But please don't start on that now. Not now.' She had never mourned with him. She could never mourn with him.

'No.' Frank was humble. He wanted to say, Can't you forgive me even a little after nine years? but instead he stood up. 'I'll go to bed.' He went to the door. 'And *muchas gracias* for the flat.'

'Oh, that's nothing,' Natasha's tone was still distressed and bitter. 'Whatever I've got or haven't got, I've got plenty of money.'

'Yes. Yes. Goodbye.' He stood for a moment, as if undecided, perhaps wondering whether he dared a kiss, then left.

Natasha sat on in the kitchen. The window dribbled with rain, a dismal sight. After a while, she stood up and made herself a piece of toast.

Joe sniffed the toast from his bed and thought of the breakfasts his mother had cooked him: bread, fried in the best dripping, accompanied by sausages, two eggs from their own chickens and, in the autumn, mushrooms from just below the hedgerow under the prow of the hill. The tea, a big pot of it, brewed to the moment he walked through the door, was served with fresh milk he carried in from their cows. That was why she looked after him like a king, because he had already been up two or three hours, milking thirty cows.

Joe knocked tentatively on the kitchen door. When no one answered, he pushed it gently with a guilty expression on his face. 'I'm sorry. I . . .' he mumbled, made as if to withdraw.

'No. Of course. Breakfast.' Natasha stood, wrapping her dressing-gown tightly, both startled and abstracted. 'I'll leave you to it. There's bread, corn flakes, I think.' She took a step, stopped, smiled. She must remember this was his happy day.

Joe held the door politely as she left. Slowly and carefully he put two pieces of bread into the toaster. He had loved his mother and then he had loved *her*. He couldn't pronounce her name even to himself.

The two pieces of toast popped up with such energy that they jumped right off the table. Crouching on the floor, half under the table, Joe pictured her, her flesh transparent, the veins as delicate as the veins in a flower. It had been against nature what he'd done.

The rain had woken Walter where he sat, still at his desk. His head ached but he soon forgot it as he eagerly scanned the writing in front of him. 'The lamp of the body is the eye. If your eyes are sound, you will have light for your whole body; if the eyes are bad, your whole body will be in darkness. If then the only light you have is darkness, the darkness is doubly dark.' Copied, of course, from Matthew, chapter six, verse twenty-two.

Walter left his office and descended past party detritus to the hallway, where he picked through the weight of newspapers already delivered before wedging four or five under his arm. Soon he was walking briskly towards the café where he habitually breakfasted. Realizing that rain was falling in needles from the sky, he hastily pulled his jacket over the papers and hurried along even faster, fleeing, perhaps, from double darkness.

Natasha and Joe sat opposite each other in the train. Natasha's head ached and she was in an irritable mood, which, because she was ashamed of it, made her even more irritable. Meeting Frank always had the same effect on her. Poor Joe. He sat opposite her placidly staring out of the window.

'It's stopped raining.' Joe spoke for the first time, a naïve look of glee on his face.

Natasha saw it above her newspaper and guessed that he was picturing his home-coming, the village, soft yellow stone draped in the folds of green hills, the valley through which road and stream ran amicably hand in hand. He deserved a kindly escort for that was the whole point of their association. 'Are you sure the key will be there?'

'Julie will have it off the agent in town. That's what she said.' Joe did not notice Natasha's mood. She was always a mystery to him and, besides, he had spent sixteen years trying not to notice the people around him.

Walter pulled over Frank's copy to see what he had cooked up between bouts of unconsciousness.

'Up to standard?' Annabel leaned over him as she placed a cup of coffee in exactly the right place on his desk. She liked boasting that it gave her pleasure to wait on men.

'"De Valera is to Ireland what Hitchcock is to cinema,"' read out Walter. When he first arrived at *The Cucumber* he had starred four names that must go. Frank's had been at the head of the list. 'Ask Johnny to bring in that Cork poet's piece on Ireland.'

I'm, just an old hack, thought Frank, not for the first time, when he got Walter's message that he'd already scheduled a piece on Ireland. What does it matter if they prefer some other garbage? The message had reached him in the Cockerel and it was with a jolly sense of camaraderie that Frank spotted an ex-colleague pushing through the swing doors.

'Derrick, old fruit!'

The moment Derrick had settled in with his favourite double vod and a packet of shrimp-flavoured crisps, a nod towards the lunch-hour, Frank shared with him the situation as he saw it. 'I'm for the chop, Derrick, the big E, the scrapyard, the knackers', the old folks' home, the paddock behind the house where the ragwort grows . . .'

'What's your worry, anyway?' Derrick finished his double with a look of injury. 'You've got a fucking millionairess for a wife, haven't you?'

'Got her! I haven't got a fucking hair on her head. Haven't had her for years. She stayed at the flat last night and didn't even bother to put me to bed when I knocked myself out on the door.'

'Women are a very hard-hearted sex.' This was a subject much enjoyed by Derrick, who had just been left by his wife for a younger man – younger than her, that is. But Frank hadn't finished with Natasha yet. Derrick could have his turn later. 'This morning, sober as a tax collector,' he interrupted, 'I raised the subject of my daughter and she turned on me like a barracuda spotting a bit of rotting flesh.'

'I've known that too,' mused Derrick.

'Think of it, she wouldn't even let me mention in her presence the name of my own dead daughter.'

'Typical,' muttered Derrick.

'I loved that girl. You might say she was the love of my life.'

'Daughters are like that.'

Frank noticed Derrick's gloomy chorus for the first time. 'Would you shut up?'

'Don't turn on me.'

'You've never even had a daughter.'

'I had a step-daughter. Some men are even closer to their step-daughters because . . .'

Frank decided that he had chosen the wrong confidant in this fat windbag waffling on over the table.

'What? Where are you going?' With an aggrieved expression Derrick watched his friend shuffle off. He had been hoping to cadge a few drinks off him.

Natasha and Joe left the train at the station nearest Natasha's house, where she had parked her car. She had no intention of taking Joe there: they would drive directly to his village.

Joe stared out of the window as the cloud thinned to a veil across the sun, reminding him of very early morning in the fields. He had had a companion then, Charlie, a sheep-dog with a bit of terrier and a bit of fox. That was the joke in the village. Charlie was always cheerful in the morning, eyes gleaming, tongue lolling, ready for a game whatever the hour. He had been good at bringing in the cows, too. Joe still could not bear to picture his last sight of him as the police drove him away. He had never been a clever dog, just cheerful and loyal, and although taken in by Ken, he had never recognized his new master and soon sickened and died. It would be strange not to have Charlie bounding and barking as he reached the cottage.

Frank lay on the floor beside Walter's desk. Sometimes his back hurt so much that there was no alternative.

'I can't publish this, Frank. It's a vicious attack on the Home Secretary.'

'Balls!' Owing to his position, Frank's voice had a sepulchral ring.

Walter looked down at the paper in his hand. 'You say his view on penal reform echoes George Bernard Shaw's that half of our prisoners should not be in prison and the other half should never be let out.'

'I can't see how anyone who spends ten years following in the good Lord's footsteps can possibly take politics seriously.'

'Render unto Caesar,' began Walter bravely.

'So you won't run this piece either?'

'Yes, I will,' answered Walter, resignedly.

It was raining again. The probation officer, large and rather pretty, got out of her car and looked up at the sky. 'Not much of a welcome,' she said, but she smiled encouragingly at Joe. 'I've put some things in the house,' she added, making Natasha guiltily aware that she had not even thought of buying a bottle of milk. 'And I'm told a grocer's van calls tomorrow. You must take things a day at a time.'

'That's right.' Joe stood outside his house in the rain as if he couldn't make the effort to go in. The little lawn in front, which used to be edged by neat flower-beds with wallflowers in the summer, was now overgrown with nettles. A few wild daisies and a single poppy were the only flowers. Ivy covered the low wall in front of the lane and a Virginia creeper, which had not been there before, crawled up across and beyond the first-floor windows.

'I'll have that off,' said Joe, 'and the ivy.' He turned to Julie. 'I thought people were in it.'

'A couple were, up till a year ago. We didn't know exactly when you'd be out, did we? Here's the key.' The two women were both conscious of getting very wet indeed, their hair straggling and dripping, and longed to push open the door but they curbed their impatience. Like a bride across the threshold, Joe needed to enter his new life in the right spirit. With his memories, he had every right to dawdle.

'Here we go, then.' Joe unlocked the door, peeling green paint where before it had been blue, same knocker, shaped like a cow, from a jumble sale. His place.

The two women, moved by their sense of being witnesses at this important occasion, stood back a few paces and, as Joe disappeared inside the house, exchanged a smile of almost tearful satisfaction. Several years of prison visiting had led up to this moment.

*

Natasha and Julie sat in Natasha's living room, drinking tea. Once again sunlight had driven away the rain and the room, painted a soft yellow, was luxuriously warm and bright. They sat opposite each other in plump armchairs. Their hair was beginning to dry, Natasha's smooth and dark, Julie's light brown and wispy. Now and again she patted it self-consciously.

'This is a very beautiful room.'

Natasha looked around with another's eyes and saw it was not the modest cottage she considered it. She saw the marble mantelpiece, the gilded ormolu clock, which had been her mother's, the American primitive painting, the inlaid chest bought on a trip to Paris, the curtains thickly lined against winter draughts, the tapestry cushions, the patterned rugs, the pots of flowers, which she replaced as soon as they wilted. Perhaps it had been a mistake to suggest that Julie came here for their talk. But they had both been so wet and Joe had needed to be alone.

'Do you think he'll manage?'

'He's lucky to have that lovely little cottage.'

Natasha tried to disown her own impressions, the meagre rooms, split linoleum, the smell, the chairs oily with dirt. 'Let's hope his farming friend will help him get back on the job.'

'Let's hope so. If things go well, we'll try and get him a telephone.'

'I suppose his sister will eventually put in an appearance.'

'I doubt it. I think she hoped he would never get out. Of course, he's planning to get a dog.'

'I didn't know that.'

'A lot of people who can't make relationships in the normal way find great consolation with a dog.'

Natasha, who liked cats because they had no intention of 'making a relationship', could think of nothing to say.

'Thank you for the tea and the drying out process. I should be off now. The office awaits.'

'And I should work.' Natasha stood.

'Work?' Julie seemed surprised.

'I make stained glass.' Natasha wanted to show Julie her studio, work-in-progress, the high-burn furnace of which she was so proud, but today she felt unnerved by her fat, sweet-faced guest. How could she show Julie her delicate roundels and diamonds, each one taking weeks of her time and bought, mostly, by wealthy Americans, when Julie spent all her time trying to patch together the lives of people like Joe, on the very edge of existence?

The two women stood at the doorway, where the plate-sized purple clematis flowers cast rich shadows on the wall. The rain was back again, forming little pools and rivulets on the stone-flagged path.

'Most unlike me to forget my umbrella.' Julie squashed herself into her anorak and set off gamely to the car.

Natasha, waving from the door, felt a shameful revulsion for all that was ugly in the world.

Joe stood in the front bedroom, looking out of the window. The hill still met the horizon in the way he remembered but everything else had changed. Facing him across the lane were a row of chestnut trees, about ten feet high, that had not been there before, and in the direction

41

of the village, there were two or three new houses. Inside the room, his single bed had been changed for a double and a white-painted chest of drawers stood beside his old brown cupboard. There was a carpet, too, where before there had been only boards and a small rug in the shape of a frog. Where had that rug from his childhood gone?

Joe walked to the back bedroom, which had been his mother's. The nearest field, which he had sometimes planted with wheat and sometimes used for pasture, was now sadly wild and unkempt, as if it had been used for nothing at all. To the right were his yard and shed, constructed by him from any bits and pieces he could borrow or buy cheap. It had taken him five years to make that yard into a workable farm and now, by the look of it, he'd have to start all over again.

Bending his head, Joe rattled down the uncarpeted stairs and out into the warm rain. This felt like freedom, all right. He walked briskly towards the yard. Give him a bit of time and he'd soon have everything spick and span, up and running, milking machinery gleaming, cows back in their stalls, milk tank calling every morning. He'd done it once and he'd do it again.

Chapter Five

Natasha exulted in her hotel room. She had escaped into a world whose chaos had nothing to do with her. Darkness had not cooled Manhattan. The deep canyons teemed and hissed. A hurricane was reported to be moving up from Florida, although it was far too early in the season. Air-conditioning units clung to buildings like bees' nests, humming and throbbing in the effort to translate wet heat into dry chill. Inside the walls, television sets throbbed, too, with news of murder, political gossip and imminent natural disaster. Shopkeepers considered criss-crossing their windows with brown tape.

When she left the hotel the streets were half empty. Many people had not come in for work, shops were closed, the sky was as yellow as the eyes of a cat and a hot wind blew. The wind whipped hair round her cheeks and then tore it away again so it stood out behind her like a black streak. She was prepared for the weather, clipped neatly into a silk sweater, trousers, trainers. She was prepared for rain, too, to be wet, swept away by the hurricane.

'Well, aren't we the brave ones?' Felicia, one of Natasha's oldest friends, who now ran a successful art gallery, welcomed her into an almost deserted restaurant.

'Take your pick, ladies,' said the maître d' expansively.

He was young with a quiff of dyed blond hair. 'Twenty tables cancelled this morning.'

'I chose this restaurant for its flowers,' said Felicia. 'If the so-called hurricane does sweep us away, we'll be ready strewn with funeral wreaths.'

'Peonies, lilies, lupins, marguerites, roses, ranunculas, aquilegias, zinnias,' began Natasha, looking round at the great bunches.

'Who'd ever guess you were a city girl born and bred?' Felicia nodded significantly. 'So what else are you doing in England, apart from admiring flowers?'

'I need a glass of wine before I tell you.' Was this why she had come to New York, to confess to this big, generous woman, like a peasant in her purple and orange shawl? 'I saw Frank two days ago. He's speeded up his drinking-unto-death campaign.'

'You care?'

'Oh, Felicia.'

'OK. How long were you married?'

'We're still married.' Natasha half closed her eyes and let the beautiful flowers on the table merge into a haze of colour. 'I took one of my prisoners, an ex-prisoner, to stay at the flat. Frank passed out.'

'You're still doing that prison work?'

'I took him to *The Cucumber* party as a treat. But it didn't work so well. I was upset. I saw . . .' She paused. Was it too late to confide the part that the strutting lover had played in her life?

'You saw dear old Frank,' Felicia completed helpfully.

'Yes. Of course.' Natasha frowned then leaned forward with a smile, 'Aren't you going to ask about my stained glass? Aren't you going to ask about work?'

Felicia was diverted. The wind funnelling through the depths of the streets had suddenly decided to attack the glass doors of the restaurant. First the outer door shot open and then the inner, until, in syncopation, they clapped shut again, one after the other. The under-employed waiters rushed to solve the problem but the wind was too strong playing a determined duet, until, all of a sudden, it grew tired and, with one final double clap, almost but not quite in concert, passed on.

Felicia laughed at this finale and patted Natasha's hand, which was lying on the table. 'Enjoy. Enjoy.'

'You always managed that.' Natasha heard her voice, like a bitter old maid's. 'How's Harvey?'

'Harvey is currently bonding with a rare species of seals in Iceland.'

'I thought he was serious, Felicia.'

'Have I not taught you to live in the present tense? Why, for example, are you still not divorced from Frank? Sometimes I don't think you're American at all.'

'You know why.' Natasha watched their food arriving through the dusky yellow of the approaching hurricane, saw Felicia's happy anticipation of the delights of warm scallops on a bed of spinach salad with creamed potatoes and home-baked nut bread.

'You can mourn without Frank as your husband.' After all, Felicia did not fall on her food too eagerly. She thought that it was true: Natasha, in her restraint and lack of openness, seemed English. She tried to remember if she had been like that before her years away.

Natasha considered Felicia's statement but could not make it mean anything. 'I don't feel as if I could.'

Felicia thought, So she won't let him near her but

she won't let him go either. She said, 'What makes you happy?'

'Ah, happiness.' Natasha had lost her appetite and despised herself for it. Despite the wine she had drunk she felt her body becoming cold. She waited for Felicia to tell her that Naomi had enjoyed four years of perfect happiness. That she had died happy. That it had been mere bad luck that she had turned up a few minutes late that bitter afternoon. That it was all a very long time ago.

'What is your ex-con like?'

'Joe.' Natasha tried to change back the direction of her thoughts. It was hard, even if her mind had been on him, to describe Joe in the context of Madison Avenue. He was so much part of an unrecorded English country life, a man who had no concept of himself, whose life would have been unrecognized outside one tiny village, were it not for a single act of violence.

'Why was he in prison?'

'He killed his girlfriend.'

Felicia put down her fork. 'Over the horizon. And you are involved with this man?'

Natasha felt a little flush of energy under Felicia's deliberate misunderstanding. 'Some go in for cleaning up the ozone, I go in for giving the inadequate a helping hand. Now, whether you like it or not, I'm going to tell you about this ruby glass I've discovered which will have your clients showering their floppies at you like confetti.'

'What you need is a nice, charming, cheerful lover,' advised Felicia, tucking in with gusto.

*

The wind, fast and furious, blew Natasha against the side of the canyon, and there she clung, creeping cautiously downtown. Above her head, the thick marmalade-coloured sky gradually darkened, turning from bronze to purple to almost black. Then the rain came, released in an unbroken river of warm wetness that soaked Natasha to the skin in a few seconds and made it not worth worrying about any more.

Walter had invited Sheena to his office at the end of his working day. How had this happened? If asked, he would have talked of the need for a youthful approach at *The Cucumber*, the lack of a strong female presence, of his responsibility as new editor to be constantly on the look-out for fresh voices. But the truth was that when she had rung, earlier in the day, he remembered how she had looked at the party, and how she had suddenly disappeared with the hot, blue-eyed Member of Parliament.

'We're on our own.' Walter greeted her downstairs. 'It's a good time to talk.'

The tangled skein of Walter's thinking about women would have held no interest for Sheena. Her success in life was based on a simple directness, which it suited her to assume that others shared. She had guessed that Walter would not be immune to her obvious sex appeal and the obviousness was not something of which she was ashamed. 'Don't you find it strange working in a house?'

Walter was disappointed in his visitor's appearance, although since he had not fully admitted his attraction in the first place, he could not admit this either. She was smaller, plumper, her skin coarser, her face more ordinary than he remembered. Sheena noticed this reaction and answered it with her own criticisms. Even his editor's power did not entirely make up for his pinched features, deep-set eyes and intense yet diffident manner.

'I might as well tell you I've been trying to set up this series for ages.'

'Two pieces, you said?'

'When I was sixteen,' she began, in businesslike tones, 'I was date-raped.'

Walter, caught off-guard, let out a nervous sigh. He had to accept that rape was part of the contemporary editor's battery of subjects. 'Did he go to prison?'

'It gave me an interest in the rights of the victim,' continued Sheena, without answering his question. 'Rape is a bit of an exaggeration, actually. Although in the States they'd have called it that.'

'Ah,' said Walter, making an effort to respond to her look of enquiry. 'I'm sorry.'

'I was very sorry the first time I met him. Afterwards I wanted to kill him.'

'I should think so.' Walter had just noticed that Sheena's bare legs were very pretty indeed. He had sometimes imagined that the only way he would achieve a sexual experience was by acting with a wild out-of-character boldness which, unstoppable as he would then become, might well amount to date-rape.

'Instead of killing him, I talked to him.'

'Interesting.'

'Anyway, he wasn't a frightening person, except on that one occasion.'

'I can imagine.'

'I beg your pardon?' Now Sheena opened her eyes wide and leaned forward.

'I can imagine some of your feelings. So what do you want to write that the tabloids won't buy from you?'

'Rapist and victim in a small town. Follow their stories. Make people understand the stories behind the headlines. The tabloids only want the sensational stuff.'

'Would you like a drink?' asked Walter, feeling the need of one himself. Was he not editing a political weekly?

'I know what you mean. Although I told you my own story merely as background.'

Walter went to the refrigerator. 'Beer?'

'If necessary.' Sheena laughed, showing even white teeth.

As they drank their beer and talked and drank another, the light dimmed in the room for it was a cloudy, damp evening. Sheena was warm now, and her skin glowed with youth and vitality as Walter had remembered from the party. He hung over her chair.

'May I kiss you?'

Sheena looked at him upside down. 'Is it my rape that has excited you?'

'I'm afraid it could be.' Walter's hand had begun to shake and there was sweat on his upper lip.

'How old are you?'

'Thirty-four.'

Sheena raised her arms above her head until she could just touch Walter's face. 'Oh, yes. You can kiss me.'

Walter came round urgently and flung himself at her, half crouching. He hoped to lose himself in an ecstasy of sensual appetite but he was clumsy and his mouth could hardly find hers.

'I'll stand,' said Sheena, obligingly. So they stood in the middle of the room and Walter tried to wrap his height round Sheena's plump smallness and that wasn't too good either. But, all the same, his heart beat frantically and, if he liked, he could lay his hand on her neck, on her breast, clasp her waist.

It was at this grappling juncture that Annabel knocked and entered.

'I'm sorry!' she gasped, truly amazed. She had believed that Walter was probably a non-sexual being but, if anything, attracted to men.

'Fine by me.' Sheena flicked her hair back from her face.

'I thought you'd gone home.' Walter, holding his head at an odd angle, went to his desk and put on the lamp. He felt reassured by the order he saw there, by the work in progress. He felt able to glance at both women and see that Sheena was still confident and careless – certainly not crying, 'Rape!' – while Annabel's expression was studiously neutral. Nothing momentous had happened, it seemed.

'I should be off,' said Sheena, looking for her bag.

'I'll give your suggestion some thought.' Walter frowned earnestly.

Sheena smiled brightly. 'I'll be in touch.'

'In touch,' repeated Walter, before hearing the words too loud in the small room.

Frank had slumped over his corner table at the Cockerel and the landlord, bored, perhaps, with the responsibility of his celebrated drunk, dialled for an ambulance without waiting for a revival. Frank woke up to find himself in the clutches of an enthusiastic doctor. 'I have read you for years. My wife and I both read you, sometimes over each other's shoulders. I'm a devoted fan and that is why I am not going to let you walk out of this hospital.'

'You want to kill the goose that lays the traditional egg? I need a drink.'

'You do not need a drink.'

Frank lay on his hard little hospital bed and looked up at his tormentor with what he hoped was pathetic appeal. He had known this attitude before, usually, however, from women who thought to save him from himself. Both his wives had been particularly hard-working in that area. Men seldom bothered which, in his view, showed their greater intelligence.

'I am keeping you in for tests, which may take several days or longer. Probably longer.'

'No!' Frank imagined himself galvanized towards escape but all he had managed was a bleat, and he was still lying on the bed, pinioned by the gimlet-eyed determination of this medical supremo.

'Can someone bring in your things?'

'One wife is the other side of the Atlantic and the other has crossed the waters of darkness.' Frank sounded infinitely pathetic. 'I'll ring my editor,' he added. Walter would smuggle him in a bottle. Walter believed in the Christian virtue of charity and could not be childish enough to believe that good health was a duty.

Joe had been waiting for his friend, Ken, to call since eleven o'clock. He had waited the day before as well. He knew he wouldn't come earlier because of the milking and he knew he wouldn't come late in the afternoon for the same reason. So it had to be in the middle of the day. A card had come to him in prison: 'We must sort out what I owe you and discuss your future.' Although Ken had never found the time to visit Joe in any of his many prisons, Joe never doubted his friend for a minute. Small farmers, often with no help, did not have time to traipse about the countryside but Ken would be there when he was needed. Joe pictured his big face with its long side-whiskers and nose as strong and knobbly as a branch. They used to meet at the farmers' market once or twice a month, and sometimes their tractors crossed in a lane and they stopped for a gossip about the milk quota and sewage in the streams.

Ken had been in his thirties, then, a married man with two little girls, a good strong man and one of the few people outside the family and the direct village who had come to his mother's funeral. Around that time, he had called on Joe for tea a couple of times. That was before *she* arrived.

Expecting Ken every minute, Joe was nervous of leaving the house for very long. The first morning he had woken at five and walked up the hill. The ground was wet with dew and soon his cheap trainers were soaked and the stones on the track pressed through to the soles of his feet. He wanted to enjoy his freedom, but his head ached as well as his feet and, after going a little further, he realized that he had never, in all his years in the village, gone up the hill just for a walk. Usually he had driven his tractor as far as he could, probably the whole way up, and if he did any walking at all, it was for a particular purpose, strewing hay for the sheep, moving or mending a fence – although even then he'd more often than not take the tractor.

So Joe waited restlessly, moving between the little house, which still did not feel like his home, and his yard, where the tumbledown state of the buildings was too depressing for him to do more than wander, ghostlike, not touching, hardly seeing. At last, on the second day, there was a knock on the door.

'Mrs Wynne!'

A small neatly dressed woman waited. The sun had come out again and she wore a girlish summery dress, although her face was wrinkled with age.

'Yes, Joe. Can I come in?'

Joe was awkward, fumbling as he let in this old friend of his mother. He was touched that she had come and went about making her a cup of tea and providing a biscuit.

Mrs Wynne waited till they were both sitting, the expression on her face unchanging all the time, never smiling, stiff with importance. Yet Joe did not doubt she had come to welcome him.

'I have this for you.' She opened her handbag and took out a letter.

'A letter.' Joe smiled, embarrassed.

'I was asked to bring it to you. Because of my friendship with your mother.' Mrs Wynne stared at him, and the blankness on her face was exchanged for an intense curiosity. Joe saw this and flushed. 'Shall I read it to you? You see, I know what's in it already. I said I'd bring it to you because I wanted you to understand there was nothing personal and I wasn't . . .' Mrs Wynne, who sat with her hands clasped round her bag as if in fear of attack, now freed one hand and waved it in the air.

Joe watched this performance with surprise but still neither opened the letter nor handed it over. 'Ken,' he said slowly, for he began to understand that Mrs Wynne had not come in a kindly spirit. 'I am expecting Ken.'

'Ah, yes.' Mrs Wynne plonked her hand back on her bag. 'He will come. I have no doubt.' She looked up at Joe, saw his anxious face, his cheap crumpled clothes, his youthful air, much more youthful than his actual age, but her face showed no pity. 'I had better tell you what's in the letter, I think.'

Joe felt an instinctive urge to avoid whatever Mrs Wynne had to tell him. A streak of sun had come through the spattered window-panes so he stared at that for a bit and then offered his visitor another cup of tea.

'It's nearly dinner-time,' said Mrs Wynne severely, but she seemed to have lost her nerve a little for quite a few seconds elapsed before she started again. 'This is not my idea but I had to concur with the general feeling that you shouldn't have come back here, Joe.'

'What?' Joe seemed amazed, uncomprehending.

'I know you think of here as your home.' She paused for a moment, confused. 'Well it was your home. But that was a long time ago.' She stopped again as Joe stood up abruptly and then came close to her staring downwards.

'Oh, Joe.' Mrs Wynne put her hand to her throat and opened her eyes wide as if frightened. But there was also a hint of a smile around her mouth as if something of his fixed stance, his strained hostility, pleased her. 'Oh, Joe,' she repeated, in a fragile little voice. 'It's old Mrs Wynne speaking to you. I still care about you, for your mother's sake, yes, I do, despite everything.' These last words were whispered with horrible emphasis before she became brisk again. 'I am only thinking of what is best for you. You are not wanted in this village and it's not a good idea to live where you're not wanted. When you give it a little thought, I'm sure you'll agree.'

Joe did not look capable of agreeing or, indeed, disagreeing with anything. His face had become waxy pale, his eyes unfocused and unblinking, his lower jaw moving oddly and uncontrollably.

'Joe?' prompted Mrs Wynne, at the same time darting a quick look to the door.

As if coming back from a trance-like state, Joe shook his head from side to side, sat down once more on the chair and repeated earnestly, 'I'm expecting Ken.'

'Ken,' began Mrs Wynne, and then stood up in her turn. 'Well, I've tried to tell you kindly, seeing as I knew you in the happy days, but I suppose you'll just have to read the letter for yourself. They won't have you here, Joe. They think you should go to a big city somewhere. Where you can be kept an eye on. Where the police are nearer than ten miles away. I'm being cruel to be kind, telling you this. There are children to think of, little ones to think of. Young women, too. Ken's got his girls. You have to understand that they don't want living on their doorstep someone who murdered . . .' Mrs Wynne was moving out of the room and reached the door on the word 'murdered'. It was opened for her by Joe, still utterly silent, and it was the sight of his hand, shaking so hard that he could hardly turn the handle, that stopped her short. She looked up at his face and saw his eyes glistening as if he were about to cry.

The sight was so awful to her, a plea for sympathy that she had no intention of answering, that she looked away at once and then ran off, over the threshold, down the path, her bag flapping against her floral skirt, her neat sandals clip-clopping.

Joe stood watching her go. Because it was the middle of the day, the high sunlight struck down directly on to the road so that the scurrying figure was carried off on a river of brightness. He had managed to block out most of her actual words but he understood well enough the general meaning. They had talked of this in prison, debated his future, as if he could have any future outside this village. As he continued to stand at his door, hoping, perhaps, that the summer countryside would soothe him, a white van came spinning down from the left.

Seeing Joe, the driver stopped opposite him. He called from the window. 'Need anything?'

Trying to pull himself together, for here was human contact, someone who had stopped voluntarily to talk to him even if it was only to sell him groceries, Joe stepped forward. 'I could do with some potatoes.'

'Right you are.' Together they went to the back of the van and picked out a packet of biscuits and a few more items. 'You're the chap who's been let out, aren't you? Last week, there was talk of putting up a notice. Citizens' rights or something. Just talk.' The grocery man's face expressed neither disapproval nor sympathy. He seemed only interested in confirming the facts.

Muttering, 'It's my home,' Joe handed over the money.

This time he did not watch the van disappear down the bright strip of road. Galvanized by the simple transaction, he went back into his house and began to unpack his shopping. It was only when he had finished this and put some potatoes on to boil for his lunch that he came back to the living room and saw the envelope Mrs Wynne had brought him. Although he would have liked to burn it, or tear it into little pieces at very least, he had too much respect for the written word, typed as this was, to allow himself that pleasure. Nevertheless he would not open it. Pulling out a drawer in the table, he shoved the letter inside and closed it firmly. Maybe he would show it to Ken.

Chapter Six

The hurricane, which was not really a hurricane, had only huffed and puffed a little at Manhattan on its way to a flashier hit further up the coast. The wind did no more than break a few flower-pots, float into space the odd awning and give plenty of people a day off from work. But the rain deluged for several hours, until offices, churches, glass skyscrapers sparkled and stone buildings lost their grimy patina. Eventually the dark clouds rolled up and away to the north, and behind them was revealed a clear blue sky, the blue of wide countrysides, deserts, mountains, all landscapes majestic and unpopulated.

Natasha walked out of her hotel into this unusual clarity and thought of her growing-up in the big apartment on Park Avenue. She had known privilege all her life. Then, fifteen years ago, her father had left her mother to live with his assistant, a clever, attractive woman, thirty years younger than him. Four weeks later, the private plane, flying her mother to a cheer-up skiing holiday in the Rockies, had crashed. No one had survived. Her mother had been the rich one of the family. Natasha, an only child, had received everything from the newly made will. She had been twenty, and the first time she had seen her father since the divorce and after the funeral, he had asked her to make him and his new wife an allowance. She had done so and then without even waiting to finish her degree, she had left to start a new life in England.

It was a never-ending sunset as Natasha walked towards a gala evening among the increasing crowds, released from their stuffy apartments into this mild, fresh air.

Waiters, young men and women, theatrical in their appearance and gestures, flung tablecloths and juggled with glasses. Guests, in black tie or designer dresses, competitive in their understatement, were already among them, having paid upwards of a hundred dollars, eager to get their money's worth. Natasha, guest of one of the organizers who had advised her to come early or be crushed in the stampede, stared curiously at this scene, which seemed to have so little to do with her present existence.

'Natasha! So you didn't funk it. Did you see the rain? I hoped some would fail to show but, once we've put our money down, we New Yorkers are a tough lot to put off.'

Natasha turned, smiling, to her host, Gino di Stefano, romantically handsome, who was trying to clasp her and kiss her and talk to her all at once.

'You must be the most enthusiastic person!'

'The most enthusiastic. The most energetic. Proof I fit so much better into New York than Naples. Now I have twenty people dying to meet you. Half of them own galleries and the other half buy the stuff out of the galleries.'

'Oh Gino,' protested Natasha, but only feebly because that, after all, was why she was here, surely, to do business. That of course, was why everyone else was here too, to do business of one sort or another, whether directly or by climbing up the social ladder.

'And later,' said Gino, pushing her forward firmly, 'if neither of us has found someone too rich or powerful to resist, then we'll meet for fresh lobster claws and tiny tomatoes grown upside down in seaweed and a cream cake like the skirts of a ballet dancer. Take this key in case you're early.'

Natasha was very early and sat, on her own in Gino's minimalist converted loft. The walls were white, the wooden floor painted black; there were two white sofas and two black pieces of sculpture and that was all. The only colour came through the wide expanse of window, which reflected lights and movement from the city outside, living imitation of abstract art.

'It's perfect,' Natasha congratulated Gino when he eventually arrived.

'One room plus bath and kitchen. Not a date between us?'

'I'm too old for dates.'

'In this city no one is too old for a date.'

Natasha had met Gino when he had first come to New York, a penniless student, passionate and knowledgeable about southern Italian Renaissance painters.

'*Voilà*, Madame. *Ecco*, Signora!' From nowhere a table had appeared with a meal laid on it, as exquisite as a Chinese painting.

'Do sit down, Gino.'

'One call, perhaps two, and I join you.'

While Gino used his mobile in the kitchen to make at least four calls, Natasha picked at the salad and thought about success.

'Why do you do it?' She could ask Gino as he tore his way into the crabs' claws. 'Why do you work so hard?'

'Work! I haven't done a day's work in years. I am the luckiest man alive. *Cara* Natasha, you have the malaise of the rich. But I shall help you a little.'

Guessing what was coming, Natasha began to smile.

'Yes. Yes. Smile, please. A very good friend, you do not know him, a new genius called Col, we are putting together a show on the contemporary decorative arts in Europe. We could use some stained glass and we could also use some—'

'Big bucks. You shall have some, Gino. I'll talk to the trust tomorrow. And you can display a couple of pieces of mine, too. I've discovered a glass as clear and rich as quince jelly.'

'But life cannot be all art.' Gino had just returned from another bout of telephoning in the kitchen. 'I have my Col, the genius. Now I shall tell you how happy I am.'

'But if you have Col,' asked Natasha, after listening to his description of an Egyptian boy who possessed the gilded glamour of Tutankhamun, 'if you have Col, why do you need a date?'

Gino stared closely at Natasha. 'Dates are for public, Col is for me.'

Natasha could see that Gino meant what he said and felt dissatisfied by her own wish to scoff. 'So this is love?' she said.

'We are not married. We do not even live together. We are in love.' He smiled beatifically.

The cab driver who returned Natasha to her hotel managed to keep up a consistently high speed by directing his cab from side to side of the road, as if he were tacking on open seas.

'Would you mind slowing down!'

'You from London?'

'None of your fucking business. Just drive more slowly.'

'You from New York.'

Lying back and shutting her eyes, Natasha realized that in England it would be already light at this time and pictured Cleopatra hunting stealthily through the June grasses. The house and studio, in all its perfection, waited for her return, a princess's castle. Where were her own red blood cells, her fierce jungle genes? At least she had managed a 'fucking'.

'Make a right at the next intersection and stop at the second canopy.'

The hotel was very brightly lit like a ship at sea.

'A message for you, ma'am.'

Natasha took the message with her key, but she did not look at it.

Morning drifted through Natasha's consciousness like a dream. She had not drawn her curtains and the sun, turned into icy whiteness by the air-conditioning, shafted her on to the sheets, a marble effigy. She was naked, uncovered, her head with its sheaf of black hair turning restlessly from side to side. One arm stretched out, a beautiful tentacle reaching towards the bedside table.

The watch for which Natasha was searching fell off the table and her eyes opened. Her hand clutched a scrap of paper, the message from the night before. Hardly awake, she carried it in front of her eyes.

Natasha's fingers loosed and let the paper flutter downwards to her breasts where it lay just above her heart.

'I would have come before,' said Ken, 'but Mrs Wynne thought it best she spoke to you first.'

Joe's affectionate looks at his stalwart friend, a little more jowly and greyer at the edges but still the same reassuring open-air face, became tinged with anxiety.

'I don't like it, Joe, you can see that.'

Joe saw that Ken was uncomfortable, his face even redder than usual, sweat on his forehead. It was a warm morning, the sky blue enough to make your eyes water. 'We'll walk your fields,' said Ken, taking Joe's arm.

This was more how Joe had imagined it. A blackbird began to sing aggressively as they passed through the hedge and under an old lime tree, whose whiskers sprouted all the way down the trunk. 'It always sang there,' said Joe with satisfaction. 'Birds don't hold with changes.'

Ken, whose mind was set on one subject, nevertheless found himself keen to prevaricate, although not on the subject of birds. He kicked at the rough ground. 'This here is called set-aside,' he said. 'Come in since your time.'

'I did wonder,' agreed Joe, not wishing to be critical.

'You get paid to leave the ground fallow, see.'

Joe wanted to say that it seemed like a crying shame, one of his best bits of grazing gone all to waste, a thistle here as thick as his arm.

'There were orchids by the hedge there,' said Ken. 'A man from this commission thing spotted them. He wasn't half chuffed.'

63

Joe thought that the right place for flowers was in a garden. He muttered, 'I'll be needing the grazing.'

'That's as may be.' Standing in the middle of this unkempt field, which domed slightly like an upturned plate, Ken at last found the courage to say what he had in his mind. Nevertheless Joe's candid blue eyes, open, trusting smile – he was smiling at the scene, sniffing at the air like a happy dog – made his task a good deal harder. He had given his wife a promise. 'You see, Joe, a lot of the village don't know you like I do. A lot of people don't know you at all. They've come since you – you left. All they know is what they've heard. Some of them talked to that probation-officer woman who came round but they hadn't had time to think about it then. Think about what you did, if you know what I mean.'

At this point, Joe started walking away, his hands in his pockets, so that Ken had to follow him, still talking to his back, his hunched shoulders. 'You think this is your home, Joe, where you were born, where your mother lived and her parents before that. But they don't think of that. They're frightened of what you might do.'

Now Joe began to walk so much faster that Ken would have to shout or run to catch him up. Instead he stopped and looked back longingly at his tractor, in the distance, parked by the cottage. But Ken had never shirked his duty. He found Joe standing in the sloping corner of the field, shaded by old and twisted hazels.

'Do you still get deer here?'

'Too many,' said Ken. 'I have to take a gun to them.'

'They're a devil in the young corn.' Joe looked away. But he knew he had to speak. 'You know I'd never hurt anyone. You know that, Ken. You know what happened.'

'That's not the point, Joe.' Ken wondered just how honest to be and decided there was no point in avoiding the truth. 'Let's face it, Joe. I may be your friend. I am your friend. But we're not close, not really close. You're right. I look at you now and I don't think you'd harm anyone. But, then, I looked at you before and I didn't think you'd harm anyone, least of all that nice—' He stopped, seeing Joe's stricken face. 'I was more shocked than anyone just because I thought I did know you. Better than most. But I was wrong. You see what I'm getting at.'

'You don't trust me.'

'Well, it isn't exactly that. But, let's face it, Joe, I have got daughters just the age . . .' This was not what he had intended to say, although it was the nub of the matter, as far as his wife was concerned. As he pronounced these words, the ugliness of the implication struck a shocking contrast to the beauty of the summer's day.

'I'm sorry, Joe, but you have to face the facts. Much better to go where nobody knows you or what you did.'

Joe did not speak, could not have spoken, and when Ken tried to approach him, he moved away. 'You'll come to think I'm right, Joe. You'll thank me. You'll see it's for the best.'

Joe stood where he was and watched his only friend retreat back across the field, which he had turned into a wilderness. He felt the soft breeze on his face and saw the line of the hillside over the other side of the valley. Eventually, tired of standing like a stump, he lay down, pressing the long grass under his body. As he lay he heard Ken's tractor start and retreat down the lane. A little later, he heard it return and immediately sat up, unable to resist peering hopefully over the top of the shimmering grasses.

But it only stopped for a moment and then was off, soon to become unseen and finally unheard.

Joe lay back again and, fearful of the blackness that might descend if he shut his eyes, he watched the blue sky whirl above his head. He lay there so long and so quietly that a group of three deer, young and curious, rose out of the dark hollows beyond the hedge and advanced delicately towards him. Their faces, eyes wide and bright, came into the edge of Joe's vision, so close that he could see the veins in the whites, the long lashes, the sleek noses, the fluff inside their ears. He kept perfectly quiet and let them sniff, their flared nostrils just touching his shirt. As he lay, he thought of Ken taking his big twelve-bore gun to protect his corn and how he had agreed that it was the right thing to do. It *was* the right thing to do but now he could not help imagining the soft enquiring faces being blasted apart and the idea filled him with horror. He must have made a movement, a shrug, even just a frown, for suddenly the deer were yards away bounding so high in the air that, from Joe's position, they looked as if they were flying through the sky.

'I wish you a long life,' said Joe, out loud, and rubbing his eyes, he stood up. The walk back to the cottage was one of the most dismal he had ever taken. Even the blackbird seemed to be mocking him when he passed under the lime tree, and when he reached the cottage he understood why Ken had come back because an envelope and a bottle of whisky waited for him on the doorstep. He must have forgotten to deliver them and then returned, so eager to get away again that he had not even bothered to put them inside.

Joe sat at his table and opened the envelope. Inside,

there was a cheque, no note, just the sum Ken owed him, a great deal of money. Joe pulled open the drawer and took out that other envelope. He read the longish letter inside very slowly, making out the words with difficulty, not only because he could scarcely read but because what they said was so cruel. After he had finished, he went to the kitchen, found a mug and poured himself a large dose of whisky.

Chapter Seven

The aeroplane overtook time and drew a silver arc from sunrise to sunset.

Natasha looked at the portions of Frank's grey bony face that were tube free and thought that he looked dead already. A beat of fear came and went, leaving her shaking, or maybe it was just the effect of her precipitate flight across the Atlantic. She opened her bag and found a small mirror into which she peered; her face was grey, too.

A nurse touched her shoulder; in her hand she held a cup of tea. 'I was passing the machine,' she said.

Such kindness. Natasha tried to smile and began to cry instead. 'I'm just so tired,' she gulped, because she did not want this young woman to believe she loved that old man dying in the high bed. She was his wife in name only. The tears went soon enough but left a dull headache, which the tea could not cure.

'He's doing very well, you know,' said the nurse. 'By tomorrow he'll be in the general ward, touch wood.'

'Thank you,' said Natasha, unconvinced.

'He spoke earlier,' persevered the nurse.

'I'll wait, then, for him to speak again.'

Natasha leaned back in the chair and shut her eyes.

An hour or two later, Walter came in and found her

asleep. Frank's eyes, however, were open. Walter bent over him.

Frank looked in Natasha's direction: his mouth was free of tubes but his voice was low and rasping. 'She's only pretending.'

Embarrassed, Walter patted the claw-like hand, noticing the thickness of the yellow nails. 'I'll pull up a chair.'

Natasha opened her eyes and saw Frank's face blocked by *The Cucumber*'s new editor, peering intently at a copy of his paper. His orange hair glowed in the neon light. She checked her watch and saw it was eleven o'clock.

'You've been very good to Frank.'

Walter spun round guiltily. 'I just sat. I hoped you'd get my message earlier. Anyway, he's making a great recovery.'

'Ah,' said Natasha.

'You don't believe it?'

'She's had enough of me,' rasped a voice from the bed.

Natasha got out of her chair. 'I came all the way from New York.'

'A reproach, you see, a reproach.' Frank winked in a parody of flirtation,

Natasha turned away.

'I've put your piece in centre stage.' Walter bent forward just as Frank's face twitched and his eyes opened wide then closed.

A nurse appeared. 'Oh dear,' she said. 'You mustn't worry. But he needs a bit of attention.'

He always needed attention, demanded attention, thought Natasha, as she was shepherded out to a waiting room. I suppose that was why he became such an entertainer, why I loved him.

'Do you think he's having a relapse?' asked Walter, his voice tight. 'Or is it just to be expected?'

Natasha looked at him with surprise. Surely he shared her expectation of death. But no. His face wore an expression of uncertainty, as if he had allowed hope to dominate and would not easily relinquish it. 'Our daughter died, you know.' It was a hint, a reproof, a challenge.

Walter rubbed his face; she guessed it was a habit of his, a nervous rubbing out of a too-revealing expression. 'I didn't know. That's terrible.'

'Her name was Naomi. She was four. Frank behaved very badly. I've never really forgiven him for it.' Why did she tell him this? A man she did not know. Was it because he'd once tried to be a priest or because she wanted no misunderstandings at Frank's deathbed?

'Would you like me to stay?' Walter looked at his watch.

'Stay!' exclaimed Natasha, realizing that she had absolutely assumed he would stay, although now she saw it was not something to be taken for granted since he was only a working colleague, Frank's very new editor. He had already stayed up one whole night.

'Perhaps I could ring someone for you?'

'I would like you to stay,' said Natasha decisively, although her dark, almost black eyes, staring at him, were pleading. She looked down. 'Please stay.' Walter wiped his hand across his face.

A silence fell, filling the small, ugly room with a strange kind of peace, usually only achieved from the greatest intimacy.

*

Joe stared at the empty whisky bottle – Ken's one and only, over and out, gesture of friendship – and he had drunk it all, every drop, in one fell swoop, at a sitting. It had to be a sitting because he certainly couldn't stand. If it had been a bigger bottle, because this one was really quite small, he'd have drunk it all, which might have killed him. Whisky could do that, or if it didn't kill, it could maim, deform, stunt, crack open the brain. So he'd heard. But with this really quite small bottle inside him – the drinking spread over quite a few hours, a solid deliberate drinking, with no undue haste about it because, after all, he had nowhere to go, no one to see, no pressing engagements, you might say – it had a merely dulling effect. Dull, duller, dullest.

Joe felt his arms and his chest and his head, clasping the top of his head, as if he felt an egg. Dull, his whole body had been dulled. He did not smile but his face lifted a bit with the satisfaction of this achievement.

Darkness had come as he sat at his table, and the bright lights of a car passing up the lane caught the sides of the bottle, making them gleam. Joe pictured the green banks, the shadowy hedges and, down in the middle of the village, that geat sycamore tree that had clapped its branches together like cymbals on the very dark winter night sixteen years ago. The image entered his head and with it a sudden curiosity. Was it still there, standing in the grassy circle, or had someone taken a chain-saw to it? Decided it was dangerous, hacked it down, chopped off the limbs first, one by one, its bushy top, and finally struck at its torso until only a stump remained, a picnic spot, perhaps, a table where children and old ladies like Mrs Wynne in their frocks and lies could unwrap their sandwiches.

With a cry, Joe sprang to his feet, knocked against the

table, fell to the floor and scrambled up again. It was horrible to think that a great old tree like that could be tortured and massacred and used like an old bit of furniture.

Holding the table, the chair, the walls, Joe reached the front door and flung it open. The night air, the mildness, the sweetness of it, caused him to stop there, gasping and swaying. Forgetting his mission in defence of the sycamore, Joe dropped down and sat on his doorstep, the same spot where his mother used to top and tail gooseberries on a summer afternoon. Tears trickled down his face which, now and again, like a blubbering child, he licked into his mouth.

Another car passed up the lane, the headlights bright and close. Joe felt confused: two cars in such a short space of time was too many. Something must be going on. Hoisting himself up again, he crossed his tiny front garden, reached the gate where the smell of the honeysuckle stopped him for a moment, and then stepped into the road where the hard tarmac rose to slap his feet in an unfriendly manner.

But now he had remembered the tree again and set off, with a forward gait, like a man leaning against the wind, down the hill. Very soon, he saw more lights, not from a car but from the houses clustered behind the green. He was distracted and frowned stupidly because he did not want to think of all those people, living behind the lights, who were planning to throw him out of his own home. Mrs Wynne's cottage was the only cottage actually on the green, her neat front garden lit by a carriage lamp.

Stamp, stamp. Deliberately putting down his feet to maximum effect, Joe fixed his heart on the tree and saw, in an instant, that all his fears were unfounded and that its great branches crested in a wave of leaves wider and higher than before, so wide that a man could take his time walking all the way round and never know what was going on on one side while he was on the other. It was more like a grove of trees than a single shoot; it was a massed rank of a tree, a celebration of unstunted growth, of triumph over evil. It was a god among trees, a full-scale wonder!

Carried away with relief and excitement, Joe began bowing and then turning, as a man bows and turns to the moon, and, as he became giddy, walking round the tree, bowing and turning at intervals. What arms! What a stout neck! What a lovely sprouting! So still, too, not a rustle, crack or pop! Round the tree went Joe and round himself as well until the whole experience became too much to contain in an upright position – let the tree be the upright one of the two of them – and he fell backwards on the grass, where he lay spreadeagled, staring up, even more impressed by the splendid survivor above him.

'That's what I do call strong!' he shouted suddenly.

It was most unfortunate chance that brought Mrs Wynne, torch in hand, out from her house and down her neat garden path at exactly that moment. She was shocked, startled and immediately comprehending, although she put her hand to her heart as if she feared a Caliban, or worse. She called to an unseen person at the door, 'Don't come out, Eileen! I'm coming back in! There's something out here!'

Blissfully unaware of the panic he had caused, Joe continued to lie, staring upwards with such concentration into the unfathomable layers of leaves that he did not hear or see a car come from the drive that led to the manor, nor hear it stop and a man approach him cautiouly.

'What! Eh? All right there?' The voice wished to help, an elderly man after an agreeable supper party, with his wife leaning out of the window sleepily. They were not from the village.

The voice came to Joe from a distance, not powerful enough to remove him from his trance. 'All right, are you? No help needed? What . . .'

'He's probably drunk, George,' called the woman in the car.

'Most probably.' He raised his voice. 'Do you need any help? Drive you somewhere?'

'No!' called his wife.

At last Joe rolled over and sat up blinking. 'I was . . . I was . . . looking at the tree.'

The elderly man retreated to look up at the sycamore. 'It's a fine tree and you've a fine night for looking at it. On the other hand, the dew can make the grass very wet, most uncomfortable.'

'George!' protested his wife.

But the elderly man seemed only goaded further into his role of Good Samaritan. He came close to Joe and held out a hand. 'Do you need a pull up?'

'I don't need nothing,' muttered Joe. 'I need to be left to myself. I were doing no harm to no one.'

'I'll be off, then.' The man headed back to his car, with a disappointed look over his shoulder.

Joe lay down again and soon became oblivious to the sounds behind him.

'I told you we needed a new car,' said the woman, as the car motor turned and died, turned and died. 'We'll have to go back to poor Henry and Susan, get them out of bed. Although they may still be washing up – they only have a cleaning lady once a week, you know, despite living in that big house.'

The car motor turned and died, turned and died. Mrs Wynne's door opened a crack, two faces peered, conferred, and the door shut briskly. The faces reappeared at a window.

'Damn and blast!' The car motor clicked in a desultory manner. 'Bugger and damnation!' bellowed the old man.

The curtain of the cottage, which had dropped down, twitched and bounced as if propelled by a special excitement within.

There was a shocked silence as the words echoed in the night. Another sound, distant but approaching fast, came to take its place. The car sped down the hill, a white car with a stripe, lights dazzling. The door of the cottage opened wide.

'It's the police!' cried the wife. 'They'll get us started.'

Behind her, in the dark shadows of the tree, Joe rose and pressed himself against its broad trunk. The police! On licence. Drunk. Drunk. On licence. Perhaps he was invisible. Perhaps he would turn into a tree if he willed it hard enough.

Natasha and Walter sat opposite each other in an all-night café. 'Nothing will happen in your absence,' the nurse had assured them. 'Mr Halliday's condition is stable.'

'Stable!' Natasha took refuge in irony. 'When was Frank ever stable?'

'What were you doing in New York?'

'Seeing old friends. Trying to sell my stained glass.'

'Stained glass?'

'I make it. It's a good hobby for a rich woman.'

'Oh,' said Walter, bewildered first by her sharp tone and then by the self-deprecating smile that accompanied it. He began to eat hungrily.

'I suppose you've seen a lot of stained glass in your time?'

Walter put down his knife and fork. 'You mean in church.' Instinct warned him that this apparently composed stranger was planning to pass the time until her husband recovered (or died) with intrusive questions. Not any old questions, about his editorial point of view, about his politics, his literary tastes, but of the no-holds-barred variety, of the sort that he most dreaded, and most studiously avoided, about his past, his religious ecstasies and agonies. He could see it in her eyes.

'How old were you when you gave up your studies for the priesthood?' Natasha leaned forward persuasively. She needed to know about other people's lives. How other people's lives worked.

'I suppose Frank has talked to you.' Walter loaded his fork with a lump of sausage, a strip of bacon and a semi-glutinous chunk of egg white. 'There's nothing like a lapsed Irish Catholic to pursue the subject. I tried to tell him he should question his own motives not mine.' Walter put the forkful into his mouth.

But Natasha was not to be fobbed off. 'It's a platitude, I guess, but where is the link between a fisher of men, a shepherd of the flock, a representative of belief, virtue – virtue, yes, I mean virtue, goodness, truth, beauty – and a journalist!' Her voice escaped her control, became shrill. Hearing herself, she began to apologize. 'I'm over-wrought.'

'Frank was – is – a pretty terrific journalist.' Surely her passion was inspired by Frank's deficiencies.

'You feel we must only talk of Frank. Perhaps you're right. It is his big night.' She looked down at her untouched food. 'I'm not really so tough. I just want to understand. I'm not tough at all.'

'No.'

'Don't think me such a fool either,' said Natasha. 'I've been brave for so many years. I don't really mean to pry into your personal life. But I am interested. I've never had any spiritual life myself. I just wondered how, having had so much – at least, I presume you had so much – such a support system, a scaffolding you could bear to give it up. To become a journalist, Frank's profession. You're right, I was thinking of Frank. Never mind.'

'Pressure,' muttered Walter. 'Unbearable pressure. Also,' he gathered strength, 'I have not given it up. Furthermore,' he sat up straighter and pushed his plate away, 'Frank's journalism has a big effect on all kinds of things. You mustn't think because he drinks too much and—'

'A good effect?' interrupted Natasha.

'Sometimes good, sometimes bad. That's what journalists, good journalists, are all about. They ask questions, they're free, independent. A journalist who starts with answers isn't a good journalist.'

'Frank started with all kind of views, rigid views.'

'That's his game, his disguise. Frank has no views he couldn't have lost tomorrow. That's his tragedy. Certainly his talent.'

'No views. No standards. No principles. Ready to jump in any direction?'

'Roughly, yes.' There was a pause. 'Journalists can espouse causes,' Walter said eventually. 'Editors direct newspapers.'

'You're describing a job, but I was talking about belief.'

'Priesthood is a job, too,' said Walter, in a sulky voice.

'I see!' Natasha fell back in her chair, with an expression of disappointment.

'If you must know,' cried Walter, face flushed suddenly red, 'I had a complete breakdown on my twenty-seventh birthday!' So she had got it out of him, after all. He was so tired, agitated by Frank's illness. 'I was in hospital for six months, convinced I was possessed by the Devil – perhaps I was but the Devil was rather out of fashion with my superiors at the time – I hardly slept, ate, talked. My spiritual life, as you call it, was very lively, very lively indeed. After the Devil receded, the Angel Gabriel appeared and ordered me to fly to Egypt – fly, as in escape, you understand, on a donkey if possible. After the angel let me drop I had an intimate relationship with the Little Flower, as St Theresa of Lisieux is commonly known by the faithful, although in my case she was more like a cross between Julia Roberts and a paratrooper. She gave me no rest, no rest at all.' Walter stopped abruptly. He hadn't sounded off like this for years. Why did he sound so raw, so enraged? Surely he was supposed to be over that.

'Please go on,' said Natasha, quietly.

'Please go on!' Walter was actually smiling. 'You may be an American but you can't listen to the ranting confessions of a madman and then simply say, "Go on." It just isn't done.' He looked at her. 'Or are you one of those decadent vampire women who thrive on bad blood?'

'I like it when people talk seriously.'

'Oh, my God!'

'If that reaction indicates disagreement – that is, you don't enjoy serious conversations – then maybe that is the reason you became a journalist, since you didn't lose your faith.'

'Maybe,' said Walter wearily. 'I was working on a Catholic weekly until I joined *The Cucumber*.'

'Frank didn't tell me that.'

'He probably didn't guess you would find me so absorbing.'

'Please don't be angry.'

'If you knew how exhausted I am.'

'I'm torturing you. Sleep deprivation. Outlawed by the UN Convention for Human Rights.'

'By the Geneva Conventions, I think. Shall we go?'

'Yes.' Natasha stood. 'Go together.'

They went out into the dark and Natasha, who was not usually a demonstrative person, took Walter's arm as if afraid he might escape.

'You see, now I feel able to think more kindly about Frank.'

'I don't see why interrogating me,' said Walter, walking briskly and well beyond being careful of his companion's feelings, 'should make you feel more sympathetic to your husband.'

'It reminds me that he did his best to hide his frailties.'

'You like that?' asked Walter.

Natasha looked at him suspiciously, but the street lamps were bright enough to see that his face wore no irony. 'Will you come back to the hospital with me?'

Chapter Eight

The stars glittered hard and high above Mrs Wynne's cottage but nobody had time to admire them. Besides, there were her carriage lamp and lights from two cars to bring everyone down to earth. Half a dozen people clustered there, including two large policemen, like father and son so identically broad were their faces, their hips, their shoes. Neither spoke. Nor did the elderly gentleman and his wife, although the former made valiant efforts of the 'If I may' variety.

Eileen, Mrs Wynne's friend, could not even get a preliminary word in because Mrs Wynne was in full spate, 'And then I heard the yellings in such language . . .'

'Would you please repeat the words to us, madam,' interrupted the older policeman politely. 'Slowly, as my colleague's shorthand's a bit rusty in the dark.'

'Ha, ha!' tittered Eileen nervously, before being silenced by a look from her friend.

'He screamed out in this dreadful loud—'

'Just the words, please, ma'am.'

'I absolutely must set the record straight.' At last, the elderly gentleman intervened, but was immediately cut off by his wife.

'Don't get involved in it, George.'

'You'll take my statement in the station I have no doubt.' Mrs Wynne grabbed her chance again. 'Once you've locked him up safely where he belongs.' She gave a meaningful nod in the direction of the police car. They all followed her glance and, for a moment, every eye was fixed on the figure slumped in the back seat. Then the elderly man roused himself again.

'I appreciate you have a special duty to protect the public, particularly when a previous conviction of such seriousness is involved. I myself am chairman of our village Neighbourhood Watch.'

'If we had one here,' interrupted Mrs Wynne excitedly, 'it would never have got as far as this, murderers wandering freely, threatening to kill.'

'It was I whose voice you heard, what,' said the elderly man, tipping his hat to Mrs Wynne in a courteous gesture. 'The young man was drunk, certainly, but he was entirely unthreatening. In fact, he was lying flat out under the tree, so quiet, so still, so very unthreatening that I was worried for his health and stopped our car. It was I who lost my temper and shouted, a most unfortunate habit which does nothing but harm.'

'Thank you, Colonel.' The older policeman stepped forward and the younger clipped shut his notebook. 'But he was drunk, in your view.'

'Drunk. Certainly. But not disorderly.' The Colonel, weaving a little and ignoring his wife who was trying to take his arm, headed off. Passing the police car, he tapped on the window, 'Good luck, old chap!'

'We'll be off, too.' The policemen put on their hats. 'Goodnight to you, ladies.'

'I wouldn't be surprised if the Colonel weren't drunk

too, coming from the manor at this hour and behaving so oddly,' commented Mrs Wynne, as the women watched the two cars departing. 'His wife didn't like his behaviour, you could see that.'

'Women always have more sense,' agreed Eileen.

'And it's women who pay the price.' Mrs Wynne turned to go back to her cottage. 'She had a young daughter, the girl he murdered, think of it. She must be nineteen or twenty now. Imagine what she feels about her mother's murderer on the rampage.'

'On the rampage,' repeated Eileen. 'I think I'll have a hot-water bottle even though it's such a warm night.'

'I was a friend of Joe's mother,' said Mrs Wynne, hand on the gate, 'but, if you take my point, I never knew his father.'

'He's still alive.' Natasha sat down in the ugly little waiting room, which now had another inhabitant, a large woman, perhaps Arab, who had the deaf and dumb look of someone in a foreign country.

'Perhaps you should find a doctor?' suggested Walter.

'You said you had a question for me?'

'Indeed.' Walter's tiredness had been exchanged for the clarity of mind he usually enjoyed in the early hours of the morning. 'Why did you marry Frank?'

'It would have been a miracle if I hadn't married him.'

'And yet you were so different.'

'Don't you want to hear the reasons? He was old,' she began ticking off her fingers, 'he was English, he was witty, he was clever, he was sexy, he was kind – at least, so I thought. How many's that so far?'

'You're counting,' said Walter. Were these the reasons why a rich, young, beautiful woman usually chose a husband?

'He was successful, he'd been married once before, he was incurious – about me that is. I'm up to nine. Do you want more?'

'You haven't mentioned his drinking.'

'I hardly drank myself so that didn't seem very important.'

'And his appearance. Did you like the way he looked?'

'I didn't notice that either. I noticed all the things I told you. I hardly knew whether he was short, tall, dark, fair. I suppose I must have been in love with him.' Natasha laughed, making the deaf and dumb woman jump. 'Sorry. I laugh because it's easier than crying. Isn't that how the saying goes?'

Walter continued to look sober. 'A lot of things can be blamed on love.'

'You know about that, do you?' She peered at him, as if surprised.

'In my case, spiritual love,' said Walter.

'It probably all comes to the same thing. And that didn't work out too well either.'

'But I didn't regret it. Not in my blackest moments.'

'I regret marrying Frank every day. I don't blame myself, I'm quite self-forgiving after years of analysis. But I regret it. Perhaps it would have been different if Naomi had lived.'

'Oh,' said Walter, looking down at his fingers, as if the

freckles were new to him. How could he have a conversation about a child's death? A mother's love. His own mother had died nearly ten years ago. He pictured Mary cradling the corpse of Jesus.

'Naomi was born with a heart defect,' said Natasha, in a matter-of-fact voice. 'They tried to put it right. They failed. A child with a sick heart. A mother heartsick. End of story.'

Having no words, Walter merely looked grave but the silence was broken at once by a loud guttural cry, 'Child! Sick!' A figure of many layers, the alien mother, stood in the middle of the room and began to wail. Natasha went to her, put her arms round her, while Walter hovered uncertainly. It was a welcome diversion. Their conversation had taken them too far too quickly.

A nurse appeared and took away the woman, reduced now to choked sobbing.

'Let's hope that her child lives and Frank dies,' said Natasha, sitting down again.

'Please.' Walter held up his hand in protest, then used it to wipe the distress off his face. 'You don't have to strike a bargain.'

'I don't have to!' She was suddenly fierce. 'But I want to. Why shouldn't I? Frank's been trying to kill himself for years.'

'I just don't think living or dying is like that.' Walter frowned unhappily. Did she want a lecture on the afterlife?

'Oh, really. Oh, *really*.' Her voice was strident. 'What is it like, then? You tell me. Do. Please! I'm waiting. All ears.'

'I can't. I'm sorry. I'm being too serious.'

'It's a serious matter, don't you think?' She was mocking him, perhaps, or mocking herself.

'I've never been close to children. No brothers or sisters, no children myself, no friends to get to know their children. I can't imagine what you felt, what you feel, I don't understand your anger.'

They both became quiet. A few minutes passed. 'I suppose if Frank's not going to die,' said Natasha eventually, 'then there's no point in us sitting here. Maybe I will go and look for a doctor. I don't think Frank's a wicked man, you know.'

'I'll go,' offered Walter, keen for action.

'Just think of me as wounded,' said Natasha. 'If you can bear to think about me at all.'

Joe sat at the table with his big hand resting on the Formica surface, thinking that he might just as well go back to prison and be done with it.

In another room, a police officer talked to a sleepy Julie on the telephone.

'I hoped there'd be no trouble.' Julie sighed.

'The woman who phoned us talked of a letter. A petition. It's a small village. Stuck out on its own. We were only there so quick because we were in the area for another call.'

'But he didn't commit an offence?'

'He was very drunk.'

'So you said.' Julie was becoming exasperated by the heavy deliberation. 'Did he resist arrest for example?'

'No. No. Mumbled something about thinking he was

a tree and got into the car. Hasn't said a word since. We might as well keep him in, though, overnight. Take him back in the morning.'

'That wouldn't help him much. Being seen escorted back by the police, I mean.'

'Depends on how you look at it. Show we've got our eye on him, wouldn't it?'

Julie frowned. 'I couldn't persuade you to get him back tonight?'

'No can do. We'll have him back in the morning.'

Julie heaved her bulk into a more comfortable position in her bed. Joe should never have got drunk. Rule one. She'd warned him a million times. 'Thank you, Officer.' He was putting down the receiver when she added, 'He's not a bad man, you know.'

'That's not what it says on his record.'

Chapter Nine

Light pressed hard on Natasha's eyelids as if trying to force them open and help her escape her dream. She struggled. Frank's flat. Frank's bed, Frank nearly but not quite dead, it was hardly surprising that he had come to her in the night and tried to seduce her just as he had when she was a girl. He had been enticing, charming, bullying, his intensity both alarming and unexpected, wanting her body but wooing her mind. How unfair that he should try to take her again, now, when she had learned to stay free.

There were no curtains in Frank's bedroom – Natasha remembered their battles about that, symbols of cowardice and fear, as he called them. Yet he had been scared of everything.

Natasha was nearly awake now, out of his clutches, mind clearing, body hardening. She fought against him, his fingers, his tongue, as she should have when she first met him. 'Ah!' Natasha sat up with instant recall as the telephone rang. The hospital. 'Yes?' Surely she had dreamed of him, eyes lustful, fingers probing, sex stiff, while he passed out of this world. Certainly he had died. 'Yes?'

But the woman's voice at the other end of the line was not talking about death. It talked of finding her number through a cleaner, of an emergency but not of a hospital

disconcerted to discover that his passenger had a voice and was unwilling to respond. This did not surprise Joe, who had far more experience of questions being unanswered than answered. 'I drank that bottle of whisky last night,' he said, wonderingly. 'No wonder my head aches.'

The policeman glanced in his rear-view mirror. He was so fair and young he hardly needed to shave and he fought against an instinctive fear of the powerful murderer in his car. He must remember to find out whether he had tortured and raped his victim before murdering her. 'You're lucky you're going back.'

'I am going, then?' Joe pressed his face closer to the window that he had not dared wind down, although it was so hot. He allowed himself to see the heavy green trees again, the overhanging hedgerows standing on their steep banks.

'You are – for now,' said the policeman, with the half-formed thought in his mind that it was an odd thing that, just a few days ago, this man had been imprisoned as a danger to society, or to women and children, as he thought of it, and now he was out in the open, as free as anyone else.

'Are you local, like?' asked Joe, almost chatty. When might he ever talk to anyone again? And this gaoler was just a boy, taking him home, moreover. His headache began to lift.

The young policeman frowned. It seemed to him that he shouldn't be asked questions like that by a man like this. 'We're nearly there,' he compromised. There were rights and duties and responsibilities, he thought, in a muddled sort of way, and next time he came near his passenger the man might be in handcuffs. You knew where you were with a man in handcuffs.

Now they had reached the hill above the village and Joe, like an animal sensing home, began to lift his head and shift in his seat. 'I didn't lock up,' he remembered suddenly. 'I can't blame anyone for that. That's what drink does to a man.'

'Perhaps someone locked it for you,' suggested the driver, feeling more kindly now that his mission was nearly complete. 'Your house is the first on the right?'

'That's it! That's it!' Joe leaned forward, eagerly pointing past the policeman's face.

'OK. OK. Mind you don't take my ear off.' It was not quite a joke.

'I beg your pardon.' Joe sat back. But the moment they reached the house he tumbled out energetically.

Joe stood in the lane, the brilliant sunlight shadowed by the mobile of the trees above, and thought that he had survived sixteen years in far worse conditions without friends – he knew all about hatred, spite, jealousy, petty meanness. He should have learned by now to expect nothing better, even from people who used to call themselves friends.

'That's me away,' called the policeman, eyes on the road. If anyone had asked him what Joe looked like he could have answered 'big and dark', but the man's face was a perfect blank: apart from that one quick glance in the rear-view mirror, he had never even looked at his passenger.

Joe walked briskly to his door. For a moment he surveyed the cow-shaped knocker, then he turned the handle and pushed. The door shifted a little, then stopped.

He pushed harder but only managed to move it by an inch or two. Puzzled, he went round to the back door and into the little kitchen. It was the smell that was worst, strange for a farming man to be so disconcerted by the smell of cow manure, but then this was piled high in his living room. Not too long since either, by the steaming look of it. They must have brought it in a wheelbarrow, trailed it through the kitchen – he could see where bits had fallen on the lino – and then dumped it on the carpet in front of his fireplace.

Joe stood in the kitchen and tried to think what to do. Perhaps he should be thankful it wasn't pig or dog shit. Head down so that he could see no spectators – if there were such, mocking his discomfiture – Joe set off towards the old farm buildings, now partly fallen in. He was remembering how his mother had always insisted he leave off his dirty shoes at the door to the cottage.

Natasha had lost her way. When she finally arrived at Joe's village, she parked her car a hundred yards up from his cottage and laid her head back on the seat. She shut her eyes, then opened them again and held up her hands to see if they shook as much as she thought. They did. This wreck of a woman had come to console and stabilize. She smiled wryly.

Natasha knocked on Joe's front door. Once, twice, a third time, and then she went round to the back.

It was about two o'clock, the sky almost perfectly blue. Joe, at the far end of the overgrown patch that once must have been his garden, was a dark silhouette, patting and moulding something with a fork. Natasha walked up towards him, feeling the long grass brushing seed heads against her bare legs and carefully avoiding the thistles and nettles. There are no nettles in America. She remembered when Frank had first introduced her to them, picking up a long plant and drawing it across her arm. It had been to teach her about ordinary human pain, he had told her, she was too cerebral, Stoic, contained. She must learn to scream out. But she had not. She had gazed at her white skin as it tingled with a harsh red rash and tried to understand why Frank, who said he adored her, worshipped her, should want to hurt her. Then she had found no answer except to distrust his love. Now she wondered whether it was because she had come too close to him, become too much part of himself. He always liked hurting himself.

She was soon near enough to Joe to see that he had just made a neat stack of manure. A dense halo of flies circled greedily above it. She stood at some distance. 'Joe!'

He turned round, stiffly on guard, face white, unshaven, eyes fearful. At first he seemed not to recognize her but then his expression lightened slightly. He dug the half-broken fork in the top of the pile and came towards her.

'When it's rotted down a bit, it'll be good for the garden.'

'Just the stuff,' agreed Natasha, although it didn't look at all like the stuff she put on her garden. 'I've come to see how you're getting on. Lord, it's hot.' She started walking back to the house.

Joe dragged behind her and was still several paces away when she reached the door. 'Perhaps you'd like to stretch your legs?' he asked.

'I'm desperate for a glass of water.'

Joe stood still, folded arms expressing resignation to the inevitable, while Natasha pushed opened the door and went inside. He was not surprised when she re-emerged without any water. 'Oh, Joe!' She looked more horror-struck than even he had expected.

'Perhaps we should take that walk,' said Natasha, recovering herself a little. 'Or would you like me to drive you somewhere?'

'I don't smell too nice for a car.'

They turned left, away from the village, walking side by side; it was very still, very hot, no cars on the little lane and the verges overflowing with grasses whitened by the sun.

'Do you know who did it?' asked Natasha, eventually. She stopped by a gate to a field and stared over a partially ripened cornfield.

'There was a letter before. Mrs Wynne brought it.' Joe put his hand in his pocket and pulled out a scrumpled piece of paper which, when Natasha took hold of it, smelt strongly of cow muck. She read it.

'Oh dear.'

'It's the way of the world.'

'Yes. I'm afraid so. They think you might hurt them of their children. Some of them really think so. Where can we sit down?'

'I don't know.' He had cleared the muck from the house and that was that for him.

'I'm no expert in this sort of thing,' said Natasha, nearly as helpless as him. 'Julie's in court today, that's the problem. But if someone shovelled shit through my door I'd call the police. You've served your time, after all, so you've the same rights as any other citizen.' She began to become enthusiastic. 'Just because of what you did all those years ago, you can't sit down and take anything people feel like throwing at you. I mean, do you know any of these signatures on this petition? Who are they?'

'I do know one or two,' said Joe mildly. He turned away in embarrassment from Natasha's unusually flushed and anxious face. Call the police, she'd said. She'd seen him in prison. She should understand.

'Doesn't it make you angry?' cried Natasha.

'The field at the back of my house – my house, my field – we could go there.'

'You don't have to hide.'

'No. But I thought you wanted to sit. You'll have to watch for thistles, though.'

They walked back down the lane and Natasha was angry with herself, who didn't know what to do, with Joe, who was so supine, such a dead weight, and with these names at the end of this neatly typed letter still in her hand, who required Joe to leave his home and only means of livelihood and go to some place where he would be an unrecognizable alien. 'If it were me,' she said, 'I'd go down to the village and confront them.'

'I'm on licence.' Joe ducked his head and walked.

They reached Natasha's car, parked in front of Joe's house. 'Are you content to be a pariah, then? Is that the position?' Natasha looked at herself in the car window and saw, with displeasure, her sweaty, tumbled reflection.

Joe did not answer her question; he probably did not know the word pariah.

'Where is everybody? It's like a ghost village. Where are all these people who feel themselves threatened by you?'

Joe lifted his shoulders in a polite shrug. He pointed. 'It's a nice field. Six and a half acres. I used to have the cows in it. But Ken's just left it. Something called set-aside that I call waste.'

'Ken? There was a Ken on that letter.'

'He used to be my friend. He gave me the whisky.'

'He made you drunk?'

'It was a present.' Joe began to walk in the direction of the field, round the side of the house.

Natasha leaned against her car and wondered if she had the strength to follow him. Almost no sleep for two nights – or was it three? She looked up at the sky, at Joe's determinedly retreating figure, perhaps, to sit in a field for the rest of his life, and she knew that she was avoiding the hospital, the place waiting for her at Frank's bedside. With new energy, she chased after Joe, coming close to his smell, and announced, in a bossy, maternal voice. 'It's really no good putting it off, Joe. We've just got to get a bucket of water and start cleaning up the living room.'

Joe responded at once, turned back and said he was sure he could find what they needed in his sheds.

'There!' exclaimed Natasha. 'That's much better. In fact, it's almost habitable.'

They had been working to clean up Joe's house for two hours or more and, in the process, Natasha had managed to throw out a great many of the furnishings that had so depressed her on her first visit. They lay – a carpet, lino, mats, chairs, a small sofa, a five-year-old calendar, curtains, a cushion – in an insalubrious pile outside the back door.

'I could wash them and dry them in the sun,' said Joe. 'Like I do my shirt.'

'Burn them,' advised Natasha briskly. 'Make a huge bonfire and burn them.'

Joe looked troubled. 'But how do I get more?'

'For now, you've got a table and chair, a bed upstairs.'

Joe seemed to wish to add a remark about curtains, but was too grateful to Natasha to voice what might be construed as a reproach.

'I shall report to Julie first thing tomorrow morning,' continued Natasha and, for the first time in hours, her face dropped as if burdened with an intractable thought. It was Frank again, his need, her duty, but Joe took the blame.

'It's getting late.'

Natasha turned to see the sun, massing out in flaming streamers along the horizon. 'Yes. Yes. The heat's gone out of the air.' She turned back again but spoke absently. 'You'll need to finish the job with bleach and proper cleaning stuff.' She wanted to tell him it was a cruel world, cruel to both of them; perhaps even put her arms round him and say, 'Be sturdy, be brave, look on the bright side.' But when she faced him, she saw her own unhappiness reflected and could manage nothing more than a smile.

Joe followed her to the car, now in shade. He pointed down the hill. 'Carry on down and you'll see a great tree. You can drive round it and be going back the right way again. That's what I did with my tractor. Or sometimes I carried on up the hill. There's a view from the hill—' He stopped, aware that Natasha wasn't listening.

'Well, then.' She got into her car.

Joe stood and watched her go. She must be very

hungry, he thought. They had stopped only for tea and biscuits and now she had that long, long drive back to London, all on her own.

Natasha saw the big tree as a guide-post, without taking in its size and majesty, saw the entrance to the manor, a cottage with its neat garden and other cottages and houses sprinkled along the road beyond. There was a church tower too, beyond the entrance to what looked like a larger house. This, then, was the village, tucked neatly under the hillside, that was determined to reject Joe.

As she circled the sycamore, a woman and a man came towards her, emerging from a track that seemed to curl upwards. They had pleasant, kindly faces, were arm in arm, old enough to be retired but young enough to go for a long walk and come back more cheerful than they left.

Natasha stopped her car. She remembered a name from the letter to Joe. 'I wonder if you know where a Mrs Wynne lives?'

The woman smiled; she wore glasses, which glinted in the evening sun. 'Just behind you. But I think she's been taken off to see her grandchildren today.'

'It was just an off-chance.'

'If we can give her a message—' but Natasha had driven on, round the other side of the tree, back up the hill, past Joe, a dark shadow in his doorway. She drove fast, unthinking. After a mile or two, she pressed in a tape of music.

Chapter Ten

It was dark when Natasha arrived outside the hospital. The streets and pavements around were filled with the noxious weight of a hot day's traffic. Natasha walked very slowly from her car, smoothed her skirt, smoothed her hair, rested, eyes closed for a moment, at the entrance. She opened her eyes again and looked up at the sky, but all she could see was a swaddling of murky gases and orange fumes. She made her way to Frank's bedside.

At about midnight Walter appeared. His hair was untidy, his eyes blinked stupidly.

'Don't you ever sleep?' asked Natasha, who was preparing to leave. She touched his shoulder lightly.

'Three or four hours,' said Walter. 'I used to be an insomniac. I would lie awake all night long. Then I discovered I could sleep three or four hours when I was worn out.'

'It's very nice of you to come back. I'm just leaving. There's no change.'

They walked out together through the greenish hallways.

'I wondered what your emergency was.'

'It's a long story.' They had reached the wide glass door to the street. 'So, are you working now? Or eating?

Or walking? Or are you worn out enough for your three or four hours?'

'I don't know. I'll come with you a bit. It's such a warm night.'

'I'm going to Frank's flat.'

They walked along side by side, the pavement still busy, cafés and restaurants open, and people sitting outside the closed pubs.

'Where do you live?' asked Natasha.

'I have a room, a flat, I suppose.' Walter frowned and was silent. In truth, he lived mostly in the office. 'It's not far from *The Cucumber*.'

'So we're going in the same sort of direction.' They walked in silence until a drunk, lurching out from a wall, caused Walter to cry, 'Look out!' He pulled at Natasha's arm.

The man staggered away.

'Did you think he was going to hurt me?'

'He was out of control.'

Natasha considered. 'Do you remember the man I brought to *The Cucumber*'s party?'

'The murderer.'

'Don't call him that.' She paused. 'I suppose Frank told you about him, described him like that. Well, that's who I was helping today. He's having trouble fitting back into his village. At least, other people, the villagers, are making trouble for him. When I arrived, he'd just finished shovelling muck out of his living room. I helped him clean up. I'm surprised you haven't smelt me.'

Walter stared at the expensive clothes, the perfect haircut.

'I've been visiting him in prison for three years.'

'Who did he kill?' asked Walter.

'A girlfriend. A *crime passionelle*. He found her in bed with her ex-husband. Not that he ever mentioned it. Looking back, I can't think what we talked about. I expect I chattered brightly.'

'He's a handsome man.'

'Very. He's like rock. He hardly speaks. His life would be so much easier if he could speak.'

'Do you think he was always like that? Or is it since the murder and being in prison?'

'I don't know.' Natasha shook her head in a dissatisfied way. 'Here we are.' She stopped abruptly.

They both stared up at the red-brick and stone building. Natasha took out her key and went up to the door.

'Does he frighten you?' asked Walter, following her closely.

'Joe, frighten me?' Natasha continued quickly before she could really examine the question. 'No, no. Of course not. Why should he?' She opened the door with an aggressive turn in the lock.

'He did kill someone,' said Walter mildly, still close.

'Years ago.' They started up the stairs and entered the flat.

'Some people would be frightened,' Walter persisted. 'It's only natural. He's broken the boundaries of normal human behaviour.'

'I don't look at it like that.' Natasha went into the kitchen. 'Something terrible happened to him.'

'To him?'

'And, as a response, he did something terrible.' She searched in the kitchen for food, opened cupboards, the fridge, the bread-bin, while Walter stood watching. Her expression became more irritable, her eyes darker. 'I'm so hungry!' she wailed, like a child. But Walter didn't seem to hear.

'So you can't understand why he's having trouble with the villagers?'

'No. It's shameful. Shameful.' She glanced at Walter and, seeing his assessingly cool expression, added spitefully, 'In a Christian society – a religion based on forgiveness – your religion.'

'Oh, I wasn't speaking for myself.'

'I can quite believe that! Do you ever? That's the point.' She turned away again. 'At least we can have tomato soup.'

Surprised by her anger, Walter watched without offering to help, as she clumsily opened the tin and, banging pans, eventually had it on the stove. 'Sit down, please,' she said, placing soup bowls on the table.

As soon as they were both seated, Walter began again, 'I wasn't talking about forgiveness. I was talking about natural, ordinary human fear. I was wondering if you were frightened of him. It's possible, I should guess, to feel sympathy or forgiveness, if you want to call it that – and still feel fear. Your friend is a big strong man.'

'I'm too tired to think. I'm sorry I shouted.'

'You didn't shout. You were angry but you didn't shout.'

'Didn't I? Anyway, I'm too tired to think. Or eat. I'm apologizing again. Let yourself out, will you?' She left the room so suddenly that Walter merely stared. Slowly, meditatively, he ate first his soup and then hers, even though he thought it had an aged, musty taste. Could she not understand, he wondered, that he was a survivor of too many principles, that he had nearly been submerged by the great weight of belief?

Yet he would not want her to think badly of him. Or of his religion. He could forgive a murderer but he didn't want one as a friend. He was a refugee from religion, that's what he was. Any port in a storm. Walter pushed away both plates and propped his elbows on the table and his head on his hands. Gradually his head sank lower.

Natasha, who had slept for an hour or two and then woken, found him there, eyes closed. 'Why don't men like going to bed?' she said. 'Or is it just journalists?'

Walter, who had been dreaming of a castle surrounded by rose briars, opened his eyes blearily.

'Everything's out of order at the moment, I do believe,' she continued. 'I'm cut off from my home, back in this flat, which I gave to Frank, hoping never to see him again. I guess that's what I hoped.'

Walter looked at his watch. 'God!' He staggered to his feet.

They had parted again. Natasha went back to bed and this time she slept till she was woken by the sun and a bluebottle buzzing around the room. It would be another hot day.

Walter was having a second meeting in his office with Sheena.

'It's not that they don't want to tell their story,' she said, 'but that they want to be paid for it.'

'The tabloids have the money.'

'There's this one man,' continued Sheena, undeterred, 'who is living with his mother in her caravan near Didcot –

mothers always forgive their sons, you know, fathers very seldom. He gave me this piece of advice, as if I needed it.' She smiled cheerfully, 'He said a rapist, murderer, whatever, should never go to a place like Didcot where there's no one like them. "I stick out like a sore thumb," were his exact words. I jotted them down. "What you should do," he confided in me, with a decisive stare, "What you should do is go to the East End of London and join all the other villains. You've got a chance then." Good copy, don't you think?'

Walter, hand wiping across his face, was assailed by a longing to slide the hand inside Sheena's skirt and between her thighs. 'I was being informed about the problems of a murderer settling into a village only yesterday,' he said.

'Didn't I tell you it was the theme of the moment?'

'I thought today's theme was security. Rehabilitation in the community thoroughly out of fashion.' He paused. 'Would you like to come out for lunch?'

Sheena was pleased by this invitation. There were so few unmarried men in her acquaintance, at least men of power and influence, that she enjoyed a delightful sense of virtuousness as they walked past Annabel's disapproval and out into the street.

'There's a French restaurant two streets away,' said Walter diffidently. 'I very seldom go out to lunch but I'm told it's good.'

'I'm honoured.'

Talking energetically of the inadequacies of society, of education, prison and politics, Walter and Sheena did not meet each other's eyes over the chicken. Soon their coffee cups were empty, the bill paid.

'How about a bit of sex?' enquired Sheena.

'No.' Walter gulped. 'Yes.'

'So where shall we go?'

She is a casual seducer, thought Walter. Yet why should she not be? In the heat of his emotions, he tried to recall the meaning of words like 'purity', which had always seemed so important. 'I have a room nearby,' he said. 'But I should let Annabel know.'

'Know what?' Sheena began to laugh.

'Know I'm going to be—' Walter stopped, confused. 'Late' was what he had been going to say. But how late would he be? How long did it take?

'Don't look so miserable,' mocked Sheena, as they both stood.

'I've got a very busy afternoon.' He was backtracking, backsliding or returning to the straight and narrow.

'Of course!' agreed Sheena, tucking her arm in his. 'Which direction?'

The flat, when they arrived, showed all the signs of an uncaring male occupant. Sheena's spirits fell, although she disguised this from Walter by plumping the cushions on an unsprung sofa. Half a biscuit bounced away.

'Good. Good.' Walter looked about wildly, as if this were an area unknown to him. Now and again his eyes veered towards an open door through which an unmade bed was visible. As Sheena turned her back to throw open a window – the room smelt stale with an odour of burnt toast the most respectable component – Walter glanced at his watch.

'Caught you!' cried Sheena, whisking round. She sat on the sofa. 'I do enjoy your company.'

'Thank you.' Walter cheered up enough to come and sit beside her. Her proximity had the effect of reactivating his lust. He laid his hand on her knee.

She felt the hot touch, which soon began to tremble, and was flattered by this proof of her powers of attraction. It even excited her. She thought that he was like a young boy and she the experienced older woman. She took his hand and put it on the flesh at the top of her breasts. 'How does this feel?'

'Nice.' Walter could not overlook the foolishness of his position or the venal quality of this experience and yet he wished to proceed to wherever Sheena might take him. Daringly, he slid three fingertips inside her neckline. As he did so he pictured the Virgin Mary offering her baby the dark rosebud of her nipple. He found himself able to be both shocked by such sacrilegious application of a holy image and even keener to progress further. Was this debauchery?

'Do you want to hold my breast properly?' asked Sheena, with the expression of an air hostess who offers a packet of peanuts.

'Yes,' whispered Walter. He watched as Sheena dextrously unhooked her bra and carefully lifted out each breast over the scoop neck of her T-shirt. They were so perfect, so smoothly rounded.

'Go on, touch!' urged Sheena.

Walter touched. It was not true that he had never made love to a woman, even if he had never lost his virginity. At the age of sixteen he had been much drawn to a handsome girl called Kirsteen; they had shared a liking for difficult puzzles that spread over a whole table-top. They had sat together one wet afternoon, picking up and setting down little pieces; occasionally, their fingers brushed, inducing a prickly sensation in the tips. Walter could still recall his terror as the holes in the puzzle gradually became smaller. When there was only one small ragged gap – a little tear in the ozone, as Kirsteen had called it – desperation had encouraged Walter to beg for a kiss. They had kissed.

'Do you want me to touch you?' asked Sheena.

'I don't know. Yes.'

Reverence thought Walter, he had always felt reverence for a woman's body, but reverence made lust a guilty secret and it was clear that Sheena held no reverence for her own body or for his. Her hands, reaching for him, were friendly, practical, arousing.

'You're standing back from all this, aren't you?' asked Sheena.

'I suppose so. Just a little. I'm sorry.'

'You must learn to let go.'

Walter knew she meant well but found that her certainty made him want to ask why. Perhaps he knew the answer: he must let go to satisfy the needs of his body. But why was that so important? He moved away a little, but the hands followed him, the breasts, the lips.

'I think I've lost you,' said Sheena, not without regret.

'Yes.' Walter tried to look as if he had just been cut off on the telephone.

They rearranged themselves and Sheena went to the bathroom. 'I'll come back to the office with you,' she announced on her return.

This was not Walter's intention and, although he was determined not to be bullied, he wanted to repay her generosity. 'It strikes me,' he said, standing, 'that there might be a story in this murderer my friend knows. It might be worth following up.'

'Instead of my rapists, you mean?'

Chapter Eleven

The sun was hot enough to make the heads of the stinging nettles droop. Julie sat on Joe's one chair, which was placed at the back door of the cottage to catch any breeze. She wiped her perspiring face while Joe hovered. 'I suppose I'll just write to the vicar again and the people in the manor.'

'I never went to church,' said Joe. 'My mother fell out with the vicar – the last vicar but one – when I was a lad.'

'Well, the present incumbent didn't hold that against you.' Julie looked at her watch. 'Maybe I will go down to the manor now. Perhaps,' she glanced up, 'you should come too.'

'Oh, no!' Joe began to wring his hands.

'You've got to get used to the idea that you're a free man, otherwise no one will treat you like one. Come on, Joe, I'll cancel my next appointment, you give yourself a wash and shave.'

Joe allowed himself to be pushed up to the bathroom while Julie got on to her mobile. Soon they were walking down the hill together, Joe with the stiffness of the condemned man, Julie with the confident stride of a woman who is doing right for another.

The manor, a friendly, stone-built house, stood at the end of a short, curving driveway. 'Mrs Hamilton won't like me coming round just like this,' protested Joe.

'You're not a child. You're a man, approaching middle age. You used to help in her garden. She knows you.'

They stood in front of the large oak door and Julie pulled the bell chain. 'Mrs Hamilton likes the side door. It's nearer the kitchen, see.'

'Thank you.' They went to the side door where the more modern bell set off a cacophony of barking.

'Dogs. But I wouldn't know them any more. Likewise, they wouldn't know me.' Joe seemed curiously cheered, or maybe only hopeful that there would be no one at home to receive him.

Julie put up her hand as if to ring the bell again, then hesitated. It was clear that she was losing her nerve. Her T-shirt, voluminously lilac, was beginning to show patches of sweat. 'Christ, it's steamy!'

'We could come back another time.'

'Good afternoon.' Mrs Hamilton came round the side of the house carrying a large basket filled with dry washing. 'I thought I heard someone ringing.' She came closer, identified her visitors and put down the washing. 'Well, Joe, I heard you were back.' Her voice did not express any particular disapproval but neither did it hold any warmth. She did not invite them in.

'You remember I had a little chat with you a year ago,' said Julie.

'That's right.' The sun baked deep into the stone walls on which three or four butterflies flapped their wings lazily. 'I told you I hoped Joe would settle in. I still hope so. I think it's this idea of registering paedophiles that's got people worked up. They think they've got a right to interfere. I'm not saying they're wrong.'

'Joe isn't a paedophile.' said Julie.

'I know. But I suppose it's the same principle.' Mrs Hamilton spoke vaguely into the air before turning to Joe quite kindly. 'Some friends of ours, having dinner here the other night, they tried to help you.' She turned back to Julie. 'I didn't sign that letter, you know. It seemed like a witch-hunt to me.'

'I couldn't agree more.' Julie stared first at her feet, which were swollen, and then longingly at the door and the imagined cool beyond. Still no invitation came. She sighed. 'Perhaps something more positive on Joe's behalf is called for.'

Mrs Hamilton thought, but before she could deliver judgement Joe had stepped closer to the wall, so gently that the butterflies, senses dulled by the heat, did not budge. 'Mother's favourite was Red Admiral but I always went for the Painted Ladies. You used to have a lot of Painted Ladies, on the lavender by the pool.'

Both the women stared at him. 'Well, I'll have a think,' said Mrs Hamilton. 'I'm no longer chairman of the parish council, you know. I wouldn't try too hard, Miss, er. Time is on Joe's side. People will see he isn't an ogre. If he manages to avoid another performance like the other night's.' Mrs Hamilton picked up her basket and it was clear that the interview was at an end.

Joe and Julie walked away. 'Better than I expected,' Julie whispered.

'I used to shell peas with her when I was little. She gave me homemade lemonade, made with real lemons. I never liked it much.'

'There you are.' They began to walk up the hill, taking the side round the sycamore that avoided Mrs Wynne's cottage.

Joe glanced at the tree and then away quickly. It was a foolish secret between him and the tree that, for one evening, they had become united. 'If I do stay, I'll have to have a dog.'

'As long as it's not a Rottweiler.' Julie was snappish because her fingers were swollen now, too, and her whole body ached and she still had to drive back to Bristol and, if possible, fit in a prison visit to another client, the self-styled Razor Edge. She took an unselfish breath. 'What you've got to combine, Joe, is lying low with showing your face. Sounds contradictory, but that's life.'

A terrible restless day and night sleeplessness had taken hold of Natasha. She was trapped in London, reluctant witness to Frank's final suffering. Now, even the hospital admitted he was dying. The doctor who had wanted to save him said, 'You can't stay here twenty-four hours a day, Mrs Halliday. It could be weeks.' At last she thought of ringing up one of his journalist drinking friends, whose number she found in the flat.

'Poor old Frank!' said Derrick, with little sign of distress in his voice. 'Speaking as a man who only eschews the hop to favour the grape and the grape for the potato, I can say that Frank was to moderation what a hare is to a tortoise.'

'Yes,' said Natasha, 'but perhaps you wouldn't mind visiting him in hospital?'

'Conscious, is he?'

'He's alive.'

A visit was arranged and Natasha picked up the telephone again, and, in a strange, impulsive mood, asked to speak to Walter.

Walter, with Annabel at his elbow, the first attempt at a letters page spread in front of him and one of his young journalists waiting for a verdict, was not hearing Natasha's hurried words too clearly.

'Do I want Frank's flat? He's not dead, is he?'

'I'd like you to have it, own it. It would be fitting.'

'Fitting,' repeated Walter, frowning. He pushed the papers on his desk aside, and gave an undirected look of appeal.

'I have to go home for a couple of days. To sleep mainly. There is nothing I can do.'

The peonies had fallen in Natasha's garden, their blood-red petals splayed across the path that ran beside the flowerbed. Natasha gathered up a pile in her hands and smelt their sweetness. She could see the head from which they'd come, the sepals quivering like the filaments of a light without the bulb. She took her cupped handful inside and everywhere she went there were beautiful things to see: the plates on her kitchen dresser shone out as blue and white as sky and clouds; the walls were a yellow as soft as the old wood of the table. She tipped the petals into a glass bowl, and poured water over them so that the red was caught in exploding bubbles.

When she walked through the corridor to the drawing room, she saw a view of the garden, the wood beyond, darkening now as the summer grew heavier and the sun sank behind the trees. It was, as always, perfection, and she placed the bowl on a marble-topped table and sat in her favourite chair.

The sun sank lower. She would have liked to sleep, but instead she began to think, and even Cleopatra, who clawed her way on to her lap, as beautiful in her purring confidence as the flowers and plates, could not stop her thoughts. She thought of her daughter. Of Frank's daughter. With the sun sinking, with Frank sinking, she allowed herself the indulgence, the luxury, the joy of remembering.

Naomi had been her greatest joy, creation, happiness. There could, would, never be a rival, she thought, with a kind of protective jealousy, because no one could arouse such love again. She thought of Naomi's face, her delicate mouth, her neat nose, her blue eyes, her bright hair, cheeks, ears, skin; she thought of her voice, the tones, the lightness, whine, lift, sweet flirtatiousness, whisper, soft, sleep half-broken mutter. She thought of limbs – each soft arm, leg, hand, small foot, finger, fingernail, toenail. She pictured her little girl's plump body, naked, smooth, glistening, sculptural, soapy, still, moving, throwing up her arms, bubbles flying off her fingertips. Her laughter. She pictured her clothed, in different outfits, spring, summer, autumn, winter, dresses, hats and a striped bathing-suit, too big, pulled down round her thighs.

The love she felt, the intimacy, the knowledge, filled her with delight. Drunk on delight, she dared to wallow, knowing it would soon all be the worse, knowing it was worth it. Frank, she thought, at first with superiority, but then, suddenly, with bitterness, an accusation as the dream began to fade, knew none of this. He had loved Naomi but had never known her. His love was all sentiment. We did not share her, Natasha thought, except in production, because Frank could think of nothing but himself. And, as she considered this, she saw again that red sun at the end of the street and herself hurrying, always hurrying, but never arriving in time.

Tears streamed down Natasha's cheeks and the cat stopped purring, dug in her claws briefly and jumped.

The telephone rang.

'Well,' said Julie, while Natasha stared stupidly at the receiver in her hand. 'Well,' said Julie again, 'I am so relieved to catch you in. It's Joe again, I'm afraid. He's part of the way through his second week. Things seemed to have settled after that early trouble . . .' Julie talked.

Natasha stood on shaking legs. 'So things have improved.' Her tears had dried, making her cheeks feel stiff.

'Potentially improved.' A large sigh wheezed through the telephone wires. 'Except now Joe won't go out of the house. Not even into the garden. He's shit-scared!' A shrieking gasp. 'That was not supposed to be a joke.'

'No,' agreed Natasha.

'He just can't take any more but I thought if you found him a nice friendly Labrador. Something the villagers would stop and coo over.'

'I don't know anything about dogs.' Natasha stood up and, looking at her perfect garden through the window, she saw heads of ground elder coming up through the roses.

Joe, unshaven, hardly washed, rather hungry, sat in his kitchen staring out of the window. He was waiting for the light to darken. Sometimes it was midnight before he dared venture out, and even then the moon or stars might shine on his pale face and into his frightened eyes. Skulking among his sheds, creeping along the hedgerows, standing under the lee of a lightly shaking wood, he looked the very image of a murderer.

The night was for sleeping, Natasha told herself, but not necessarily. She thought fleetingly of Walter. At four she finally rose and made herself breakfast. She took it to her studio, wandered round fingering the little pieces of glass, admiring her designs, open on a stand like a Bible in a church, but soon became disheartened at the sight of the cold furnace. There was no time to start it up and, beside, the whole place seemed to belong in the past. She made herself think of her friends in New York, of Felicia and Gino, how shocked they would be by this drifting lassitude. They would explain it as 'denial' of Frank's importance in her life, as an expression of sorrow that she would not or could not admit. Perhaps they were right.

At seven Natasha got into her car and drove towards Joe's village.

Sheena had a young person's easy approach to time and decided that the best chance to talk to this Natasha woman was first thing in the morning and, since she did not answer her telephone nor, it seemed, pick up messages, she decided to drive to the pretty-sounding address Walter had given her: Owl Cottage, Little Trumpington. At the very least, it would be an excuse to leave London on a beautiful morning.

Owl Cottage was not difficult to find and Sheena, bright-eyed and pleased with herself, arrived at the same time as a young woman opened the front door to put outside some dead flowers.

'Good morning!' cried Sheena. 'Walter sent me to talk to you. Sorry to barge in but your telephone's out of order.'

Paula, pretty and fair in sawn-off jeans and flip-flops, smiled at the silly London girl with her tight skirt and makeup – so early in the morning too. 'It's not me you're after – I'm the cleaner. And she's out.'

'Out,' repeated Sheena, not particularly disappointed, doubtless her prey would return. 'I couldn't make myself a coffee, could I? I'm dying of thirst.'

Walter, already in his office, took the call from the hospital and, after crossing himself, bowed his head for a few moments. Then he reached for his address book and carefully dialled Natasha's long country number.

'No, I'm afraid she's out. Just for the morning, we think.'

The voice seemed familiar. With a lowering of spirits caused by confusion and embarrassment, Walter wondered why Sheena should be in Natasha's house and could not avoid recalling that he himself had given her the address. It had been, again it was an unwelcome conclusion, a nearly vindictive act, as if he had felt Natasha deserved punishment for not properly attending to her husband's mortal illness. He was ashamed of himself and, only half absent-mindedly, put down the receiver.

Chapter Twelve

The tangled skeins of Virginia creeper, ivy and honeysuckle bulked over Joe's cottage door. It was shady on this side of the house and cool. Natasha lifted her hand for the third time and tapped the cow knocker loudly. Since there was still no answer but only an insistent bird and a far-off tractor, she went to the back door where there was no answer either. She turned the handle and went in. The room was empty. The bright sunlight filled the scarcely furnished room, cruelly revealed the scuffed floor, the dirty wallpaper, the grimy windows and peeling paintwork.

After a while it struck Natasha that it was strange that Joe should be out since the ostensible reason for her visit was his refusal to leave the cottage. Perhaps Julie was wrong. Natasha made herself a cup of coffee, cleaning the kitchen a little in the process, and sat on the single chair to wait.

An hour passed and Natasha, half asleep, heard a slight movement from upstairs. She was struck immediately by the notion that Joe was in danger, that he had attempted suicide. Death, after all, was in her mind. Springing up from her seat, she thought no more but went briskly up the stairs. There were two doors at the top, one open. Still in her fearful haste, she looked in.

There lay Joe, naked, white, asleep. He lay on his back,

one arm behind his head, his hair black against the uncovered pillow.

Natasha stared. She wondered if she had ever seen a beautiful man's body before. Certainly she had never made love to one because she had always been attracted to the cleverer, more amusing, very charming, terribly interesting. She had been the beautiful one.

Turning abruptly but silently, Natasha tiptoed downstairs. Joe was not dead. Again, she took up a waiting position on the chair.

Joe stumbled downstairs where Natasha sat primly, not looking up even as he entered.

'I thought I heard something.'

'Yes. It's me. I was waiting.'

Joe hitched up his trousers, which was all he wore. 'I'll dress.'

'I've come to help you buy a puppy.'

Joe's face took on the bewildered, stubborn look that most irritated Natasha. 'Buy a puppy,' he repeated, as if the words were meaningless.

'I know you've been wanting a dog for ages so that's why I've come.'

Joe thought a bit more, standing at the door, with his bare white feet planted firmly. 'I wouldn't do that.'

'Why ever not?'

'Buying a dog isn't right. There's always a litter and a little one no one wants.' Apparently forgetting his plan to dress, he came closer, a new earnestness in his face, 'I don't hold with buying dogs. You wouldn't buy a baby, would you?'

'You bought your cows, didn't you?' Natasha fought against the kind of helplessness she often felt when faced with Joe.

'I bred them.'

'But you must have bought some in the beginning. In any event,' Natasha roused herself. 'There's this very nice shop – that is, kennels, about ten miles away and . . .' Her voice died as Joe turned and looked out of the window.

'You could say I bought my canary. With cigarettes. I gave up smoking, see. But I didn't sell it. I left it there. It was happy hanging in the window, that's what I thought.'

'You had a canary in prison? I never knew that.'

'You and me met in the visitors' room, didn't we?'

'But you never told me. You never mentioned it.'

'There's not much to a canary. Dogs are different.'

'Exactly!' Natasha stood and tried to look brisk and unemotional, the way Julie looked. 'You get dressed and we'll be off.'

It was only when Joe had gone upstairs again that she remembered that he was supposed to be suffering from agoraphobia or at least felt unable to leave his house. It was a relief, therefore, when he approached the car with a look almost of anticipation.

'I thought we'd get a Labrador,' she said.

'Those aren't farm dogs. Those are dogs for Mrs Hamilton and her sort.'

'What do you want?' asked Natasha. 'Frankly, I can barely tell one dog from another.'

'We'll see what we'll see.'

It was obvious he knew exactly what he wanted, but Natasha decided to concentrate on finding her way to the kennels instead of enquiring. She half understood that he did not dare display enthusiasm for fear of challenging Fate, which he had plenty of reason for suspecting to be adverse where he was concered. This belief was confirmed when they arrived at the kennels and she stood by him as he watched a litter of puppies rolling across each other in perfect confidence that the world was a happy place.

'I've never seen you smile—' she began, but stopped before he should hear and become self-conscious.

Best of all, they were able to find some new-born sheep-dogs, instead of the despised Labradors. As he cradled the smallest puppy, Joe's face swapped eager sweetness for his usual dull passivity and his hands, which often hung, large and ungainly, at his side, gently stroked the puppy's head.

'I'll name him Charlie after the other,' said Joe.

Charlie was too young to leave his mother that day but, as they drove back, the atmosphere in the car was positively cheerful.

'I told you I didn't want no Labradors. Labradors are always worrying animals. Sheep, cows, chickens, they'll even chase ducks across a pond.'

'Well, then, I'm glad we found you a sheep-dog,' said Natasha contentedly.

This triumphalism lasted till they re-entered the village when Joe suddenly hunched down in his seat. 'There's her!'

Natasha looked and, seeing a little old lady with nearly white hair, exclaimed, 'Mrs Wynne, I suppose. You can't be scared of her.'

'Who said I was scared?'

This vision cast such a gloom over their entrance to the

cottage that Natasha soon made a resolution and, without stopping for tea and toast, and without explanation to Joe, returned to where they had passed the old lady. There she was, now in her front garden, carefully dead-heading a rose-bush. At Natasha'a approach, she looked up, pursed her lips and was about to turn away when Natasha called, 'Good morning, Mrs Wynne.'

Forced to respond, she murmured, 'Good morning,' while making a lively bid to reach her front door.

Natasha quickened her pace. 'I wonder if you'd mind having a word?' A regard for proper manners made Mrs Wynne indecisive and gave Natasha the chance to block her escape. 'It's quite a chore dead-heading at this time of year.'

'Oh, yes.'

Natasha saw she must continue bold without provocation. 'I've just been buying a dog for Joe.'

'A dog!' Now, there was a reaction, however speedily subdued.

'Don't you approve, then?'

'It's none of my business, is it?'

'That's not what I've heard.' Natasha heard herself pronounce these words and wondered at finding herself in confrontation with a nice old lady surrounded by her own summer flowers. 'I'm sorry, Mrs Wynne, to come at you like this but I do need to talk to you about Joe. Perhaps we could sit down somewhere.' She glanced at the house.

'No,' announced Mrs Wynne, her cheeks suddenly pink. 'It's my house. You should be ashamed of yourself. And you an American too!'

This was better, the enemy declaring herself. 'I don't want to upset you . . .'

'It's not what I want, it's what the village wants.' She put her hand on her heart as if in appeal, but her eyes flashed with warlike energy.

Natasha told herself that bunions and wrinkles are no excuse for a vengeful spirit. 'You speak for the village, do you? I understand there's a parish council—'

'And the chairman put his name on!'

'In his official capacity?'

'He put his name on. That's all I know. He's not wanted here. You'll see I'm right. He should never have come back! Buying him dogs!' Now she turned and determinedly headed for her door. Equally determined, Natasha followed and was close when the old lady faced her again and cried out, with a new viciousness, as if proximity to her home gave her confidence, 'It was a woman like you he murdered. An educated woman. And if she didn't behave as she should then she didn't deserve what she got neither. And just the daughter left behind. Not more than four or five years old. Now, imagine if you had a daughter that age!'

As the door shut between them, a blood-red passion filled Natasha, and she felt rather than heard a voice screaming from her mouth. 'How dare you talk like that? What do you know of anything? A mean little shrew like you! What do you know of daughters? Or life? Or death?' Words she had scarcely used before, 'Christianity', 'forgiveness', 'revenge' issued in explosions of accusation and rage, but the door did not reopen. Silent and trembling, Natasha walked back down the neat garden path and out into the road. She realized she was crying and wiped her eyes furiously.

'Can we help?' Beside the great rattling tree, stood the couple Natasha had stopped on their way back from a walk.

'I'm sorry. It's nothing.' To her horror, Natasha found she had begun to cry much harder, unstoppably in fact.

The woman came over and put an arm round her. 'I'll make you a cup of tea.'

In this way, Natasha found herself in the heart of the village, sipping tea in a friendly kitchen. Her hostess brought her own cup to the table. 'It's about Joe Feather, isn't it?'

'Yes,' agreed Natasha. It was too complicated to explain that her anger and tears had come from closer to her heart.

'We're since his time. We feel quite ashamed about that letter, actually. Would it help if we met him?'

'At the moment, he's too unnerved to leave the house unescorted.'

'Mrs Wynne believes she's doing right, so nothing will change her. She cleans the church, arranges the flowers collects for charity and is always ready to help anyone in trouble.'

'Not quite anyone,' interrupted Natasha. 'Did you hear about the cow muck?'

Mrs Fordyce had not heard about the cow muck and professed herself almost unable to believe it. 'Twelve years ago we left South Africa to avoid behaviour like this. I'll tell you what, I'll get him to do some mowing, that will make him visible in a nice domestic setting.'

*

Sheena drove back to London and Natasha drove back to her house in the country where Walter, at last, contacted her.

'Frank died this morning,' he told her. He told her that it had been sudden, without pain, that there had been a friend with him, another journalist. He did not tell her that this journalist had been drunk and banished from the hospital.

Natasha listened carefully. She thought that his voice was the most attractive part of Walter. It was deep, soft, tender. She hardly needed to listen to the words because she had known the message they brought for years. 'Thank you,' she said. 'Of course I must drive to London.'

'There are papers to be signed.'

'I wish I wasn't so tired.' She stared at the curtains, which were drawn against the sun. 'I'll see if there's a train.'

'He doesn't have any other family?' asked Walter.

'Not unless he was keeping them secret.'

Natasha sat in the cool room. She forced herself to picture Frank's raw face, his white bristly hair, which had once been fair. She thought of his wasted body, now wrapped in its last shroud. She waited for emotion: any emotion, rage, despair, pity, nostalgia, love, a very little love would have done. But nothing came, just an immense, overwhelming exhaustion. She closed her eyes. Joe's face appeared and then his naked white body as she had seen it on the bed. She might have been looking down on him at the very moment Frank's spirit left his body. That phrase – 'the spirit leaving the body'. She had tried so hard to imagine Naomi's spirit still in existence. She certainly didn't want her to meet her father in some spiritual region from which she was shut out. Now tears came into Natasha's eyes.

Her sorrow, she thought dazedly, sitting up and rubbing her face, was all reserved for Naomi. She continued to weep listlessly, the tears sliding down her cheeks. All her anger with Frank had come to this. Perhaps it was a kind of mourning. At least she could not hate him any more.

Natasha stood up and began to walk about the dim room. Hardly conscious of her movements, she sometimes bumped into her chair arms, sometimes sat down for a second or two before rising again. Her head buzzed and ached with so much she did not want to think about. Least of all could she face the arrangements for Frank's funeral. A quick visit to the crematorium should do it, she thought, with the spurting energy of spitefulness. But found, in another change of mood, that she had shamed herself. They had loved each other once.

Ducking out from this, she thought of Joe but, in trying to record the success of finding good Mrs Fordyce, she was struck only by the essential hopelessness of the situation. It seemed that his very innocence had caused him to commit his crime and would be the cause of his victimization. He was blind, deaf and dumb, utterly ignorant of himself and of everyone around him. Not innocence, she corrected herself, but ignorance. Could he be blamed for that?

Frank, too, however brilliant, however unlike Joe, had also been ignorant. Why, otherwise, would he have rated Naomi and herself so low in the scheme of his everyday life? He had changed nothing for them, no daily habit, no habit of thought or idea. And yet he had loved Naomi so much that her death had toppled him down deeper and deeper into the bleak consolation of alcohol.

Natasha sat down abruptly. The most terrible thing was to be alone. The most terrible thing was to be without love.

Chapter Thirteen

A great sweep of light came through the glass window behind Frank's desk. Walter had sent Natasha clippings of Frank's obituaries; there were many, all admiring. Even his drinking inspired reminiscences of wit and charm. How could a man have so many obituaries and so few friends? thought Natasha. She sat in his flat at his desk, her silhouette edged in sunlight, and not only was there this sheaf of laudatory press but also a stack of letters. These were addressed to her, although she knew few of the writers, many of whom seemed to know Frank better than she did. Some spoke warmly of his first wife, as if her talents somehow resounded to the second wife's credit.

Out of one envelope a small newspaper clipping fell, which she read before the accompanying letter. 'Village of Fear'. The headline at first confused her. What did Frank have to do with this? She read on:

> A small village in the West Country is living in fear of a convicted murderer who has returned to live on his own in the cottage which once belonged to his mother. It stands only a few hundred yards from the spot on which he brutally strangled a young mother while her young daughter, Amy, looked on. A neigh-

bour who was living there at the time told the *Western Echo*, 'We are all too frightened to go out of our houses.'

After this Natasha was not surprised to see a photograph of Mrs Wynne, holding up her hands as if to ward off approaching danger.

'There are children in this village,' said three-times-granny Mrs Wynne, 'whose mothers dare not let them play in their gardens. A man like that should be kept where someone can keep their eye on him, best of all in prison.' It seems that the police have already had him back in prison once when he was found in the middle of the village green, drunk and yelling obscenities. The feeling in the village is growing daily. As Mrs Wynne put it, 'They should act before something terrible happens, not when it's too late.'

Natasha put down the clipping by an obituary. 'I will not condone morality,' had been one of the sayings with which Frank had wooed her.

Natasha picked up the telephone.

'Yes?' Walter sat at his desk. He was very well brushed and washed and wore his priestly dark suit and tie. He was bidden to lunch with the Home Secretary. He was expectant, confident: he had an agenda of six points he wished to raise and they were ordering themselves constantly in his mind. 'Yes?' he enquired again, brusquely.

'It's Natasha.' She paused.

Walter frowned. 'How can I help you?'

'Oh, it's not that,' said Natasha. 'I was merely wondering

if you still recall that I offered you this apartment. I'm seeing a solicitor today.'

Walter did not recall. Apartments were of no importance to him. Nor possessions. Nor material objects of any sort. That, at least, was something he had brought forward from his past of which he could be proud. 'May I ring you this afternoon?'

Sheena failed to reach Walter altogether but she managed to extract Natasha's London telephone number from Annabel.

'Sheena who?' asked Natasha, who had just finished acknowledging a fifteenth letter of condolence.

Sheena did not think her surname relevant but obliged in the interests of cordial relations. 'We did meet, at *The Cucumber*'s party.'

Natasha conceded that that was possible, and Sheena felt able to introduce the subject of the ex-prisoner.

'Ex-inmate,' corrected Natasha but, at the same time, unburied the clipping from the local newspaper.

Sheena's voice, bright and loud, presented her plans for an article or even a series of articles. 'It's Walter's idea, to be honest. I had something much more racy in mind.'

'All Joe wants is to live his life quietly and privately.'

'I see that.' Sheena's tone was respectful.

Natasha fingered the newspaper. 'We could have a cup of tea and talk.'

At four thirty Natasha, who had taken the trouble to go out and buy a packet of chocolate biscuits, opened the door to Sheena. They stared at each other. Sheena saw a white face, sharply framed by black hair, in which the smile, painted wide and pink, looked as if it belonged somewhere else. Natasha saw a voluptuously bosomed girl in a tight suit.

They sat down together in the kitchen. Between them lay the neatly clipped article from the local newspaper.

'Well,' said Sheena, after giving it the once-over, 'that's blown the gaffe! Walter never told me about that.'

'It's only just happened. I can't believe anyone could be so irresponsible.

'They think they're being responsible.'

There was a pause. Natasha poured Sheena more tea. 'Do you know Walter Harris well?' she asked.

'Oh, yes.' Long hair was shaken round plump shoulders. 'Extremely well.'

Walter was half-way through his allotted lunch-time with the Home Secretary, his private secretary and a press officer. They sat in the dining room of the House of Commons where Walter's agenda must compete with the attentions, always welcomed by his host, of their fellow diners who hardly seemed to sit still for a moment.

Worse than the minister's sharp eyes flicking from one ingratiating caller to another was his determination to speak of Frank Halliday. 'A brilliant mind,' he repeated, more than once. 'If it were possible I would come to his funeral. I read every one of his obituaries. A real character . . . an old-style journalist . . . You don't get them like that any more . . .'

As the clichés rolled out, delivered, however, with a glow of real affection, Walter began to find words in urgent need of pronunciation, words like 'drunk', 'lecherous', 'untrustworthy'. With some difficulty he controlled them, and began once more on his second point. 'Do you have any plans to expand the community-service sentencing for young offenders?'

This time the Home Secretary did not even make an attempt at an answer but handed it at once to his secretary, who began on a long litany of new programmes, every one of which Walter had already read in a briefing note. He began to think that, after all, Frank was the best subject, for at least it gave a personal note to the lunch.

Joe had a caller. It was the Reverend Almeric Cooper, although, since his dog collar was hidden under a polo-neck sweater, Joe did not guess his status or the reason he had come on a visit. This put them at cross purposes.

'May I come in?' asked Almeric Cooper.

Joe stood aside reluctantly. The vicar, who was used to visiting all kinds of homes, often uninvited, could not hide his surprise at the nearly unfurnished state of the front rooms but nevertheless persevered through to the kitchen, where he sat at the table with the air of a man who has little time to spare. 'Now let's see about all this,' he said, taking out the *Western Echo*, unfolding it to a particular place and then laying it flat on the table. He put on reading glasses and, as Joe came near, took them off again. 'I need to know the truth. You'll understand that. Were you really so drunk?'

Joe put a finger on the newspaper. 'What's this?'

The vicar looked at Joe, bewildered for a moment. 'Do you mean you haven't seen it?' He saw that that was indeed so and sat back on his chair. 'If I say it a hundred times, it's communication that's lacking – E. M. Forster's *Only Connect*.' He paused, seeing Joe's face on him.

'What's been written? Is it about me?'

'I'm afraid so, old fellow. Read it for yourself.'

Too ashamed to admit his lack of skill in that direction, Joe started the laborious task.

Mr Cooper looked at his watch. 'The point is,' he interrupted, to both their relief, 'the one thing you need is to keep out of trouble, but you seem to have stirred up a hornets' nest.'

'Yes,' agreed Joe. 'You're not from the police, then?'

'The police!' The priest laughed loudly. 'A policeman of souls, perhaps, but not of bodies. I'm your local vicar. Didn't your probation officer tell you I was coming?'

'No,' said Joe, wondering how this could have happened since he had no telephone.

'I'm on your side. Or let's say on the side of right. You have a right to live here as long as you don't do anything wrong. Getting drunk, no point in denying it, was a step in the wrong direction.'

'Yes.'

'Good. Good. I'll see what I can do with Mrs Wynne. She's the keenest member of my congregation.' He was on his feet. 'Like me to send you some furniture, a rug, curtains? Nothing new, mind you.'

'Thank you,' said Joe, his fate, as always, in the hands of others.

'Well done. There's not much in this. It should blow over. Excellent!' He was gone.

*

It was Amy's best friend's mother who saw the piece in the *Western Echo* and sent it on to her at university. 'They put her name in too, poor girl.'

Amy's friend, who was called Jemima, did not produce such a bombshell without much thought and advice from various sources. She even approached her moral tutor, who had not previously known of Amy's tragic background. The consensus, after two days of deliberation, was that Amy might well discover the reappearance of her mother's murderer for herself and that therefore it was best to prepare her by producing the newspaper. Jemima, who was studying psychology, felt the telling was a challenge to her skills and became intensely excited as the hour neared when she had decided, over tea and toast, to break the news.

Amy, a large, fair girl who seemed to have inherited nothing from her mother, did not wait for the toast. 'What's the matter Jem? I've never seen you in such a state.'

They were walking through a shopping precinct, which Jemima thought inappropriate background for her news but she found herself beyond control. 'Oh, Amy, Amy! It's too dreadful for words!' She burst into tears.

So Amy found herself comforting her friend as the news of Joe's release from prison and his terrorization of a small village gradually emerged. The newspaper was taken out from its concealing plastic bag and they took themselves across to a garden square where Jemima's tears would cause less comment. 'It's the thought of him being so near,' she moaned.

'It's hardly very near,' said Amy, lifting her eyes from the article.

'But he's dangerous!' cried Jemima.

'I wonder if Dad knows,' said Amy. 'I always assumed the prison, the Home Office, whatever it is, would let us know.'

About to wail again, Jemima was struck by Amy's extraordinary calm. She was paler, perhaps, her usually wide blue eyes a little narrower, but her voice was steady; her hands, still holding the clipping, did not tremble. 'There isn't a picture of him, just this old woman.'

'Would you have recognized him if there had been?'

'I don't know. I was very young. And he may have changed a lot.'

Jemima, who had already heard the story of the murder and had a clear picture of Joe as demonically dark, nevertheless longed to pursue this question further. She hesitated, however, aware that her motives might be construed as merely shameful curiosity; on the other hand, she told herself, it was essential that Amy should talk through this crisis and not repress it with all the dire reactions that might follow. 'Doesn't it frighten you,' she asked, 'that he's out and about again? You seem so calm.'

'I don't know,' said Amy, after a pause. 'I don't know what to think. But I can't see why he should want to murder me.'

'Oh!' responded Jemima faintly.

'You see, until that night,' Amy expanded, 'my memory of him is of a friendly man, not speaking much and when he did, with a strong West Country accent. I can remember him holding me very gently. I remember him showing me some calves. I remember his dog not being allowed into our house and lying panting on the doorstep. Of course, I never knew he was my mother's lover. I was much too young. I only found that out a few years ago when I read the reports of the trial. I don't think my dad ever wanted me to know that. He would have been quite happy if I'd believed it was a random act of violence. Anyway, I've told you the story already.'

'Yes,' agreed Jemima, in a hushed voice.

'He must have gone mad.'

'But what if he went mad again?'

'I suppose it would be quite unlikely that the same circumstances would recur.' Amy looked up at the thin trees above her head, through which she could see purplish clouds scudding across the sky. She wondered whether to confide in Jemima that she had sometimes felt that her mother had been at least partly the cause of her own death and then decided against it. Then she thought of her dad, of whom she was very fond, and of her step-mother, whom she called Mum, and her step-brother and step-sister, whom she loved dearly. They were her happy family and it seemed a great pity that they had to know this news at all. She looked down at the newspaper again, and this time studied the photograph.

'I remember that old woman. I used to go to tea in her cottage and she gave me biscuits still warm from the oven. We'd only been there five months when it happened.'

Jemima said nothing. She felt confused, for this meeting had not developed as she had expected. The drama and terror that had caused her excitement and tears seemed to have turned into something different, seemed to have entered an area disconcertingly like real life, where heightened emotion must take second place to more rational judgement. Yet glancing again at the newspaper clipping resting on Amy's lap, and rereading its lurid headline, she thought that there could be nothing more dramatic than this. So perhaps it was something in Amy's nature which refused to admit what was happening: her mother's murderer at large and once again threatening.

'I presume they wouldn't have let him out of prison if he was considered dangerous,' commented Amy, as if reading her thoughts.

'Well . . .' Jemima hesitated. It would not be the act of a friend to remind her of how often one read about ex-prisoners reoffending the moment they were out of prison. 'What are you going to do about it?'

'Do?' Amy considered. She knew what she wished. She wished she hadn't broken up with her boyfriend, who held her in his arms so confidently. 'I suppose I'll ring Dad.'

'Yes,' said Jemima, relieved. 'That sounds sensible.'

'But, on the other hand,' Amy rubbed her nose childishly with a finger, 'I might just do nothing.'

Chapter Fourteen

On the morning of Frank's funeral, Natasha walked very slowly round the outside paths of the Chelsea Physic Garden. She had done the same following Naomi's death but then it had been to strew her daughter's ashes over the lavender, the linden and the vervain. She looked at those plants now, imagining the magic of their medicinal power, their blue-green intensity increased by Naomi's youthful properties.

Helen Fordyce and Susan Hamilton stood watching Joe through Mrs Fordyce's window. They both held a cup of coffee and wore the expressions of mothers at a horse show, hoping but not expecting that their offspring will perform well. 'He turned up early,' said Mrs Fordyce. 'That must be a good sign.'

'He was always a willing worker.'

'Of course, I'm so new to the village.'

'The way Henry sees it, I'm new too.' Mrs Hamilton laughed.

'Men are like that.' Mrs Fordyce joined the laughter. She was thinking that, from Joe's point of view, it was the greatest bit of luck that Susan had dropped by just now for a cup of coffee. She could see for herself how carefully Joe went up and down their little lawn, how seriously he turned the corners, how tenderly he lifted the border plants before mowing under them. This could not be the man supposed to be terrorizing the village. Again, both women stared through the window and were rewarded by the sight of three children's heads passing rapidly behind the wall as they bicycled along the hedge.

'There!' said Mrs Fordyce. 'The Wilkins' children with a friend, cheerfully going about their business.'

'It's always been a happy village for children to grow up in,' said Mrs Hamilton, giving just a whiff of *double entendre*. But, meanwhile, up and down went Joe with his lawn-mower, instilling confidence in all who saw him. The ladies returned to their chairs.

The day was warm, although the blue of the preceding days had been overtaken by a sullen grey. Joe, already in shirt-sleeves, rolled them to his elbows and now and again paused to swat at a crown of flies encircling his head. He had stopped for this reason when a woman's face appeared over the wall. She seemed to be standing on tiptoe, or even jumping a little, for every now and again she fell back an inch or two.

'Can you direct me to Joe Feather's house?' she shouted. Joe stared at her gravely. She was young, darkish-skinned, bright eyes, a sharp-looking girl, he thought, not the sort from hereabouts.

'Well, can you?' She thrust herself up again and called impatiently.

'He's not in,' said Joe, beginning to mow again.

'What?' cried the girl.

'He's gone off!' bellowed Joe.

Sheena dropped back into the lane and, brushing her hands together, started to walk to her car. She was undeterred by the information provided by this large, handsome man because she did not believe him; from what Natasha had told her, Joe would not and could not leave the village, which soon led her to conclude that her informant was the very man she was looking for. Why else should he lie?

Mrs Hamilton was just leaving when Sheena walked briskly up Mrs Fordyce's short driveway. Both women watched her politely but impersonally, as you do someone who is collecting for charity.

'I'm not a Jehovah's Witness!' she cried cheerfully. 'In fact, I'm looking for Joe.'

'Joe!' repeated Mrs Fordyce, looking involuntarily in the direction of her lawn. 'Well, I don't know. What's it about?'

'I'm a journalist, and I'm doing a piece on injustice,' said Sheena.

'Injustice?' murmured Mrs Hamilton. 'I'd better be getting along.'

So Sheena was left with Mrs Fordyce, who asked her in but with an almost severe expression on her face. As soon as they were both inside she produced the local newspaper from a hall table and said, quite forcefully, 'You're not the idiot who wrote this, are you?'

'Oh, no!' Out came Sheena's cheerful laugh again. 'I want to help Joe, not write rubbish.'

'In that case I'll make you a cup of coffee.'

Joe was coming to the end of his morning just as some outsize drops of rain began to fall. Looking up at the sky, he saw that a great deal more were to follow and, after wheeling the mower into a shed, hastily made his way to the kitchen door. Mrs Fordyce had promised to pay him in cash, which was what he needed to buy potatoes and bread from the grocery van. The rain poured down as Joe knocked on the kitchen door.

'Ah, Joe! You certainly finished just in time.'

Water ran off Joe's head and shoulders, plastering his shirt to his chest, turning his black hair to ringlets.

So this is Joe, thought Sheena. God, he's beautiful.

The funeral was over. Natasha had intended Frank's flesh and bones to join those of the anonymous departed, which waited for a general conflagration. But, following her walk in the Physic Garden, she had relented. Now she and Walter sat in Frank's flat; between them the table was laid with smoked salmon, lemon, thin slices of brown bread, a bottle of good white wine. Outside the rain splashed and splattered. They had talked of Frank during the journey back from the crematorium, and Natasha had told Walter, without irony, that now Frank was dead, she felt more able to take pity on him and might even scatter his ashes in the same place as Naomi's. The confidence had made them shy with each other.

'I mean it about this flat,' said Natasha, eventually. 'I want you to have it.'

'I can't do that.'

'Because of its value, you mean? Perhaps you don't know, but I'm far too rich for that to matter.'

Walter wanted to talk about the psychological strings attached, to say she was hardly more than a stranger, but he did not wish to insult her.

'Surely you, as a Christian, allow me the right to pare myself down a bit – in preparation for the needle's eye?'

'You want me to be the object of your charity?'

'There has to be an object. Perhaps by agreeing to become that object, you yourself are performing an act of charity.' Natasha pushed away her plate of untouched food. 'I suppose you're afraid I'll cling to you. I suppose I am clinging to you. But I wouldn't do it if I thought it was a problem for you. You see, as I understand it, nothing affects you very deeply, least of all me. That's why I can give you the flat without it meaning too much. I want to get rid of it quickly because I want to get rid of anything to do with Frank and I like the idea of you benefiting from it. Isn't that enough?'

Walter felt the wine slowing his thoughts. He wanted to say something about not liking the idea of being part of her plan to reduce Frank to nothing. Was this what she called taking pity? But instead he asked, 'But what about me? About gratitude?'

'Gratitude? I don't want gratitude.'

'But what if I want to give it?'

'You can, I suppose. But you don't need to.'

'You look at it entirely from your point of view. Try to put yourself in my position.'

'I can't. I'm too tired. Why do you make giving so difficult?'

Walter saw that the wine was affecting her, too. Her voice was child-like and petulant. She put her head in her hands, and when she next spoke, Walter could not make out the words. Perhaps she was crying. On the whole he rather hoped so. He looked, surreptitiously, at his watch. It was time he went. His comment page was still only roughed out. 'Do you mind if I make a call?'

'Be my guest.' Natasha did not remove her head from her hands.

Walter went towards the table where Frank used to sit at his typewriter, and pulled out his mobile. Natasha, lifting her head, eyes glassy, watched him galvanize into decision-making. He made two or three calls, walking up and down now, his voice brisk and confident. When he came to her, she was ready with a calm smile. 'Thank you so much for everything you have done to make this day and the days before easier. I don't know how I should have coped without you. I should have said before, that is the reason for giving you the flat, a thank-you. Quite simple, really.'

To Walter, whose mind was on the news that the Prince of Wales wished to write a piece for *The Cucumber*, this did seem simple. She wanted to thank him in a rich person's way. He would think about it later.

Sheena was one of the many callers during Walter's unprecedented three-hour absence from the office. Naturally, Annabel gave her short shrift. 'Mr Harris is unavailable for the rest of the day.'

'Thanks for nothing.'

Sheena, who was sitting in Joe's small sitting room, clamped shut her mobile telephone. Joe, hovering on the other side of the road, started, and then bent down to the fireplace. He had made a fire in the grate; as the rain continued to pour down, it was a sign of hospitality with which he had surprised himself. His mother has always liked a fire, even in the summer, not that this miserable flicker of sticks could give much comfort.

'Cow,' added Sheena. She looked at Joe. His extreme, almost melodramatic, good looks still disconcerted her. She was used to feeling sexual passion aroused by a handsome face, by a well-made body, but how could you feel attracted by a murderer? It was disconcerting, too, that he was so silent and that he stood so far above her, not just because of his height but because there was only one chair. She had never conducted an interview under such circumstances. In fact, if she had been honest with herself, she must have admitted that she had never held any communication with a man of any age or description without an undertow of flirtation encouraged by her. Only its absence was remarkable.

'Fuck.'

Joe looked at her quickly and then away. Her air of foreignness, more pronounced in the dim light, and her very short skirt made him especially nervous. His mother's ghost seemed to enter the little room and warn him against girls who were no better than they should be. His hands began to sweat and his face reddened. He wished he hadn't lit the fire and gave it a kick with his sodden trainer.

Holding her pad with one hand, Sheena scrabbled in her handbag. 'Let's hope this one works.' She produced another pen. She wrote at the top of the page. 'Ready now. Name?'

Joe told himself he was not in prison and didn't have to answer. It was that Mrs Fordyce who had got him into this. He jangled her coins in his pocket. 'You said you weren't going to use my name.'

'This is for my information only.'

'You know my name.'

'Fine.' Sheena crossed her legs. 'Date of birth?'

144

Joe could see no harm in telling her this.

'And when did your offence take place?'

'My offence?' Joe considered. 'The night the clocks went back. That was the start of it.'

'I see. In the autumn, then, of which year?'

'The year after my mother passed on.'

Sheena wondered if this method of answering was a deliberate effort to be obstructive or merely a peasant's approach to information. She decided on the latter, and also that it was rather fascinating. 'It took place here in the village, I understand.'

'I'm not telling about that. You said up at Mrs Fordyce's it was the coming out of prison you wanted me to tell about.'

This was a long sentence. Sheena gave him a business-like smile. 'Right. Sorry. Just background.'

Joe decided he did not like this word background and walked over to the window. It was still curtained from the outside with a mixture of creepers. He'd definitely have them off tomorrow, he thought, no problem.

'How long have you been out?'

'Ten days,' replied Joe, almost absent-mindedly.

'And what help have you been given by the social services?'

'I don't want no help.'

'Money?'

'I'm not talking about money to you.'

'I bet Mrs Halliday gave you money.' Sheena leaned forward. 'She's loaded.'

'I don't want no money from her. I can look after myself.'

'I see. What is your means of livelihood?'

145

'I'm a farmer!' His voice was defiant, for the first time, animated.

'A farmer.' Sheena wrote down the word with extreme care and then gazed at it assessingly.

'That's what I am – if they'd let me be.' Joe reverted to his expression of dull hostility.

'And how much land do you have?'

'That's not for you to ask nor for me to answer.'

It seemed that Joe was affronted. 'I'm sorry,' said Sheena, looking down rather despairingly at her notebook.

'Before, I had twenty-seven cows, sometimes even thirty,' Joe relented slightly. 'But Ken had them off me and he's not told me anything. I'm a dairy farmer who hasn't any cows, although I've got the quota and that's what counts.'

'Good,' said Sheena, writing quickly. 'So you'd like help with getting your cows back?'

'Not likely. I did it all before and I'll do it all again. If they let me.'

'They?'

'Them – them that want me away. Or back inside.'

This was more like it. Sheena scribbled furiously. 'But how can they stop you? You've served your sentence. You're free.'

'I'm on licence.' Now Joe took a couple of steps towards her. 'I'm on a lead. Like a dog. They can pull me in any time they like. I'll never be free.'

'So you're free and not free,' said Sheena, head down, so that she missed the first proper look Joe had given her.

'That's right. Free and not free. How can a man live that way? Well, I've just got to.' This remark seemed to be addressed to himself and started a new train of thought.

'That's enough now, I should say. I've got things to do more than talking. The rain's gone over. You'll be all right to go now.' He came up close and stood over the chair.

Sheena felt his animal presence, smelt his sweat, and crossed her legs more tightly as she stowed away her notebook in her bag. A man like this, she thought, could kill easily, hardly know he was doing it, kill almost without meaning to. Perhaps that was how he had done it before and, if he had done it once, perhaps he could do it again, whatever that Natasha Halliday said. She wished, momentarily, before quelling the thought, that she was not trying to write a piece with a high moral tone but something downmarket and swashbuckling on the lines that girl had invented for the local rag. Now that she had actually met him, she could sell the story for a mint. 'My Afternoon With a Murderer: He was towering over me, a strange glint in his eye . . .' Yes. That would be very easy to write.

Joe escorted Sheena to the front door, unlocked the door carefully, shook her hand and then turned inside in instant dismissal. Wherever had he put that cheque left for him by Ken? He hurried to the cupboard where he kept his meagre ration of food, to the drawer in the table – there were few enough places to look. For a few moments he worried he had used it to light the fire but at last he was triumphant. On a shelf in the bathroom! That was a lot of money, that was, his dues earned by the sweat of his brow, and no one could take it from him.

Chapter Fifteen

Raindrops began to crackle on the car roof. Natasha lifted her shaking hands off the steering-wheel. She sat, where she'd landed up, facing the wrong way on the road, headlights beaming into sinuous tree-trunks. She had just missed running into the back of a parked lorry and, ramming on her brakes, set the car spinning. Apart from the truck, the road had been, and still was, totally deserted.

'I am lucky not to be dead,' said Natasha to herself, and then, in that shocked second, began to wonder. Why, after all, was she so very lucky? What bound her to the world? Not family, not friends. Her work, then? She was proud of her work but it was not as if she had the reward of knowing she earned her living.

The rain was bouncing on the road in front of her. Finding her hands more in control, Natasha turned the car till it was facing the right way. It brought her close behind the lorry that had nearly been the cause of her death and, for the first time, she wondered why it was parked at one in the morning where there was no sign of a house, a garage or even a lay-by. Perhaps it had broken down or perhaps on this wide straight stretch the driver had felt an overwhelming need for sleep. That, she decided, was the most likely explanation because, otherwise, surely he would have stepped out of his cabin by now and climbed to see who had approached him, lights blazing, and then slewed round with a squeal of brakes. He might have felt guilty as the cause of it all. Or he might have thought, here was someone who could help him in his predicament, although it would be surprising if he did not carry a mobile telephone. Searching for what she knew of the habits of lorry drivers, Natasha found she could recall only stories of rape and murder, acts of violence committed against single, unprotected women who had broken down.

But she had not broken down. She could drive away at any time and would do so the moment her head stopped spinning and her legs no longer felt like jelly. But what if an innocent-looking man, no black beard or ape-like jaw, came towards her in the beam of her car lights and asked for help, perhaps begged for a lift. What would she do then? Would she assume him an honest man or a murderer? How could she be, at the same time, both icy calm and completely hysterical? The rain was trickling down her windscreen, distorting her view.

To her own surprise, she found that this image of the murdering lorry driver was scaring enough to make her scalp prickle, which suggested, surely, that she did not want to die. An example of human programming, instinctive and therefore meaningless, or something more? She should question Walter on the subject.

She put her hand on the gear lever and made the connection: Joe. On just such a dark night as this, he had left his home and murdered a young woman, younger than her but not, perhaps, very different. This was the nightmare she tried to deny.

'Are you all right, Miss?'

The voice, with a narrow, stubbled face, was close up to her window. He had approached from the dark rain beside her, not, as she imagined, in the beams of the car. Her mouth opened but she managed to suppress the scream.

'I know about murderers,' she told herself, as the thin face stared. I have personal experience. They do not murder without reason or very, very seldom. The newspapers only report the random horror and very seldom the intimate nature of murder. Eighty-five per cent of murders take place between family members or people who are very well known to each other.

'I was out of my cab when I saw your lights. I must have forgotten to put on my hazards.'

'I'm all right.' She forced out the words and then, her body acting without her will, she put the car in gear, pressed her foot on the accelerator and sped off down the road. Her final image was of a man's bewildered face, mouth and eyes agape.

Driving at sixty miles an hour, round the tightest corners, in the darkest night, Natasha fled from the danger of death, despite being convinced, first, that there was no danger and, second, that she had no reason to live.

After about half an hour, when she was not more than ten miles or so from her home, she slowed down again and tried to calm herself. She admitted that Frank's death had caused her such despair because it had severed her last link with Naomi. She had needed him even in their alienation.

Pulling over to the side of the road, Natasha gave way to a paroxysm of weeping. At this secret hour of the night, it had the unreality of a dream that could be discounted in the morning. Tears running down her face, she became aware of lights and noise and, suddenly, there was the same lorry rolling past her and screeching and hissing to a stop just in front of her.

'Oh, my God! Oh, my God!' Muttering aloud, rubbing her fists into her wet and swollen eyes, Natasha rammed the car into gear and sped past the lorry just as its driver jumped down from the cab. Now she was certain he was a murderer. Death, of all sorts, seemed very close to her as she covered the remainder of the distance to her house. Abandoning the car, she unlocked the door with shaking hands, entered, drew the curtains, switched on the light and ran to the telephone.

'Felicia! Oh, Felicia. You're in. You're not out!'

'Who is it? Natasha. What's the matter? Of course I'm not out. I told you I had this massive work panic. Oh, today. The funeral.'

'It's all death. All. All! Death. Murder!'

'Where are you?'

'At home. I'm being followed. A lorry driver . . . I—'

'But where *are* you?'

'I told you. At home. This truck.'

'And are the doors locked?'

'Of course the doors are locked.'

'So no one can get in?'

'Of course no one can get in. You know how careful I've always been about security.'

Natasha's panic began to be diluted by childish irritation. Could not Felicia see that she was out of control, needed warm comforting not an interrogation?

'I just wanted to establish you were safe,' continued Felicia, as if she'd read Natasha's thought, 'before I rushed to call Interpol. Now sit down.'

151

'How do you know I'm standing?'

'I can *hear* you're standing. Look, Natasha, we all have a murderer outside our front door who desires to catch us. The secret is to have the door bolted so he can't get in.'

'You're talking about New York. Not the English countryside.' But she sat down all the same and subdued her panic enough to take a deep breath.

'This is the day of your husband's funeral. You had to have some reaction, even a control freak like you.'

'I did not imagine the lorry driver and I don't need insulting.' With gratitude, Natasha heard her voice sounding more weak than hysterical.

'Well, would he have caught up with you by now?'

'I guess so. He wouldn't have known when I turned off anyway.'

Natasha began to admit to herself that her terror of a 'murderer' was about everything but the scrawny and surprised lorry driver.

'So how was the funeral?'

'I don't know. I can't remember. Horrible. Lots of journalists. Frank's admirers, I suppose. Two cousins. It passed.'

'What have you been doing since?'

'I gave lunch to Frank's editor, then I . . .' Natasha's voice faded away. Outside her window a few night birds sang a mocking chorus before falling silent again. Then she had gone back to the Physic Garden and let her tears fall in an unseen corner over insignificant plants and herbs so that even she did not have to decide for whom she cried.

'Tell me to be brave, Felicia.'

'Be brave, Natasha.'

'You didn't add it.'

'What didn't I add?'

'But not too brave.'

'But not too brave, Natasha.' Now they both smiled.

Sheena woke suddenly and sat up in bed. She was usually a heavy sleeper, despite sharing a flat with four other people, two of whom returned at intervals during the night. She assumed that she had heard one of them and called out, 'Tod!' No one answered. She listened to the absolute silence. Even the busy main road was quiet, apart from the very occasional vehicle. That must make it between four and five in the morning.

Sheena went to the bathroom and looked dizzily at the orange swirls on the shower curtain. Why had she woken? Something on her mind. Joe on her mind. She kept writing in her head the big-selling piece. In her mind, the price rose higher and higher, her name splashed inch-big across the top, job offers, staff job offers, the end of this frightening freelance round, never knowing whether she would be able to pay the rent of this crummy flat or crawl home to Mum. And, as her mum pointed out, she was lucky to have a mum to crawl home to. Worse than that, and something Sheena hated to admit, was her habit of sleeping with men she thought might be of use to her. If only she had a nice steady boyfriend, but whenever she met a hopeful applicant the thought of settling down depressed her more than anything else.

Sheena walked speedily back to her room, saw the light was beginning to come through the thin curtains and picked up the telephone. What was the point of having friends on the night desk if you couldn't consult them when everyone else was asleep?

'Oh, Sheena.' The young man's voice was hardly enthusiastic. 'I didn't know you had a night job.'

'I haven't. I've got something on my mind.'

'Something more than the usual, you mean?'

Sheena managed to mimic an appreciative snort before continuing. 'It might be quite a story. There's this man who murdered his girlfriend.'

'Sounds like a good start.'

'Anyway, now he's out of prison and he's absolutely off the wall.'

'Dangerous?'

'If you've done it once and you are round the twist, I guess the odds are for it.' An image of Joe's face in the rain came to Sheena. 'He's like a cross between Daniel Day-Lewis and Ralph Fiennes.' There was a pause.

'That's all there is to it, then, is it?'

Sheena hesitated. 'He kind of made a pass at me. Scary.'

'You'd have to get back in there. Get something seriously threatening.'

'Set him up, you mean?' Sheena sounded shocked.

'You'd be saving all the others.'

'All the others,' repeated Sheena.

'The ones that won't get murdered because you got there first and blew the whistle.' The voice was beginning to sound impatient. 'Look, I'm only a night-desk editor. You asked me. I told you. It doesn't sound to me as if you've got the bottle. Why should you? Stick with social gossip, it's safer. Now, I'm busy.' He put down the phone.

Sheena sat in the bed and pulled the covers to her chin. She shivered. She had been frightened by Joe, there was no doubt about it. A girl had to go where the story was. If only she hadn't been such a fool as to try the other approach on *The Cucumber*'s weirdo editor. The more she thought about their couple of hours together, his sexual hang-ups – Jesus, what hang-ups! – the odder he seemed. Now if anyone had told her *he* was a murderer she wouldn't have been at all surprised. But she could have managed him, whereas this Joe, well, there was something unmanageable about him, Sheena thought, becoming quite excited at the idea. Something alien, that was it. And that had to make him a danger to society, a big man like that.

Giving up any idea of sleep, Sheena lay under her not-very-clean duvet and listened to the increasing volume of traffic outside her window. Lorries, buses, vans, cars, motorcycles, police cars, ambulances. She heard them all individually and soon the hard light filled her little room.

The milkman came soon after dawn. Joe liked to hear him come, the rattle and then the clink on the doorstep. He padded downstairs to bring in his bottles to the kitchen.

'Birds of a feather, eh!' Joe stared in surprise at the pink face in the uncurtained window. The Reverend Almeric Cooper believed in starting God's work as early as possible because, as he was fond of announcing, 'Man's work is sure to get done, whatever the time of day.'

By the time Joe had realized who his visitor was, the vicar was inside with a black sack in either hand and a chair on his head. 'No helpers today,' he puffed, 'so I thought you'd better have the stuff first thing. There's more in the car.'

Joe went to the road, where the trees cut off the first streaks of sun through mauve and pink clouds. He took out a television, a table, a rolled-up carpet, bundled curtains.

'Glad to get rid of some of this junk!' said Almeric heartily. 'I'll just dump them for you to arrange, although I wouldn't mind a cup of tea before I'm off.'

Joe, who had hardly spoken, made the tea with the fresh milk and, for the first time since the morning of his arrival, sat across the table without fear. 'It's very good of you.'

'Quite. Getting on all right, are you? After that bit of difficulty. I've had a word with Mrs Wynne, as promised. A very active mind and not enough to fill it with, that's her trouble. Lack of occupation – that's the trouble with half our population today.' His eyes, which had been directed nowhere in particular, flicked towards Joe. 'You're getting on in that department, are you? Farmyard. Buildings. Garden. Plenty to do for an able-bodied chap like you?' The sentence ended with a definite question mark.

'I mowed that Mrs Fordyce's lawn,' said Joe defensively.

'Very good. Well done.' The priest began to walk to the front door, peered through the window, from the inside this time. 'I'd take off some of that Virginia creeper, if I were you. Gives the wrong impression, hanging all over the window like that. As if you had something to hide. Got some shears, have you?'

Not waiting to listen to Joe's half-hearted murmur about the shed, he was off to the car, casting over his shoulder a last bracing cry, 'I'll be back to see you've done it and sorted yourself out. Jolly good.'

Later that day, Julie, as usual in a hurry, drove fast into the village and was thrilled to find Joe up a ladder at the front of his house. 'Well, Joe, good afternoon!' she eased her bulk out of her too-small car.

'It needed a cut,' he replied, coming down to greet her with the embarrassed air of a well-behaved child.

'And just look at this.' Julie came inside.

'The vicar brought some stuff. The telly's a bit dodgy, the picture anyway, but the sound's OK.'

'You probably need an aerial.' Julie sat down with relief. 'Now, there's things to sort out. I've got your money, your cards.'

'As Julie talked, Joe's mind wandered, for once in pleasant regions. It had been exciting plunging around in the sheds, finding things he'd forgotten existed. He'd always liked things, as he put it to himself, spades, buckets, wooden posts, rolls of barbed wire, hammers. They stayed where you put them, no nasty surprises, no bad feelings. You could rely on things. Tomorrow he'd start cleaning them in a more organized way, pull them all out in the yard, see what he'd got, and in a few days' time he might even tackle that old tractor and the harrow and the rollers.

'Now, I've talked to Ken,' continued Julie, 'and he says he gave you what he owed you and that the fields are yours whenever you say the word.' This was an extremely edited version of her real conversation with Ken, who had made it clear that, in his view, Joe should take the money and disappear into some metropolitan vacuum.

Julie saw that Ken's name had banished Joe's cheerful expression. 'He did give you the money he owed? Is that right? Because you'd better show me or we'll end up in trouble with the DSS. Ken seemed to suggest you were a rich man.'

'It belongs to the farm, not me.' Joe spoke with the air of a man who has had the last word.

Chapter Sixteen

Each summer day Natasha spent in her garden. She bent, she bowed, she knelt, she plunged her hands in dark damp soil at the back of the beds, raked her fork through dry crumbly earth at the front. She buried her face in the soft sweetness of overblown roses before snipping them off neatly so that their heads rolled into her basket leaving behind the admirably tight furls of new buds. She wrenched the ground elder up by its roots, cut back her hedge of rosemary, tied up the delicate tendrils of late-flowering clematis, which seemed to grow under her fingers.

'That's right,' approved Paula. 'Get your hands dirty, make your back ache, that'll do you all the good in the world.'

In the evenings, not so extended now as the sun dropped earlier and the dew spread along the grass, Natasha went into her workroom. She drew only, designs inspired by what she saw about her. A cobweb slung between two stalks, a grasshopper pretending it wasn't there, a leaf bowling along in the wind, an eyebrow-shaped moon one evening when she had worked late. These things were her friends, she told herself, better than friends.

She felt herself remote, caught in a fragile bubble that might break if she ventured too far. Late at night she rang

Felicia, who asked whether she was mourning as she should and advised her to read Freud on how to survive the death of someone you were very angry with. As Natasha didn't contradict her, she continued, 'It isn't, as it turns out, so different from the death of someone you love because in both cases you hold on to your feelings till they make you crazy.'

'I don't feel crazy,' said Natasha, after consideration deciding not to confide in Felicia her notions about the friends in the garden. 'I feel quite calm and, even, in a melancholy sort of way, happy.'

'That sounds like clinical depression to me,' said Felicia.

Finding the girl who had written the article about Joe was no problem for Sheena. She plucked her from the local paper's office and, as they sat together in a coffee bar, she soon had all the information. This included the surname of the murdered woman's daughter and the university where she was studying.

'I thought I'd leave her out of it. But some sub put her name in. Bad enough having your mother murdered.'

'It certainly is,' agreed Sheena, while inwardly rehearsing the argument that this Amy had a right to be informed of Joe's reappearance and the exact state of play. Vaguely, she recalled a 'victim's charter', or something similar, which probably made it her duty to visit Southampton as soon as possible.

Amy was playing tennis with a steady kind of strength that made up for its lack of elegance. She wore baggy flowered shorts and her sturdy legs were flushed from the exercise. Her opponent was a dark, stringy boy, who was not a boyfriend and who played tennis as if it were squash, dashing about and slamming the ball with all his might. Now and again they stopped and went to drink from a bottle of water because it was another hot day.

Sheena, who had spent several hours tracking Amy down, hovered about in the thin shade of a birch tree. She felt conspicuous in this university area, confused, irritable, jealous, patronizing and not in control. There had been no chance for her to go to university. Besides that, Amy did not look good casting for the role of victim that had been assigned to her. The boy, too, whom Sheena assumed to be a boyfriend, was quite fierce and hawk-eyed. Remembering Joe's passivity, Sheena, with half-formulated anxiety, felt that Amy was, let's say, not defenceless.

The sun began to lower; Amy took up the bottle; they had finished their game and began to walk away. Sheena, who had been sitting on the grass, short shapely legs uncovered to the warmth, rose abruptly and hurried after them. Her level of determination had been eroded.

Amy said goodbye to her friend. 'Let's have a return match soon.'

Sheena, tripping along behind, saw her chance. 'Amy!'

Amy turned, smiling. The smile remained, even when she saw an unknown face. Sheena, on the other hand, looked in need of help. 'I wonder if we could have a talk.'

Amy swung her bottle as she turned her wrist to look at her watch. 'What's it about?'

'Your mother.' Sheena blushed with the lack of finesse.

'My mother? What about my mother?'

Sheena understood that there was a misunderstanding

and felt herself blushing more. 'Your mother who died.' Seeing the shocked surprise on Amy's face, she added, 'Please.'

But Amy seemed to have recovered herself. She assessed Sheena from an extra six inches of height, plus the healthy after-glow of a game of tennis, a better education and a better accent. 'You're a journalist, aren't you?'

'Sure. I'm writing a story for *The Cucumber*.'

'*The Cucumber*,' Amy repeated, apparently impressed. 'We get that in the JCR.'

'It's a serious piece about penal reform.'

Amy began to walk, not angrily but with the look of someone who found walking easier than standing still and expected other people, if they were really keen, to keep up with her. 'I'm afraid I'm not interested. I mean, I don't want to talk to you about her. It's all a very long time ago.'

'Yes, indeed.' Sheena bustled. They were on a pedestrian precinct now, and the shops were shutting, glass doors bolting on books and shoes and clothes. Out of the corner of her eye, Sheena saw a jacket she really fancied and for half a second was diverted from the matter in hand.

Amy turned to face her. 'I think you're sort of following me, and, without being rude, I really don't want to talk to you.' She shifted her feet, heavy and solid in their trainers. Sheena thought she was like a horse, even a carthorse. She produced the local newspaper's article from her pocket.

'I expect you know about this.'

Amy stared at her. She was really surprised that this girl, just about her own age, should be behaving so badly. 'Look, it's nothing to do with you. It's pretty upsetting for me. So please leave me alone.'

'I just want to talk. For background.'

'But I don't want to. It's my life. I don't know you. Please, go away.'

'I can't go away. I'm a reporter.' They stood facing each other. The big fair girl and the small dark girl. 'It's my life, too.'

Amy stopped trying to think. She was bigger and wore trainers. 'Well, I'm just going to run away and you'll never catch me.' Putting down the bottle, she ran.

Sheena watched her go, disconsolately at first until she began to think how she could phrase this meeting: 'Victim's distraught daughter flees.'

Amy, gaining confidence in her energy, hardly slowed until she reached her rooms, where she found Jemima in whom she confided. Jemima was sympathetic but, after Amy had described the attack and the chase and the escape, could not resist commenting, 'You never did tell your father, did you, that he's out? And I really think you should.'

'No!' Amy went into the bathroom and locked the door.

Natasha had just put down the telephone to Felicia when it rang again. 'Something you forgot?' It did not occur to her that anyone else would ring at one in the morning.

'It's Walter,' said Walter, scrabbling his fingers through his hair. 'I've just realized how late it is. At least, I suppose I thought you were the sort of person who never slept. Like me. Were you asleep?'

'No,' said Natasha, aware that she was smiling. 'I was speaking to a friend in America.'

'Finished speaking, I trust?' For the first time, Walter

considered Natasha's life outside their meetings. He concluded at once that she had been speaking to a lover.

'Yes. My best friend. We speak a lot at the moment.'

'Your best friend,' repeated Walter stupidly, also beginning to smile. There was a silence.

'How are you?' asked Natasha.

'Fine. I've just got out this week's edition. I'm in the office. It's a good moment. I felt like talking. It's been a long time. Since Frank's funeral. How are you?'

'Good. I'm doing a lot of gardening. Getting my hands dirty on a regular basis.'

'I can't imagine you with dirty hands.'

There was another pause as both thought this was the silliest conversation ever and both their smiles broadened. Natasha, who was sitting in an armchair, draped her legs over the side, which was something she never did. 'Who have you replaced Frank with?' she asked.

'Of course, he's irreplaceable. I'm going to try different people in the slot. Actually, I'm tempted to take the page myself.' This was something he had not even known he thought until the words came out of his mouth.

'You're the editor.'

'But I'm not much of a journalist. OK for editorials but a whole page might be beyond me. Or beyond my readers.'

'How about a diary?'

'Guests do that.' Another silence. 'I don't suppose you'd give me lunch in the country?'

'A picnic?'

'Oh, yes. Definitely. A picnic. What a superb idea. Where's the nearest station?'

This arrangement, so unexpected, took their breath away and the conversation came to an end quickly. The night that held them apart had only a few more hours to run.

Natasha went to her bed, lay on it wrapped in a shawl and watched the light gradually spread over her misty, tranquil garden. She walked out, then, over the dewy lawn, catching blades of grass between her naked toes. She shivered at the freshness of the air, at the sharp stillness where the birds had not yet started to sing and a falling rose made a soft sloughing sound. As the globe of the sun appeared behind a dark silhouette of trees, a breeze rose too, and she thought suddenly, with as much eagerness as if it had been forbidden and now was allowed, of new-ground coffee, with hot milk and crusty bread. She went inside to her kitchen and shocked a sleepy Cleopatra by the enthusiasm with which she went about making her breakfast.

Walter, hardly knowing what he was doing, opened his Jesus drawer and took out his notes and some of the manuscript. He read through them, shuffling the pages about, amazing himself by the wonderful things he found there. He read aloud passages he had forgotten writing and which now seemed full of profundities, and soon he had left his own pages behind and turned to texts that seemed filled with light: 'Faith is the substance of things hoped for, the evidence of things not seen . . .' He turned again. 'And there appeared a great wonder in heaven; a woman clothed with the sun, and the moon under her feet, and upon her head a crown of twelve stars.'

*

Dressed all in white, Natasha crossed and recrossed her pale green lawn. She had pulled a wooden table and two chairs under the one big tree in her garden, a tulip tree, whose thick, knotted trunk produced leaves as light as tissue.

Natasha finished her carrying, tablecloth, plates, glasses, cutlery and sat under the leaves, layer upon layer of them but still fine enough to filter a green sun on to the tablecloth and her white dress. She sat with her hands in her lap, not as if she were waiting but as if her place there, in the quiet hum of her midday garden, was enough in itself. Filled with anticipation, she hardly wanted the moment to end.

A car turned noisily into her narrow driveway. Walter's voice talked to the driver; the car left. Natasha continued to sit. She remembered how she had always run to Frank, daring him to talk her down and he always had. She must have wanted it, she thought kindly, as she heard Walter ring her doorbell, even though she had left the door wide open. Should she shout now?

Cleopatra, brushing over Walter's feet, his scuffed suede shoes, paraded across the lawn to where Natasha sat, fixed in her own time. Walter followed.

'I've arrived!' he cried, with nervous joyousness. 'I can't remember when I last took a day out. If I'd known the world looked like this, I'd have done it more often. Good morning.' He came close to Natasha and hovered over her.

She stared up at him, dark eyes slit for she could not see him properly any more. She would not stand, or run, dance, gabble. As if to immobilize her further, the cat jumped into her lap, curled up and shut her eyes. 'It's a beautiful day.' Natasha said.

'Oh, yes!' Walter was fervent as he stared round at the well-kept garden, whose flowers dazzled with their profusion of colour in the brilliant sun. 'You've obviously got green fingers. I can see that.' He was restless, unable to take the chair opposite Natasha. 'I brought you a bottle. On the doorstep now but it would be better in the fridge. It was cold when I bought it in that friendly little town but it won't be for long. I'll tell you what, I'll bring it over for us.'

He left, back across the dried lawn, forehead sweating, heart pounding too hard, the air of unreality that surrounded Natasha too great for him to penetrate. He came back with the bottle.

At last Natasha moved, standing abruptly so that Cleopatra, affronted, dashed from her lap and climbed to a low branch of the tulip tree. Natasha laughed. 'She's not used to sharing.'

'I've never been very good with animals,' said Walter. 'I just don't see their point.' He didn't seem very good with bottles either as he struggled to open the champagne. 'A few years ago,' he continued, 'I spent a great deal of time trying to discover whether St Francis had a real affection for animals or whether it was a myth.' He set the still unopened bottle on the table and contemplated the cat, who contemplated him with narrowed, unblinking eyes.

'And was it?'

'What?'

'A myth.'

'Oh, I never discovered either way. I commissioned an

article, however – it was during the period I edited a religious weekly – and we had a very lively correspondence. Cat lovers, in general, believed their pet understood the meaning of life.'

'Well, I don't believe that,' Natasha eyed the bottle doubtingly, 'but I do believe that animals, birds, fish, flowers, trees,' she waved her arm about, 'are part of the natural order.'

'The natural order,' repeated Walter gloomily. 'I'm not too good at that either.'

Natasha laughed again, feeling as she did so that this gaiety was curious. 'I expect it's about love,' she said. 'People enjoy loving and caring for something that can't answer back, or not much anyway.' She watched Walter take a step away and give a rather wild look to the house. 'Let me open the champagne,' she added, 'and then I'll get us lunch.'

In silence Walter watched her expert handling of the bottle until he remembered the offering he had brought her of the latest edition of *The Cucumber*, which he pulled from his pocket and laid on the table. 'There's a piece that might interest you, written by our Home Secretary, in case you've forgotten, arguing that individual responsibility must be shared by society.'

'What does that mean?' asked Natasha, pouring very large glasses of champagne. She, who had thought she longed to talk to Walter, now pictured how nice it would be if they both sat silently in their chairs, sipping their drinks and listening to the buzz and hum of this English country garden. Quite far away she could hear the sort of very large machinery moving through the fields that suggested they had started harvesting.

'It could mean, although I don't think it does,' said Walter, frowning, 'that your friend, the murderer, should not be left to look after his own problems but that they should be shared by those around him.'

'That's perfectly right and proper.' Natasha frowned, too, because she very much did not want the spectre of Joe to enter her little idyll. 'You sit down and I'll get the food.'

Walter sat and watched her go, slim and white, out from the shade into the glare. Without knowing quite what he was doing, he followed, in through the hall, and came up behind her into the kitchen. She heard his footsteps and hesitated, although not turning round to face him. He put his arms around her, hugging her clumsily.

Natasha gave that strange laugh and tried to twist her head to see him. But Walter pressed her closer and spoke into her black hair. 'I'm in love with you.' His voice was muffled and distorted but Natasha heard it and held her breath.

Slowly, they faced each other and laid their cheeks together. Was it only a seeking of comfort? Why had he spoken of love?

Natasha took hold of Walter's hand and, forgetting lunch and garden, led him to a sofa in the cool living room. They sat closely, side pressing side.

'You're kind to me.' Walter put his hand to Natasha's face.

'It's not that. But I won't say any more.' She smiled at him.

Walter gasped, 'No. No. Don't say anything. I'm quite happy as it is. Anything more and I might have a heart-attack.'

'I'm happy too,' said Natasha.

Chapter Seventeen

It was a cooler day and Joe wore a hand-knitted sweater, which was too small and scarcely covered his elbows. Sheena found him rootling about in his sheds. Until he saw Sheena, there was a busy purposefulness about his actions. Already he had crusty buckets and tools lined up against a wall. He emerged backwards, dragging a bale of very musty straw. As he dropped it down, a large rat, followed by four or five smaller ones dashed across the yard.

'A-aaah!' screeched Sheena, jumping from foot to foot in horror. She felt half-way certain that two or three had shot up her legs and into her skirt. She screamed again.

'They're only rats,' said Joe idly. 'They're no fonder of you than you are of them. The whole place is streaming with them.'

'Can't you get a cat?' Sheena was calming down a little, although backing several yards further from the shed in case another family broke cover.

'I said not to come back, didn't I?'

Sheena shimmied nervously under Joe's accusing gaze. 'I haven't come to interview you. I've come to help.'

'Help chase out these here rats and sluice out this yard and scrub down the muck from the walls?'

She had never heard him say so much and so loudly, as

if the physical exercise had strengthened him or, perhaps, the feeling that he was a farmer standing in his own farmyard. 'I don't think I'd be very good at that!' Sheena tried to laugh. 'I could make us a cup of tea.'

Without answering, Joe disappeared back into the shed. Sheena looked around a little wildly – she was certainly not going to follow him into the rat-infested dark – and saw two young boys arrive by the wall bordering the road that led down to Joe's cottage.

'I know he's there!' cried one excitedly.

'Who's she?' shouted the other, spotting Sheena.

'I'm not deaf, you know.' Pleased to have a new purpose, Sheena advanced towards the wall where the boys, after preparing, apparently, to flee, waited warily.

'Are you a friend of him?' One stabbed a plump finger in the direction of the shed.

'What's it to you?' replied Sheena.

'You know what he's done?' said the other, a weasel-faced creature with knowing eyes.

'I can see you can't wait to tell me.'

'He's a murderer!' Although the voice was lowered conspiratorially, the accent was triumphant.

'So what's that to you?' The boys gaped; they looked at each other with shocked disbelief. Sheena almost laughed at their expression.

'He murdered a girl!'

'In this village!' corroborated his companion.

'Just down the road.'

'We live there!'

'It happened in our own house!' they gloated in chorus.

'What do you think should happen to him, then?'

Recalling her journalistic mission, Sheena approached the wall.

The two boys recoiled, clung to their bikes, means of escape. 'It's obvious, in it?'

'Not to me,' said Sheena, with a virtuous expression.

'He should be hanged, shouldn't he?' It seemed that both boys cried exultantly together, and at just that moment Joe re-emerged from the shed. Sheena only knew it because mouthing, 'Look out! Here he comes!' the two boys leaped on their bikes and whirled off down the hill.

'Your admirers,' said Sheena, attempting humour.

'They've moved into village since my time. They ride past my windows all hours.'

'I suppose they're on holiday.'

'Could be.'

'What's that you've found?' Sheena moved a little closer and thought, with faster beating heart, that it was like stalking a wild animal.

'A nice piece of lino. Never been used.' Joe spoke carelessly, as if trying to disguise the pride of ownership. 'Might do for the kitchen.'

'That *is* a good idea,' said Sheena. 'Are you going to try it now?'

'Maybe I will.'

With Sheena following two steps behind, Joe crossed the yard and entered the cottage. 'Hold down this end,' he instructed, unrolling the heavy and none-too-clean material. Sheena crouched uncomfortably in her tight skirt and wondered why he had accepted her after all. Perhaps he was lonely, she thought, or perhaps he was already harbouring secret desires for her person.

The afternoon passed with a sense of purpose that Joe

had not known before. Sheena, bending and smiling and eventually removing her cramping shoes, thought of herself as on assignment, as a war reporter goes to a dangerous front, and didn't notice she was having a rather good time. Joe had opened the doors back and front and a breeze aired the house, bringing the smells of new-mown grass, the sound of birdsong and the occasional passing car.

After the lino had been cut and laid, Sheena sat on the step with a packet of cigarettes. He did not smoke, Joe explained, but coming out with a cup of tea, he stood beside her, staring out over the fields. 'That's my field,' he said, eventually.

Sheena was unsure how to respond. Even she could hear the depth of emotion contained in his words. But Joe seemed content to announce ownership into silence.

Sheena looked at her watch. With so much progress made, she was loath to leave. 'How about a walk?'

'Where? Where do you want to walk?'

'I don't know.' Sheena waved her hand. 'Up the hill. In your field.'

'You haven't got the shoes for it. It rained last night.'

But they did walk. Sheena left her shoes behind and said she liked the feel of the damp ground, the tickling grass. Because her skirt was so tight, she couldn't climb the gates but Joe opened them politely. 'First lesson,' he said. 'Close gates behind you.'

'Even if there're no animals in the field,' quipped Sheena.

'There'll be animals soon enough.' Joe tugged out something growing at his feet. 'Once I get rid of this ragwort.' He stopped abruptly. They had reached the middle of the dome-shaped field so that he stood raised up, the blue and white sky above him, the hedges around, and just visible beyond, some rooftops and the church spire. Sheena, bending to investigate a prickle in her foot, saw him from below, rising like a statue into the sky. Then his black curls flapped as he turned to face her. 'You see, I've got plans.'

'Plans,' repeated Sheena, rubbing her foot energetically to avoid his eyes. But she had already seen the intensity and hope, and it was painful to her because she, also, had her plans.

Outwardly, Natasha and Walter's life continued the same. She stayed quietly in the country, spending less time in the garden and more in her studio as the long dry heat was broken by days of gusting wind and rain. Walter worked as hard as ever so that even Annabel did not guess that his heart pumped with love. He read, 'All flesh is as grass, and all the glory of man as the flower of the grass. The grass withereth, and the flower thereof falleth away . . .' but he felt sure Natasha was excepted.

Natasha was content. She was still too exhausted to want him at her side constantly, even if that had been possible. She liked loving him from afar, feeling a warm spurt of happiness as she walked round her garden or during the longer and longer hours she spent in her studio. She tried to explain what had happened to Felicia but her friend seemed incapable of understanding.

'You're telling me you've fallen for an ex-priest you never see?'

'I've told you, he never finished his studies for the

priesthood.' Natasha wanted to slow Felicia down. 'But he's a very serious person.'

'Serious,' repeated Felicia, as if she were not sure what the word meant. 'Well, I suppose that means he's a different sort of guy from Frank.'

'Frank had the problem of both being too serious and not serious enough.'

Feeling the discussion was losing out on the *joie-de-vivre* appropriate for the acquisition of a new lover, Felicia returned to her earlier theme. 'So are you ever going to live together?'

'He's staying in my apartment, Frank's apartment,' Natasha replied, trying not to sound defensive. This was true as of the day before. While she remained in the country, a medieval lady set in a bower of lilies, her very parfit knight had taken up a plastic bag of clothes and moved into the flat.

'Well, I suppose that's something,' admitted Felicia doubtfully. 'Are you sure this isn't all sublimated lust for your dishy murderer?'

'Felicia! Sometimes even you – '

'Joke. Just allowing my imagination to link up with my penchant for rough trade.'

Sheena came to Walter's office. As on her first visit, it was the end of the day and the room was rosy with evening sunlight. Walter rubbed his eyes and straightened his shoulders; he had almost managed to forget Sheena's existence, but now their ridiculous confrontation in his flat came back to humiliate him. Too honest, too foolish to send her away, he pushed piles of papers around his desk to confirm his status as a busy editor. 'So what have you got for me?'

'I'm deeper into this rehab story.'

They spoke together and stopped together.

'You first,' said Walter.

'I've been seeing a lot of this guy you put me on to. You know, this ex-murderer, friend, client, don't know what, of Mrs Halliday.' Sheena, not noticing Walter's reaction to Natasha's name, began to tell her story. She described how she had been to Joe's cottage half a dozen times now, how she had helped him lay his lino, paint his bedroom. How she had met his nice, sensible probation officer, how close they both were to the case, although she herself was closest of all because she had more time. How, just yesterday, she had helped Joe collect a sheep-dog puppy, and on the way they'd stopped to eat a hamburger and Joe had behaved quite like a normal person. He'd fitted in without remark.

'So where's the story, then? Where's the problem?' Walter watched as Sheena hesitated. As always, her breasts were prominent, her skirt short, her mouth glistening. Against his will, he remembered the feel of her skin, the taste of her nipples, '*The Cucumber* isn't much into pictures of paradise. Where's the snake?' He spoke severely, looking at his watch.

Sheena still hesitated. She was used to being rudely treated by men who had come close to her body so she was only slightly annoyed by Walter's tone. Besides, he was right: there was no story, unless she created one. Even Mrs Wynne had gone quiet and, after she had chased the boys away that morning, they had not come back. Joe was beginning to be accepted and two or three people shouted, 'Morning, Joe!' when they saw him out working in the yard.

'It's a tinderbox,' said Sheena, leaning forward earnestly. 'He's fine until he goes up in flames.'

'Explain.' Walter was sceptical.

'I was just keeping you informed,' said Sheena, with a certain dignity. 'This is an interim report. I thought you might give me a little advance.'

'Advance for what?' How could Walter know that Sheena was testing both of them? If *The Cucumber* were behind her, she might not, despite the lures of fame and fortune, turn to the tabloids. Sheena blinked, pulled at a long strand of dark hair.

'You look well,' said Walter abruptly. He meant it. There was something different about her, wholesome, a breath of country air, perfume of wild grasses and corn. 'Do you want a bite?'

Of course Sheena wanted a bite. But why this sudden change? Warily, she followed Walter as he speedily exited the building and headed off to the same restaurant where they had lunched before.

'Tell me more about this murderer,' asked Walter, pouring wine. But Sheena could see he wasn't truly interested in her description of their walks, Joe's renovation of his sheds in which to receive the cows he planned to buy, in the new kitchen cupboard they had bought together. How could she know that Walter was thinking of Natasha, of her pale sharp face, her white dress under the shade of the tree, of their discussions about death? He smiled inappropriately and a little wildly across the table. Sheena would certainly not be interested in the meaning of death.

'I guess we could use another bottle of wine!' cried Walter, waving a hand at the waiter.

Walter took Sheena back to his flat – that is, Natasha's flat or even, as it might be termed, Frank's flat. At least, it was Frank's bed they got into.

It's just one of those things that happens, thought Sheena, a little dismally, as Walter proved to her that he was more of a man than their last sexual encounter had suggested. She didn't quite know why she felt so dismal about this example of an activity she thoroughly approved between consenting unmarried adults, on the grounds that it gave pleasure and did no harm. Perhaps it was Walter's staring eyes, which suggested thoughts more painful than joyous.

Walter lay back, head throbbing. So that was it. The great sin, the great pleasure. Well, I have done it at last. How I love Natasha! The thought came to him involuntarily, making him smile and shut those glaring, staring eyes. Guiltily, he rolled on to his side, and opened them again. There lay Sheena, all curves and black hair. He felt for her hand, curled tightly like a child's. He put his own bony fingers round it. 'Thank you.'

Oh, fuck, thought Sheena. Why do I get myself into these situations? He doesn't care about me one tiny little bit. That she did not care about him either did not strike her as much of a consolation. She found her thoughts tangling away into images of country sky, hedges made of four sorts of leaves, flowers, berries. A tear, remarkable in one who never cried, rolled from her cheek. She took her hand out of Walter's hot grasp and laid it close to her side. The truth was, as it had always been, that she was on her own.

Walter roused himself from a doze. Guilt returned with a sensation of cramp at the backs of both legs. He grimaced and, although he had neither cried out nor moved, he felt Sheena stir at his side. There she was, no use denying it, recipient of his lust, willing or not, used and abused and now heartily disliked. The pain in his legs moved up to his stomach, where it tied itself round his entrails, pinching, squeezing. All this was merely a diversion, Walter knew it well enough.

'Excuse me.' He fled to the bathroom.

Left alone, wide awake, Sheena tried to sort out a plan of action but felt lassitude creeping over her.

Walter returned with the one idea of regaining his office. Work, work, work, it had always been the answer. But he did not mean to compound abuse by unkindness. He stood by the bed. 'Er. Sh—' He could not quite pronounce her name. 'I'm afraid I've got some urgent . . .'

Her eyelids fluttered open. In the darkness, only half lit by the street-lights through the drawn curtains, he saw her for the first time as a pretty young girl instead of Eve, the temptress. 'Oh, God.' He sat on the edge of the bed.

Sheena was thankful to see that he had already dressed, but was still overcome by this unusual lassitude. 'I suppose you want me to go,' she muttered.

Walter did not answer. He was still trying hard not to look the facts in the face: that he had declared his love for one woman and slept with another. The psychology was obvious enough.

'You could leave me behind,' suggested Sheena, who

found this comfortable berth compared favourably with her own ugly, noisy and squalid room.

'I don't think so!' Walter sounded horrified.

Sheena rolled over, expressing, if anyone had been there to understand, a complete lack of interest in the whole world. Let it turn for others.

Walter stared down at her, struggling with a desire to transfer his anger with himself on to her. He lost the struggle. 'You'll just have to go!' His voice rose. 'It's not my flat to keep you in!'

Sheena rolled back and sat up. In one way his anger was a relief for it gave her new energy to fight her corner. 'So are you going to tell me whose it is, then?'

'Mrs Halliday's!' yelled Walter, while a quiet voice reminded him of his love for her and their slow, loving Sundays in the country.

'Oh, her!' Sheena managed a derisive cackle. 'The awfully rich, awfully suffering, stick-a-ramrod-up-my-ass widow. Actually I knew all along. She gave me tea in the room next door.'

Walter felt himself shaking with a tension of rage and shame and self-humiliation, which caused him, the most peaceable of men, to raise his arm in a threatening gesture. He could already imagine what a satisfactory release it would be to smack her smooth, shiny skin. How he would exult.

Sheena cowered with a mixture of fear and satisfaction. He was just the sort of man who would enjoy spanking – or, more likely, being spanked. She should have guessed before. It did not even cross her mind that he might be really angry and intend to hurt her seriously. She had done nothing to deserve that. None the less her heart pounded.

Walter felt his arm and hand like the hammer of righteousness but still did not mean it to come down. 'You are a – a —!'

Sheena laughed. 'Go on, say a rude word.' The hand quivered above her. She did not care; her face wore an expression of glee. A ringing entered the room. Both Walter and Sheena frowned in the way people do when they try to remember where they put their mobile, if they had brought it with them, and whether they had switched it off. Walter lowered his arm and went in search of a telephone. Sheena watched curiously.

'Hi, it's me.' Walter listened to Natasha's only slightly American cadences with a warmth of feeling, a delight, which was surprising under the circumstances. She was telling him about her day, a stained-glass brooch she had designed, about how she looked forward to seeing him on Sunday. He was coming, she assumed, with a question at the end.

Walter assured her that this was the case and turning his back on the bed, listened with his ear close to the receiver.

Perhaps he hopes I will have vanished when he turns round, thought Sheena, that his good fairy will have waved her magic wand and transported me back whence I came. She had guessed, at once, that the caller was Natasha and considered how best to proceed. It was time to move, at any rate, she felt that now, and the only question was how far to embarrass Walter and whether to involve Natasha. Sheena's nature was not vindictive and she felt some female solidarity with Natasha, and even a sort of patronizing pity for a woman who had seemed at their meeting so depressingly lacklustre – although, admittedly, she'd just lost her husband. Quite honestly, they deserved each other.

Walter heard the bathroom door close behind his back and, heaving an unconscious sigh, began to pay rather more attention to Natasha. 'If it wouldn't inconvenience you, I think I'll come to London for a day or two.'

'When?' barked Walter, as if she might walk through the door at any minute.

'Next week. More probably the week after. No hurry. Just an intention.'

'Excellent!' exclaimed Walter heartily.

'In a week or two I may be ready to come out of purdah.' Although Walter was interested enough as she elaborated, a little fearfully on this subject, his concentration was divided because Sheena had reappeared and was now dressing in front of him. This was a tease, which did not take long, and at the end Sheena held out her hand.

Walter, hearing Natasha pronounce the word 'Naomi' with accustomed intensity, stared blankly at Sheena. In order to make her meaning clearer, Sheena opened her bag and took out her wallet, which she quickly proved was empty. 'Taxi money,' she mouthed.

Half standing, receiver still pressed to his ear, Walter felt in his pockets, retrieved a couple of coins, found nothing else, pulled out his pockets, widened his eyes in supplication at Sheena, who smiled sweetly but still held out her hand.

'Can I ring you back?' said Walter, despairingly, but Sheena had now had her fun and, with a backward wave and a hoofer's high kick, made her exit.

Joe was poring over a copy of the *Farmer's Weekly*. He had once managed to get hold of a copy in prison. It had lasted him for years, not only because he read with such difficulty, but because he studied every article every photograph, every tiny piece of information, whether it was a graph showing the fall in the price of beef or a forecast of wheat yields in a year long past.

Now he had the newspaper open at a picture of a prize-winning home-built bale accumulator, and the puppy lay curled up in a cardboard box at his feet. It wasn't right, of course, to have a working dog in the living room, would give him ideas above his station, but he hadn't been able to resist the appeal in his baby brown eyes. Getting soft, that's what he was.

'Charlie, you're going to make a fool of me, that's the truth of it,' pronounced Joe, as he crouched down to tickle the silky ears.

Part Two

Chapter Eighteen

The two little girls had been playing in the stream all afternoon. They were building a dam, staggering with stones as big as they could lift, rolling and kicking them into the water until they settled with a splash, then filling in the gaps with smaller pebbles and bits of dead wood. Although it was a warm day, they wore rubber boots because they didn't like to get their feet wet; one sported a Batman T-shirt and cloak, the other a Little Grey Rabbit apron. They were serious children, intent on doing a good job for, although it was only a very small, shallow stream, they felt sure their dam would create a nice pool on the higher side.

They were making, at least in their imagination, a bathing-pool, there under the big willow and the smaller saplings. They were scarcely a few yards from the lane that circled their village, but that did not lessen the adventure, their sense of independence. The only problem was the rush of water, which dropped in a miniature waterfall not far from where they worked and still flowed fast enough to push out the smaller stones. Once a small hole was breached in their wall, it soon widened until the whole dam was in danger of collapse.

'Quick! Over there!' A flurry as one girl waded off to save the day.

'I'll put my boot in the hole! Karen! Oh! The water's gone over the top!'

'You are silly!'

The excited voices made no more sound in the little dell than the birds on the trees around them. Soon, the girl who had filled her boot with water guessed it must be tea-time and left the stream to run home.

'We're so nearly finished!' appealed Karen. 'There's only those two little gaps.'

But her friend was determined, only relenting as she ran off to cry back over her shoulder, 'We can finish off after tea, can't we?'

'Fine by me!' called Karen, using her favourite expression, and ran off to meet her mother, who was coming down the lane to fetch her.

Joe felt like cheering. After a week of fiddling, his old tractor, so out of date now that it was more like an antique, had finally sparked and decided to begin a new life. It was true, the noise it made was not altogether healthy, there was an irregularity, a rattling, wheezing and, occasionally, a clicking, like an old man who is pushing his body into unaccustomed action, but nevertheless it was alive.

Joe left the engine running and went to lean on the wall to the yard. Absently, his fingers prodded a crumbling hole; he'd have to start rebuilding soon or the rain would get in and, hey presto, there'd be no wall. A van came up the hill and slowed opposite him. 'Got the tractor going, then?'

'Just about. Thanks to you.'

*

The sun was still high enough to sprinkle light through the trees on to the stream when Karen returned. Aghast, she looked at the dam, which was reduced to a pile of stones. 'Oh dear! Oh dear!' She tut-tutted to herself and, even though her friend had not reappeared, set directly to work. After all, her mother was going to collect her as soon as she'd finished the washing-up.

The van was white, unmarked and unremarkable. The man, when he jumped out of it, his attention caught, perhaps, by the flash of the white apron under the trees, was tall and dark.

'Hello!' said Karen politely, as he approached, although her face wore a pinched look of anxiety. He was not a man she recognized and she had been well taught about strangers.

'Up we go,' said the man, and in a second he had lifted up the little girl and whisked her away to his van.

A wet mist rolled slowly over the countryside. In the night it merged with the darkness and cloud, but at dawn it was revealed floating just above the ground and below the tops of the tallest trees, a smudged stripe marking the contours of valleys and streams.

The police van came slowly down the hill. Since it did not pass through the village, no one saw its arrival or the three large police officers who sat in the back or the tense and soldier-like way they descended silently and approached the back and front of Joe's cottage. One, standing near the front door, was very young and kept nervously lifting his fingers up and down to his mouth as if trying to resist biting his nails.

'We should have been here three hours ago,' said an officer, who seemed to be in charge.

'He could be anywhere,' agreed another, jerking his head in the direction of the yard. As he spoke, Joe's face appeared at the window.

'That's him!'

From the inside the violence of the police entry was overwhelming. Joe stood, back against the wall.

'He's got a knife!' yelled one of the men, who had come in through the kitchen door.

'Joe looked at the knife in his hand. He was incapable of saying that he had been half-way through his breakfast but managed to open his fingers so that the knife fell to the ground. He did not struggle as his hands were forced behind him and cuffs fastened them together. His brain was dulled immediately by the appearance of the police, as if he were already back in the endless years of prison.

The officer began to caution him and, as the noise and confusion quietened, they all heard a high-pitched crying, almost like a baby's. The puppy had pressed himself behind the curtain, where he crouched, trembling and whining. A wet patch showed on the floor. 'Is this yours?' asked the officer.

Joe did not think this worth answering.

'Got someone to look after it?' The young policeman tried to stroke the puppy, who cowered away from him.

Joe shook his head.

'Bring him in the van, too,' said the officer impatiently, and he looked at his watch.

Mrs Fordyce, taking a stroll after church, stopped

abruptly, ran back to the van, which was about to depart. 'What is it? What's the matter?'

'Taking him in for questioning, Madam.' The van began to move, halted. 'You a friend?'

'I try to help.'

There was a bustle from back to front of the van, and the puppy was produced, wriggling and licking, through the window. 'Help him by looking after this, would you?' The van moved off conclusively and Mrs Fordyce found herself standing with a puppy in her arms. 'I'll call Julie!' she shouted, into the fresh air.

Natasha knew there was something wrong – not just because this Sunday was grey and dismal so that they could not sit in the garden, but because Walter walked from room to room, unable, it seemed, to settle.

'Have you got something on your mind or are you just acting like you've got something on your mind?'

Walter stared at her, looking exceedingly surprised. He came to her and put his fingertips on her face and hair. Natasha sat still. She was continually touched by his nervousness and child-like reverence for her. 'What is it?' she persisted, as he moved away. 'Work? Affairs of state?'

'Yes,' replied Walter, wondering whether this was bravery or cowardice. Yet there seemed no point in spoiling for both of them this unlikely new love.

'Remember, I was married to Frank.'

Walter, surprised again, blushed until he realized that she was not referring to her sexual experience but to her experience as a journalist's wife. 'There is an idea – I hope it might appeal – for an award in his memory.'

'Who can down a bottle of vodka fastest?'

'I thought, maybe, you didn't feel quite like that any more.'

'I don't. I'm sorry. Christian forgiveness overwhelmed by a wish to amuse. I'm not angry with him now. In fact, I'm beginning to think of him as a tragic figure. What sort of award?'

'We want you to be involved. Essays on social injustice?'

Natasha laughed. 'But that's so unlike Frank! He thought social injustice was another name for cowardice or, even worse, weakness.' She turned her face to the window. 'Look, the rain's stopped.'

Walter watched her animation as she stood close to the glass, like a child waiting to be let out to play, and his heart, which had calmed a little during the conversation, gave a painful throb. 'Think about it,' he said.

'Poor Frank, tortured beyond the grave,' Natasha led the way to the door, 'in the name of honouring his memory. It would appeal to his sense of irony.'

Natasha and Walter walked across the wet grass, passed through a little gate under dripping trees and down a rutty track past a patchwork of vegetable plots, old-style allotments, until the landscape opened into a wider view of hills, hedges and coppices. The sun began to shine on the beetle-browed distance and, as they walked, it spread slowly down towards them, making the sweet smells of rain on grass and bracken rise around them.

'It's steaming,' murmured Natasha, and Walter clasped her hand in his.

As the two figures receded so far from the house that they were only black figures in a landscape, the telephone began to ring in the living room. Cleopatra made her elegant way towards it, never touching the floor, but using table-tops, sofa and bookcase to arrive at the source of the noise. She put out her paw and, with the utmost delicacy, patted the receiver. At once, as if at her command, a voice spoke into the room.

'Natasha, it's Julie. A real emergency. Joe's been pulled in by the police again. The whole thing's just terrible bad luck. At the moment, they're only questioning him. They're doing their job. Quite right too. In a case like this they have to pick up obvious suspects in the area . . . although it happened miles away, down by the coast, I think.' The cat listened intelligently.

It was only natural that Walter should offer to accompany Natasha on her errand of mercy. They drove in her car. Walter's feet were uncomfortably wet from their walk but he could not help a feeling of relief that this emergency would make it impossible for him to confess his wickedness. He watched Natasha's pale, stern face, her hands set on the wheel, her eyes staring, black and concentrated.

'It's about fifteen miles,' said Natasha.

They entered a dark tunnel of trees, huge branches intertwined above their heads, the roots sliding, snake-like, down steep banks. 'Tell me more about Joe,' said Walter.

'He has his own farm. A little land. A cottage. A yard. I think I would call him a peasant farmer – although I've no idea what that means.' She laughed suddenly, showing even white teeth that Walter noticed and admired. 'Remember, I'm a rich girl from New York.'

They came out of the tunnel into a fine bright upland.

All the clouds had been smoothed out of the sky so that there was a clear dome above their heads. 'Could he be a hero?' asked Walter.

'What do you mean?' Natasha smiled again. She was happy to have Walter at her side. 'A subject for the Frank Halliday Memorial Award?'

It was only as they dipped down again and saw the small town below them, a square church tower, a railway station, spreading rows of terraced houses fanning up the side of the hill, that Walter recalled Sheena's involvement in the case.

They drove downwards and eventually discovered a low-built modern police station. 'At least the building's not threatening.' Natasha turned into the visitors' car park.

'That depends on your point of view.'

'Joe's spent sixteen years in prisons,' persisted Natasha, 'some of them very grim places indeed.' Despite her real anxiety about Joe, she also felt light-hearted, there was no use denying it. She took Walter's hand, bent his fingers round her own, and they walked hand in hand to the entrance.

Sheena walked from front to back of Joe's cottage. She banged on both doors, peered through the windows, stretching her short legs on their inevitable high heels, and then set off for the yard. The only sign of life was the tractor, which stood, nose pointed to the track, as if ready to set out for work. Back again at the cottage, Sheena peered across the field in which Joe and she had walked on her first visit and then circled about so that she could see the top of the hill on the other side of the valley. But there was no sign of a tall dark figure.

She got back into her small, battered car and drove down into the centre of the village. She was very noticeable as she stood by the large sycamore tree peering round and Mrs Wynne was the first to notice her.

'I can't say I'm happy to be proved right,' she approached purposefully, 'but no one can say I didn't warn them. Not but that's much consolation to the little girl's mother.' She stood close to Sheena, squinting up at the great tree above their heads. 'This is just where he stood, that night, when I called the police. You could see he was evil then. But they have to let him out again and then these do-gooders decide to help him. What a fool he's made of them!' She raised her eyes in the direction of Mrs Fordyce's house. 'And even Mrs Hamilton took him down a bag of her early apples, best Cox's—'

'What's he done?' interrupted Sheena.

'You haven't heard? And you a reporter! Perhaps you'd like a nice cup of tea. I know I need one. It's horrible we have to think about such things.'

Sheena and Mrs Wynne, an odd couple, sat side by side in the pretty little front lounge where every flower was plastic and every shelf decorated with ornaments and every surface with mats, round, oblong, rectangular, lacy, embroidered, woven.

'Here we are, my dear.' Mrs Wynne produced a large brown envelope. 'I hope you're not easily upset. That other reporter hardly read any of it. I just kept everything from the start, you see.' She produced a yellowing newspaper photograph of a girl with long dark hair. 'His first victim.'

She studied it, with a hint of tears in her eyes, before producing more clippings, which she handed over to Sheena.

Sheena thought of Joe's hands as they cut the lino. 'What do you mean, his *first* victim?'

'You'll come to that soon enough,' said Mrs Wynne who, despite her distress, seemed determined that her visitor should view her collection rather as if it were a family photograph album. At last she came to a clipping from that day's paper. 'Karen's Night of Torture,' read Sheena.

'Of course, it's the vicar's job to forgive sinners but that doesn't mean . . .'

Sheena read the story of the little girl's abduction. How her body had been found, naked, in a deserted shed scarcely three miles from her home, how a white van had been spotted in the area, driven by a big man with black curly hair.

'It's horrible! Did the little girl live nearby?'

'Near enough for someone behind a wheel.'

'But Joe hasn't got any transport apart from his tractor. I had to drive him myself to pick up his puppy.'

'There's ways.'

'What ways?'

'What colour is the grocery van that brings him his supplies?'

'What colour?'

'It's white, that's what it is, and the two of them are friendly enough to do a bit of borrowing one from the other.'

Sheena looked out of the window at a border of well-tended roses. Was it possible that the Joe she knew had committed this atrocity? What could she believe? Or did it even matter what she believed? Her job was to report, not to make judgements.

'I'm not saying that's how it happened, I'm just saying how it could have been done and that's one way.'

Sheena had no intention of tracking down Joe. For one thing she didn't know where he was being held, and for another she was trying very hard to re-create him as a monster and the reality might have impeded the process. But, as she crossed the green to her car, she saw Mrs Fordyce leading two dogs, one a Labrador and the other a squirming sheep-dog puppy, who kept turning round to chew his lead, and when reprimanded, lay down and kicked his feet in confident appeal.

'That's Joe's puppy!' cried Sheena, without thinking.

Mrs Fordyce looked up. 'It certainly is. You wouldn't like him, would you?'

'Oh, no! I mean, I live in a bedsitter.'

The two women eyed each other. 'You've been here with him quite a bit.' Mrs Fordyce's words, between question and rebuke, were interrupted by the puppy throwing himself at the bigger dog and both beginning to bark. 'They've taken Joe to the police station,' she shouted above the din. 'You should go.'

'I can't get the thought of that poor little girl out of my head,' said Sheena, slowly walking away. Under her arm was a large brown envelope.

Chapter Nineteen

The police station was a pale block in the picturesque old town.

'When can we see him?' asked Natasha, laying her ringed hand on the red Formica.

'You're not his probation officer, you're not his solicitor, you're not a relative.' The policeman behind the desk possessed what, in other circumstances, Natasha would have described as a kindly face, but now it was set in impervious severity.

Walter reached in his pocket and drew out a card, which he laid on the desk. 'Press,' he said.

The policeman, appearing scandalized, pushed it away with his fingertips. 'I don't know how you people get word of things. Ugly things,' he added, as if to himself.

'Why did you give him that?' Natasha whispered. She should have envisaged this scene. She had been too calm with Walter at her side. She tried to be both business-like and charming. 'I work for a charity that helps prisoners like Mr Feather. His probation officer called me out here because she's delayed.

The policeman hardly seemed to listen to Natasha as he pushed the press card fiercely along the desk-top. 'All I know is,' he said, 'and I'm not stepping out of line here because it's common knowledge already, a poor little girl has been horribly murdered and we've picked up a local man who's killed once already. I'm not saying more but that's the truth, no more, no less.' He looked directly at Walter, 'And you can quote me on that.'

'Please, no!' wailed Natasha. She took hold of Walter's jacket, stared blindly at the thread.

Walter reached for the card. 'You want us to go?'

'Check.'

'We'll go outside but you've not seen the last of us.'

They stood outside the station, Natasha still clasped against Walter. Another little girl dead. She must not think about it. The light was dimming fast and clouds were banking up over what sun remained. Across the street a row of shops, closed but illuminated, advertised, in turn, unfashionable ladies' underwear, harvest loaves in elaborately moulded coils and cut-rate flights to Alicante, Florida and South Africa.

'Did you know about this – this child?' whispered Natasha, eventually.

'It's in the papers. I read all the papers on the train. The usual gory details. True, untrue. They didn't know a suspect had been picked up when they went to press.' With an effort, Walter took Natasha's cold hand. As he did so, a bell began to ring not far away. 'Sunday evening,' he said, 'a service in some church or other.'

'We have to go somewhere. Somewhere I can think.' She looked round helplessly at the closed town.

'Think whether he could have killed her, you mean?'

'Worse than that. He said worse than that. I can't bear it . . . I can't imagine . . .'

'Imagine Joe doing it, you mean?'

She did not correct him, although it was not Joe she was thinking of. That she didn't want to imagine.

They began to walk, following the sound of the bell.

A yellow light flared from the stone porch of the church; the bell stopped ringing and a few late worshippers hurried, Natasha and Walter behind them.

Who said life as an investigative journalist would be easy? Sheena rallied herself as she got lost for the second time and found herself back at the same infuriating roundabout with the only signpost directing her to Merrydown Industrial Estate. The town had to be a mile or two away, if she headed in the right direction. She cast a look over her shoulder and, seeing the large envelope on the back seat, took heart. She had a scoop in her grasp. 'My Friend, the Murderer'. Pity it couldn't be 'My Lover'. She flushed suddenly. Of course she hadn't yet decided to write that sort of piece.

Joe sat unmoving on his chair. He had turned to stone.

The other side of the first door, which separated him from the world, one policeman said to the other, 'If he showed remorse you'd have some sympathy.'

'Why they ever stopped hanging men like him, I'll never know,' contributed the other.

'It's so wrong it makes you weep.'

'If this wasn't a law-abiding country, he'd be dead before now.'

'Or have the decency to do it himself.'

The two men moved off down the corridor, one

looking at his watch because he was coming to the end of his duty rota and the other intent on a cup of tea. A lot of tea had been consumed since Joe came into the police station.

Sheena had decided she would find the police station more easily if she parked her car and proceeded on foot. She hurried through empty streets, thinking how she could never bear to live in such a dead, no-hoper place. When her path was crossed by a wave of contented, even exuberant people, some humming, one singing, she slowed her pace and stared amazed. Religious services had never been on her agenda. Then she saw Walter and Natasha.

They walked, close together, hand in hand. In Sheena's eyes, they exuded the same air of smug virtue as those other passers-by, so inanely free of care. Her first instinct, as images of her coupling and her parting with Walter presented themselves, was to run up to him, fling her arms round his neck and give him a smacking kiss.

Walter, indeed soothed by the service was encouraging Natasha with the first law in journalistic door-stepping. 'We must make it absolutely clear we're there to stay. And, unless we're given news of Joe, we're prepared to stay for ever. It's a game of bluff.'

Natasha smiled at his vehemence. The hour inside the church had given her time to recognize that Naomi's spirit was peaceful now and could not be dragged out to fuel this new horror. She must try to concentrate on doing right by Joe and leave her own emotions out of it. She glanced at Walter's concentrated face and squeezed his hand gratefully. This was called growing up, she supposed.

Sheena advanced. She would not act, she thought, with a pleased sense of her own maturity. She would wait for Walter's greeting and then react.

But it was Natasha who spotted Sheena and stopped. 'Look. There's that reporter.'

Walter looked. What shaming panic took hold of him so completely that he, a man approaching middle age, a clever, thoughtful man, at the sight of this young, ignorant girl, hardly more than a child, turned tail in the most ignominious way, and literally ran back the way he'd come? Natasha turned to stare. Sheena stood where she was, amazed. She could not have imagined this, that he would be so terrified, disgusted – she did not know what – at her appearance that he would not even say a polite hello, or any sort of hello.

But Walter, all reason gone, tore along the pavement and, reaching the church porch, still lit and welcoming, rushed headlong inside, as if seeking sanctuary from a dozen Saracens. He crouched on a pew, perhaps praying.

As a result of Walter's avoidance technique the two women were left standing close together. Natasha, who had started as if to follow him, now stood with a dazed expression.

'That's a first!' exclaimed Sheena. She began to think of laughing, but a look at Natasha's face made her change her mind. 'Perhaps he was taken short,' she said instead.

'I guess he was running away from you,' said Natasha slowly.

'I guess you're right. I came about Joe.'

'Joe?' Natasha came close to her. 'How did you know about Joe?'

It was dark now on the narrow pavement, overhung by

old houses bulging upwards. A silhouette of distant hills beyond the edge of the town appeared in front of the western sky where the absent sun still threw up a glow. Neither woman could see the other's face clearly, nor did they want to. 'Perhaps we should talk about Joe,' continued Natasha, in a small, matter-of-fact voice.

It's as if she wants to banish Walter from existence, thought Sheena, which, come to think of it, seems to be what he plans for himself too. Perhaps they are well suited to each other. 'Fine by me.' She shrugged. 'Although I can't see talking's much use.'

Talking, they walked round the empty town, their steps, Natasha's long, Sheena's short and quick, echoing round the old streets.

'I didn't get to see him,' admitted Natasha.

'It's a horrible thing. A little girl like that.' Sheena paused, took hold of Natasha's arm. 'You're so certain he couldn't have done it?'

'Of course he couldn't have!' Natasha cried out.

'I don't know him as well as you. But the village where the girl lived seems a long way from Joe's village.'

'It's vengeance, only vengeance. Stupid people. With so much real misery why should they invent more?' Natasha spoke firmly but, since Walter's flight, she could no longer think properly about Joe and her words sounded hollow even to herself. Why were they walking round the streets like this instead of returning to the police station?

Round they walked. Long. Short. For the second evening, a cold mist rose and came with them, winding down the streets.

'He'll be let out immediately,' said Natasha, contradicting the confidence with a long shiver. 'Autumn's coming.'

'You're so absolutely completely certain he's not guilty?' repeated Sheena. It was, after all, the only important question.

It was at this moment that a figure, jerking like a marionette, swung out from the shadows of an alleyway. 'Why are you talking about me?' it cried, in a hoarse and unnaturally high-pitched voice. 'As if someone like you could understand anything – anything!'

'Walter,' began Natasha, too feebly to stop his tirade.

'You're vile, like something crawled out of an urban swamp!' He stabbed a bony finger at Sheena, who stood her ground, hands on hips. 'And what rough beast, its hour come round at last, slouches towards Bethlehem to be born?' His voice lowered and rumbled in revulsion. 'You are the devil's serpent, which defiles and corrupts everything it touches.'

'You liked touching me well enough before,' interposed Sheena briskly, taking a step closer.

'No closer!' cried Walter, holding up his hands as if to ward her off.

Farce, melodrama, both were present, and yet Walter's anguish, ridiculous though he seemed, was real for both women.

'All this because you do a little bit of not very inventive screwing,' said Sheena, 'and that's trying to be kind.'

'Putrid!' shouted Walter.

'Oh, no,' whispered Natasha, looking around as if for somewhere to sit down.

'I was pleased to see you,' Sheena announced, 'I forgave your revolting self-obsession, your rudeness. When I saw you on the street, I thought, What a bit of luck. That's lucky.' Her words began to run together as her excitement grew. 'I thought, he may not be much of a lover, and ungrateful at that, but he's a great editor and, since I've got a great story, we might be able to get together in a more productive way.'

'Whore!' shouted Walter, shaking his fist like an Old Testament prophet.

'Quite. Whore. Quite. Well, you'll be glad to hear you've made up my mind in a particular direction, the subject of which, now in police custody, you seem to have quite forgotten, and about which I shall not confide in you now because I'm off.' And so she was, only pausing to hiss at Natasha in passing, 'I wouldn't touch him with a barge-pole, sweetie. A pathetic prick.'

Walter was shaking so hard he felt it necessary to lean against the wall. Natasha watched tiredly, unhappily, curiously. She had not been married to an alcoholic for nothing. 'You've been drinking, haven't you?' She moved nearer.

'I'm so ashamed. So ashamed. If you knew.'

'You're not as crazy as you seem, are you? You went into that pub, knocked back some Dutch courage.'

'I'm such a disaster.'

Natasha smelt the whisky on his breath and sighed. 'Drink doesn't suit you. So, you slept with that – with Sheena. I expect she was willing enough. It's not the end of everything. Men do that sort of thing all the time. So do women.'

'You don't understand. I've never – And you. Oh, it's all so humiliating, so worthless. How could I when it's you . . .'

Natasha watched Walter, sliding weakly against the wall. It was cowardly of him to take such pathetic refuge.

She made up her mind. 'I'll drive you home. To my home.'

Walter followed obediently, grateful for her attention.

Sheena's long, dark drive back to London gave her plenty of time to relive her conversation with Natasha and her absurd shouting-match with Walter. Two things emerged clearly. First, Natasha, despite having known Joe over several years, could not put her hand on her heart and swear that he would be incapable of committing a second dreadful crime. Her protests, though passionate, had been unconvincing, as if she were not even willing to consider the possibility of his guilt. As for that crazy Walter, he would never, ever print an article written by her now, even though he owed her one, having given her one.

The whole thing was such a mess, Sheena thought, angrily pressing the accelerator as far as it would go on her poor old car, and unless she took action, she would be the loser, used and thrown aside. Sheena had not eaten all day so her rage and exhaustion churned in an empty stomach, a light head. By the time she reached her room, rocking with weekend revelry from the surrounding tenants, she was capable of doing anything as long as it put her back in some sort of control.

Telephoning her friend at the newspaper was almost an anticlimax. 'Hi. It's Sheena. You know that murderer I told you about, the one who came back to his village . . .'

Joe lay on his bed in the police station. It must be well into the night because there had been no movement outside for some time. He was glad of that, glad of the peace and silence of night. In prison hardly an hour passed without some clamorous noise, the slamming of doors without handles, the turning of heavy keys, heavy feet patrolling.

Walter and Natasha lay side by side in bed. Outside, the familiar owl hooted far enough into the purple night to be soothing. Walter had stopped shaking, had stopped apologizing and both had just about run out of energy for analysis or explanation.

'I don't think we've come together for sex,' said Natasha, sadly. She wished she could make a joke about it but Walter's self-flagellation over Sheena seemed too raw for anything but the greatest seriousness. She remembered one of Frank's first remarks to her. 'Sex proves God has a sense of humour.' He had been standing in a party, near the bar, of course, addressing any pretty woman who passed by without leaving his post. She had been the one who stayed.

'Have you always been perfect?' murmured Walter.

Perfect? thought Natasha. When I've abandoned Joe to look after you? Does that make me perfect? But all she said was, 'No.' He had not wanted even that answer, she knew. Frank had never made her better than she was. There was the owl again, not so soothing – challenging, mocking, haunting. Yet eventually she slept. Curled into this hot stranger's arms.

Walter lay awake listening to Natasha's soft breathing, the sound of forgiveness. He searched for words:

He that has light within his own clear breast
May sit i' th' centre and enjoy bright day;

> *But he that hides a dark soul and foul thoughts*
> *Benighted walks under the midday sun.*

Lulled by the quietness of night, Joe allowed his numbness to lift a little and, with physical pain, reaching through his stomach and heart, he pictured what he had left behind, the tractor, ticking over nicely, his house, windows bright, dreary creeper banished, Charlie, snuggled up in his cardboard box.

At first light, Natasha opened her eyes and saw Walter by the window, looking at a small square paper. She had slept well for a few hours and her head felt clear. It was a deep joy to realize that she did not regret letting Walter into her life. He is stringent with himself, she thought. That's why his episode with Sheena was so horrible to him. 'What are you doing?' she asked.

'It's the train timetable,' Walter jumped guiltily. 'I have to get to the office.'

'Good.' Natasha smiled. She would not mind his going. In fact, she would be glad to see him re-enter the world where he felt powerful.

'Good, really?' Walter stood over her and she was amazed by the brightness in his face. She smiled. Reassured, he continued, 'There's a train at five.'

'That's fine. I love you.' Had she spoken out loud, just then, as he left her?

He seemed not to have heard. 'You don't mind, then?'

'No. No.' She lay comfortably.

'What I mean is, I need you to drive me to the station.'

The sun had not yet risen when Natasha, mackintosh

over nightdress, smudged through the dew-wet lawn to her car. Walter had produced a pad from his pocket, which he studied as she drove. If we were married it would be like this, thought Natasha. And if Naomi had lived she would be thirteen. What would she have made of a step-father like Walter? Aged eleven. Growing into puberty, looking at men with new eyes. Two dreams, each as unreal as the other. All the same, she liked the thought enough not to banish it immediately.

The train was in the station when they arrived. 'Thanks.' Walter put his stubbly face briefly against hers and ran. Natasha saw his mobile phone in his pocket, jumping about, in danger of jumping right out. She turned the car and drove into the first slivers of the sun. Soon she must consider the vile accusation laid against Joe. But not yet, not in this fragile dawning.

Walter, head aching dreadfully, remembered a talk he had once had with a priest who told him that his conscience was too 'nice'. It had been a warning of what was to come. Now he was changed or, at least, changing.

Chapter Twenty

It was part of Walter's job to see all the papers, however disreputable. 'MY ESCORT THE MURDERER: Sheena Williams shares the details of her intimate relationship with a convicted murderer.' Walter read, and wondered, as he sat at his desk with a cup of coffee provided by Annabel, how they had arrived at that word 'escort'. He could imagine that 'lover' had hovered temptingly above the truth. 'Intimate relationship' could only mean two or three visits on a fairly formal basis, a journalist investigates. Or was that quite true?

He himself had only met Sheena a few times before they had found themselves in very intimate relations indeed. Sheena, it was hard to avoid the thought, could not be trusted to keep herself to herself, even with a convicted murderer, and this one, he remembered, was very handsome.

With the stoic look of a man undergoing a penitential rite, Walter read the rest of the two-page article, which was accompanied by a large bosomy photograph of Sheena and a small but terrifying mug-shot of Joe, in which he appeared to have no nose, a thin line for a mouth and huge bushy eyebrows. Walter tried to estimate whether the paper had doctored the photograph or whether the police cameras were defacing enough already. He read with attention because he wanted to see how they introduced the fact that Joe was now in police custody being questioned about a more frightful murder than the first. A great deal more shocking, thought Walter gloomily, if graduations in murder were proper, which he, unlike the present law, indeed believed. And there it was, the tentatively presented peg to hang the story on: 'Joseph Feather is now held for questioning over the murder of five-year-old Karen Oldstock.' Around this information was Sheena's story – not badly written, thought Walter, the journalist, although one never knew how much an editor had been involved.

She had spoken to the original victim's daughter of whom there was a somewhat blurred photograph, and several women in the village, one of whom had been Joe's mother's closest friend. As these things go, it was a well-researched picture of a man and his surroundings. Anyone reading it would be absolutely certain that Joe Feather should never have been let out of prison. There was also a dramatic undertone to the first-person narrative, which could be crudely summarized as 'I went into the lion's den and escaped by the skin of my teeth.' No real evidence was given that the lion had roared in her direction but the physical description – of his huge height and strength, his black hair, his fierce blue eyes, his great broad hands (which had, undeniably, strangled his victim sixteen years previously) – all gave the impression of a creature more beast than man on whom any taming process would be necessarily superficial. Somewhere, too, was slipped in his illiteracy, as if that put him outside the pale of human communication. Perhaps it did. Perhaps he *had* attacked this little girl. The world was filled with cruel, unlikely events.

Walter sighed and flipped through some other pages. Sure enough, there was an article asking for tougher conditions before the release of dangerous criminals. No one, presumably, was in the least bothered that this sort of prejudging by association could quite clearly prejudice Joe's fair trial. Was this a story for *The Cucumber*, a combative story about the morals of journalism?

Walter frowned. In a shameful corner of his mind, he hoped that Joe was guilty because then justice could take its rightful course and Sheena's odious story would become irrelevant.

Sheena stared at her article with slightly less pride and pleasure than she had expected. The photograph, which she had posed for only the day before, seemed to show a vapid, vulgar person, not the intrepid investigative journalist she had expected. Maybe she had been wrong to wear such a tight T-shirt – but that was her style, pride in the body beautiful. Nevertheless, she was surprised to see her breasts figuring quite so prominently.

Neither was the text altogether satisfactory for it had been much edited and rearranged, losing in the process the sensitive bits (as she described them to herself), descriptions of the countryside, Joe's love for his puppy, his hardworking ambition for his farm – all the bits, in fact, that she had put in as a sop to her never-very-active conscience. She could not disguise from herself that, stripped of subtleties and softening colour, and with the addition of lines such as 'I shivered as we stood beside his bed', and 'the hands of a murderer gripped my shoulder', it was a cruel, callous act of betrayal. Joe had trusted her.

In order to dispel such an unwelcome thought, Sheena made several telephone calls in which she exulted along the lines of 'Two full pages in the *Daily* —! The big time at last! Enough to pay the rent for three months.' Her friends were particularly impressed by the last statement, and few enquired as to the subject of the article.

Dressing quickly, in an unusually baggy shirt, and placing two copies of the newspaper in her bag, Sheena set out for lunch in a new trendy café round the corner. There were sure to be aspiring writers there who would die for two whole pages in a national newspaper.

'But why ever did the stupid girl do it?' cried Natasha, her indignation vibrating over the telephone. This felt like simple energy, simple emotion.

Walter reminded himself that money, as a reason for doing things, had never entered Natasha's life. 'I expect she's convinced herself that she's acting as a watchdog for the community but, actually, it's her name in lights she really wants and, even more important, a nice cheque.'

'But she *knew* Joe!'

'Quite.'

'She *befriended* him!'

'It's a cruel world.'

Despite their only recently declared love for each other, there was an air of irritation in their dialogue. Walter could not quite understand the depth of Natasha's outrage; he found Sheena's behaviour almost predictable, although he hadn't predicted it. From the journalistic point of view, Sheena's action could be interpreted as expressing a serious commitment to her profession.

Natasha expected more from Walter, more active disapproval, perhaps a plan to counteract the dreadful effect
that this bit of self-interest must have on the 'poor,
innocent victim'. She used those words about Joe as if the
strength of her passion must convince more than just
Walter.

'Poor? Innocent? Victim?' repeated Walter, as if each
question mark deserved an answer.

'There are many ways to be a victim!' cried Natasha. I
must not make this a trial of his love, she thought. I must
remain calm as he likes to see me. He cannot understand
the confusions of past stories. He cannot be expected to
understand how I feel the death of this little girl. To him,
she is only a page in a newspaper. 'Yes, victim,' she said.
'There is no reason why Joe can't be both convicted
murderer and victim. Even a prisoner does not lose his
rights and he's served his time.'

'Yes,' agreed Walter. 'If he's innocent, he'll be freed,
despite this odious, possibly lying, article. I want to say to
you, I regret ever having allowed Sheena to enter our lives.'
He added, with more energy, 'Annabel warned me against
her.'

'Annabel!'

'Sorry. Again.' The defensiveness could not be disguised, or the wish to forget all this mucky business. As he
spoke to her, he had begun to edit an abstruse article on
Malawi, a subject on which his knowledge was minimal.

'I'm not sure "sorry" is enough. Don't you have libel
laws in this country?'

'If you can pin down the lies.' Walter ran a hard line
through two paragraphs before adding, 'Were there any
lies?'

Again, Natasha succeeded in checking herself. She had no right to tell him what to do. She could not even ask him to run an article. 'Not exactly lies,' she admitted. 'At least, not important ones.'

'The priest who received me into the Catholic Church had a favourite saying, which he brought out when the going became tough.' Walter pushed away the article. 'He used to advise, "We must watch and pray." At first I found it irritating but later on it became useful.'

'I suppose I watch and you pray,' Natasha commented coldly.

'Congratulations,' said the policeman, laying Sheena's article in front of Joe. 'You're famous.' It was the same policeman who had once driven him to his village and he seemed to relish this evidence of his captive's degenerative qualities.

Joe stared at the picture of Sheena without immediate recognition. Nor did he attempt to read the print, for reasons his tormentor could not have guessed.

'Know her, don't you?' prompted the policeman.

Now Joe recognized Sheena. 'She's a friend,' he muttered, regretting it at once as the policeman smiled sarcastically.

'With friends like that, who needs enemies?'

'It's nothing to do with me.'

'Nothing to do with you!' The policeman thought how he would describe to his wife the bare-faced, hard-hearted, cool-as-a-cucumber behaviour of this monster dressed up as a man. 'Nothing to do with you!' he repeated, prodding the newspaper with his finger, for it enraged him that Joe would not read it. 'I suppose it's nothing to do with you either that an innocent little girl has been tortured and murdered!'

Joe stood up. His height and breadth in that small room made the policeman, despite his belligerence, take a step back towards the door. 'Don't shout at me. You haven't the right.' He turned his face to the wall.

Snatching up the newspaper, the righteous arm of the law left the room.

Joe did not read Sheena's article but there were many who did: all the inhabitants of his village, for example. Those who had previously been unaware of the existence of a murderer in their midst were introduced to the information with especial shock. Sheena had described, in graphic detail, Joe's attack on the young mother sixteen years ago, and there was also a photograph of the cottage where it had taken place, 'looking just as it does now', as the villagers put it to themselves, imagining, perhaps, that such a ghastly deed should have blown the stone walls asunder. Few entertained the possibility that Joe might be innocent of a second atrocity.

Amy sat in the hairdresser's salon where she had a vacation job as a receptionist. It was the sort of genteel establishment where the *Daily* — would not be expected to make an appearance. So it was the worst of bad luck that the paper was discarded on her desk and that Amy, in a dull moment, flipped through it.

She was looking at the photograph of Sheena, wondering in a slightly patronizing way why any girl could possibly want to look so ridiculous, when she noticed, on the facing page, a small photograph of her mother – the same shot she had kept by her bedside for many years. Quickly reading a few lines, Amy realized the subject of the article.

The lavatory at Ici Sophie, as the hairdresser's called itself, was very small and suffered from high ambitions and overuse. There was floral wallpaper in shades of fuchsia, pot-pourri in unidentifiable odours, shell pictures, a bowl of soaps in further shades of pink, a hand-cream dispenser, a ruched blind behind shiny curtains and a soft carpet that wriggled underfoot.

Amy sat in this little bit of fantasy and read and reread the article. All the details of her mother's murder were there, including a long and emotional description of her own involvement. Now she recognized the ridiculous girl as the same pushy reporter who had chased her from the tennis court last term. She read the words that she was supposed to have said with the knowledge that she had not spoken them but a sense that they were the truth all the same. *'I hate him! I loathe him! He's a monster! He's wrecked my life!'*

She had never allowed herself to say such things, or even think them. With a child's strong will, she had pushed tragedy behind her and got on with the present. She prided herself on her cheerful control, hardworking, capable, conscientious. Yet again Amy read the article, slowly, word for word, and then lifted the lavatory seat and vomited. *'I hate him! I loathe him! He's a monster! He took away my mother!*

Amy went downstairs, found the owner of the hairdresser's and, saying she was ill, which indeed she looked, left for home. The house was deserted, as she had known it would be, children at school, father and step-mother at work. She entered the bathroom, opened the cabinet above the basin and took out a bottle. Not long ago, a boy had nearly succeeded in killing himself by swallowing thirty paracetamol. Even as Amy took off the bottle-top and methodically, glass of water in hand, began to swallow the pills one by one, she remembered how amazed she had been by that despairing boy's action and how proud that she had survived the worst trauma in the world without even suffering serious depression.

It was as if reading that disgusting article had brought her face to face, for the first time, with an unavoidable truth: she could not spend her life in a world where her mother had been murdered. It was neither fear nor hatred of the black-haired man that propelled her forward now, taking carefully pill after pill, forcing her unwilling throat to swallow. If she had still felt such strong emotions, it would have given her reason to live. On the contrary, she was overwhelmed by a nothingness, which left her with only one course of action. Her mother was dead and she must follow her.

After swallowing most of the pills, Amy's sense of purpose was dissolved by a drowsiness and a longing to rest. She crept to her bedroom and, taking up her mother's photograph, crawled with it under her duvet. It was a dark, soft place to be and she shut her eyes.

Chapter Twenty-one

The room was forty floors up, walled with glass on three sides, so that Sheena felt as if she were in a helicopter. A blind was lowered across one window and its half-open slats painted stripes across the frank, open face on the other side of the desk. He was a young man and Sheena was equally amazed at his boy-next-door appearance and her presence across the desk in his office, the office of the editor of the *Daily* —. She was a courtier rewarded by an interview with her king, who found him without any grandeur or dignity.

'This is good stuff,' he was saying, in his light, easy voice. 'That's why I asked you here.' A lock of well-washed hair dropped across his forehead as he bent his head over her article, which lay open on his large and, save for telephones and a yellow pad, empty desk. 'It's got further to go. You've touched a nerve. And that's what our paper's all about. Finding a nerve.' He looked at Sheena quite suddenly and directly so that she noticed that his eyes were a child-like blue. 'Fear. Fear is a very powerful emotion. The government has a duty to protect its citizens from fear. If it doesn't manage it, then it's our duty to give it a little nudge. This'll be a fucking sharp nudge.'

Sheena settled herself a little more comfortably in her

chair. This was a badge of honour. 'I did put in weeks of work,' she said modestly. 'No invention.'

'You're still a bit inexperienced,' interrupted the editor, with a charming smile. 'It's your story, of course, but I'm going to put a more experienced pen on to it.'

Sheena remembered the heavy pen that had got to work on her subtleties, and saw the way the wind was blowing. She tried to speak, but something about his smile silenced her. He couldn't be thirty, she thought, with an athlete's figure.

'Doug's been on the paper for years. Knows just what's wanted. A free lesson for you. Has your guy been charged yet?'

'No,' said Sheena, jerked back to her business.

'Well, you get down there, suss out the court scene, get back to the first victim's daughter, talk to the neighbours.'

'So I am still on it?'

'Whoever said you weren't?' A note of impatience underlined the slightly less lounging attitude that the editor had assumed. It was clear that the interview was nearly over. 'Leg-work,' he said, 'that's the secret of a good story. Anyone can write it up. That's desk work. Doug is the guy for that. Feed him the facts and he'll make them sing.'

'But . . .' began Sheena.

But the editor was on his feet and, once more agreeably boyish, took her to the door, which he opened to reveal several courtiers waiting to be admitted. Among them was Doug.

'Good story, girl,' said Doug, taking Sheena's arm,

after giving her anatomy the once-over. 'Now let's see if it's got the legs.'

The door to the editor's room closed behind them.

Summer was over. The grass continued growing but the flowers crimped and died and the sun, when it appeared, did not brighten the garden but covered everything with a dull gold, like old varnish on a painting.

Natasha wandered about distractedly. She was cold and tugged her coat about her without becoming any warmer. What was the point of all this prettiness? she thought, with disgust, and thought it more strongly when she opened the door to her studio and saw the jewel-like roundels and half-finished pieces of coloured glass. With brisk efficiency, she piled all the pieces into boxes and then left, slamming the door. Her living room was no better, the pale, elegant colours like a dreary negative of real life.

Natasha stood by the telephone, even lifted the receiver. But whom should she call? And what was the point of being loved if the lover was unassailable on a matter that was more important to her than anything else? All night long she had lain awake with the image of Joe in prison, that defenceless body which she had once seen naked, taken into a dingy cell by dingy men and held there, like a beast, without explanation or reason. This image of Joe, the pure victim, sacrificial, a garland of withering flowers about his neck, had effaced the image of the kidnapped girl, defenceless and alone.

Abandoning the telephone, Natasha stood in her well-ordered kitchen and, instead of making a cup of coffee, stared blankly out of the window, while inwardly writing an angry letter to Walter. 'You believe in the soul as having greater importance than the body, in the importance of the conscience, of right and wrong, of Christian duty, morality and kindness, yet you are the most selfish, cowardly man I have ever met. Even Frank would not duck or dive the way you do or, at least, he could admit it to himself and drink himself to death at the shame of it. You want to be good and that's about as far as it goes. Oh, yes, I know you do a bit of self-torture on the subject of body and spirit, our animal nature being such a source of terror to you. But there are much more important things than that, dear Walter, which even little boys understand. You think fucking Sheena was bad, and I can't say I exactly admire you for it, but turning your back on Joe is far, far worse. For one thing, it's the same as turning your back on me. I have made Joe my cause. You should have sprung to my defence.'

Here Natasha's angry pen halted abruptly. What was this? Walter her defender, her knight in shining armour? What age was she living in? Walter was weak. The fact that he lunched with members of the cabinet made absolutely no difference to that. He had failed to be a priest, he had succeeded in becoming an editor. That should have told her everything. There was nothing hidden in his life. He wanted to be her knight, certainly, but only so long as she woke no dragons.

Natasha looked at her watch and calculated what time it was in New York. She should close down her house, catch the afternoon flight, re-enter that other world, which she had fled so long ago but whose glamorous charms still remained an ungrubby alternative. Later, perhaps, she would summon Walter, fly him over for a day or two so that Felicia could look him over. There, he could be editor and would have no need to be hero.

Natasha put down her cup and, unhooking her keys from their neatly designated place, left the house for her car.

Julie had set aside this whole day for paperwork. A memo marked 'urgent' lay on her desk: 'No client meeting exists till it's down on paper.'

Fortified by the knowledge of a Mars Bar in one of the drawers of her desk and a packet of Rolos in another (separated, they seemed less self-indulgent) she started on client number one, a young woman who had stolen three bras and three pairs of pants from a chain store and was now spending the autumn in prison while her four children were looked after in care. Julie sighed and opened the drawer. This was the woman's third stay with HMP, and she showed no sign of linking cause and effect.

'I'm sorry to barge in like this.'

Guiltily, Julie shut the drawer. Natasha, crisply elegant as ever, stood in front of her. Reminding herself that good looks, wealth and a calm demeanour were not virtues, but that neither, on the other hand, could they be justly blamed on the owner, Julie managed her usual good-natured smile. 'This is a surprise.'

'I know. I know. I'm sorry.' Natasha already felt foolish. How could she find help in this place of honest workers, shabby and drab and, doubtless, underpaid? It was hopeless, quite hopeless, and she might have turned and left at once if Julie's professional eye had not caught her mood and taken pity.

'Please sit down,' she said kindly. 'I'm glad to be interrupted, actually. It's my paperwork day, worst day of the month.'

Natasha sat down, crossed her slim legs in their designer jeans, put her head in her hands and began to weep. Tears fell from between her fingers.

Julie sighed. She had known this before, these charity ladies who couldn't verbalize their own inner demons, although it seemed surprising in an American. In her experience, Americans were usually cleverer about working out the cause of their problems, even if they couldn't solve them. Julie cast her eyes longingly at the drawers.

Natasha wiped her eyes and looked up apologetically. She liked Julie for not trying to stop the flow but was surprised to see her pop a bit of chocolate into her mouth. Their eyes met.

'My secret vice,' Julie gave her sweet smile, 'not so secret, I suppose.' She patted her stomach and then, heaving herself from behind the desk, came round to Natasha and laid a comforting arm across her shoulder. 'I expect you needed to cry.'

'Like you needed your chocolate.' Natasha began to giggle weakly, unsure why it was so funny. 'And I thought I'd come here to talk about Joe.'

'How is Joe?' asked Julie.

'You know better than me. In captivity.' Tears and laughter drained down. At last, here was someone she could talk to. 'You saw the piece, of course. That girl wrote. I mean, do you think Joe could kill a child?'

'What I think is hardly the point, is it?' Julie returned to her chair and might have seemed officially formal except that, throwing caution to the winds, she released the rest of the Mars Bar from under a paper and began to nibble away at an end.

Natasha began to cry again, in a quietly controlled mode. She wanted to talk to Julie about Walter, if not to reveal the intimate details of his failure as a human being at least to describe her attempts at persuading him to take up Joe's cause in *The Cucumber* and his calculating reluctance. But the tears overwhelmed speech and, perhaps because of this limitation, she was struck by the idea that she was at fault in all this because her real, unavowed, vindictive aim was to punish Walter for sleeping with Sheena, whom she despised. To be forced to despise Walter by association was almost too much. He must, therefore, reclaim his good name by good works. In short, Joe's welfare was not her real motive.

'I thought I'd come here to talk about Joe,' she pronounced, forgetting she had already said exactly the same words before.

Julie finished her Mars Bar and experienced the usual defiant exhilaration accompanied by shame and remorse. Could it be that she had reserved all her pent-up emotion for a Mars Bar? And if she did, why, after all, did it matter? For were not her clients the winners, finding such a good-natured defender?

'They still haven't charged him,' she commented, choosing to ignore the subtleties of Natasha's tears. 'Of course, they don't need to charge him to put him back in prison for the rest of his life.'

'But can't we do something?' wailed Natasha, coming out of her self-absorbed trance.

There was a knock at the door. An androgynous face appeared. 'I thought you called. We're having coffee.'

'Not now thanks, Eloïse.'

Natasha considered the nature of office life, of the home comforts it provided even in such dreary surroundings against her own isolation. Against Joe's isolation. 'I'm afraid this Joe business has really got to me. It all seems such a muddle and no one seems the slightest bit interested whether he's actually done it or not.' She paused, frowned unhappily. 'At least, I suppose the parents of the little girl might be.' She paused again. 'You have the experience . . .' Her voice trailed away.

'We do take more account of the victim or the victim's relatives, I'm glad to say.' Julie's voice had the bright, professional timbre. 'The press have seen to that.'

'The press!' Natasha pictured Sheena's breasts as displayed in her article.

'And then the police like appearing on TV and that sort of thing. They've all seen a lot of films. They fancy themselves in a starring role. And why not if it helps find the murderer? The police need a bit of PR like anyone else.'

'But what if they point the finger at the wrong man?' Natasha realized she was shouting.

'The process of law will see to that. English law is very keen on presuming innocence, you know.'

Natasha saw that she was being patronized and Julie had decided to use her Americanism as a reason to withdraw. Already she had edged a pile of papers closer towards her. 'He does have a solicitor.'

'Yes. Yes. So there is nothing I can do. Perhaps I could check his cottage is properly locked before that dreadful Sheena goes rummaging around?'

'The police searched it and sealed it,' replied Julie, sounding almost cheerful. 'Best thing is to go home and await further news.'

'I want to,' said Natasha. 'You see, I had a daughter who died. I arrived too late. I wasn't there when she needed me. I tried to blame everyone else but it was me I couldn't really forgive. I know this isn't the moment to talk about myself. You're busy. It's not your business. Sorry. Besides, it's old news.'

Julie sighed, opened the drawer in which the Rolos lay waiting and then closed it again. Forcing herself to stare at Natasha's suffering face, she said, 'I'm so sorry. I've never had children, of course, but I should imagine you can never get over the loss of a child, whatever the circumstances.'

'You see, that's why I felt so sad for Joe at the beginning. Now it's different.'

Julie did not quite see but felt too tired to try to understand. 'Please go home,' she said, 'and I'll let you know as soon as there's any news.'

'Thank you. You're very kind.' Natasha stood and, as she went to the door, heard a drawer being opened briskly.

Joe stood immobile as the charge against him was read out. He watched the man's face for a second or two, wondering where he had seen it before, until he realized that it was only the expression he recognized, the same he'd seen on almost every prison officer for sixteen years: a partial blindness that enabled the gaoler to separate the prisoner from the rest of the human race. Any minute now he'd be back in prison and back with that same face, probably for the rest of his life.

Amy felt exceptionally comfortable. She knew that she was alive and that the nightmare of taking all those ugly dry pills had passed to no effect. She even knew that she was in hospital: the pale undecorated walls were quite unlike either her room in college or at home. She felt at peace and, despite a sore throat where they had fed in the tubes, rather hungry. In fact, she could hear her stomach rumbling.

A nurse came energetically into the room, consulted a chart, picked out a thermometer, approached Amy, smiling. 'That's better, then. Much better.'

'Oh, yes,' murmured Amy, before the thermometer was thrust into her mouth.

Outside, a man's anxious face stared through the square glass window, retreated and then, reappearing, opened the door. Amy smiled with her eyes and her father came in with an unusual sidling gait of humility.

Amy wanted to tell him that it was all right now, that the blankness had passed and that she knew her mother wanted her to live. She had told her so quite clearly. Tears slid slowly out of her eyes, although she did not think she felt sad. The nurse, bending calmly, wiped them away before they reached the sheet. She reassured the father with a sensible look and removed the thermometer. 'Ah-ha! Perfectly normal. All over.'

As she left the room, the father sat down and took Amy's hand. 'I'm so glad,' he said. He was like her, strong and fair.

'Yes. I'm fine. I'm sorry. It just came over me.'

'Yes. Yes.'

'That article. Anyway, I don't want to think about it. I'm very sorry about you and Mum. Alice and Billy. It was very wrong of me.'

They talked, with the light growing brighter in the room and the noise on the corridor outside increasing, and the nurse brought them both cups of tea before announcing her replacement by the day nurse, who was soon there offering them more cups of tea. It was a friendly hospital and the girl who had been stomach-pumped after that piece in the paper was nearly a celebrity.

'Well,' said the doctor, 'no reason at all why you shouldn't go home. But just remember that paracetamol is a secret killer. You were lucky.'

Amy found herself blushing, an agonizing wave of shame becoming stronger and stronger, because she could not believe she had done such a thing. Yet the doctor's serious face and serious words told her she had.

'I'll bring the car round,' Amy's father walked out, renewed spring in his stride. Down to the car park, not too slow, not quick, give Amy time enough to dress calmly and compose herself for the world. The heart of Amy's father, which had beat a fearful drum ever since he had rushed to the hospital, began to take a more normal course. Yet he thought, for his own sad, guilty moment, So long after. So very long after.

Sheena did not feel altogether happy about this current aspect of her developing career, and it showed in the belligerence with which she slammed her car door and did up the buttons of her jacket. Of course the girl had not seriously tried to commit suicide, but she could see that there was a case for not bothering her in hospital. On the other hand, she tried to convince herself, half her own friends had tried the overdose route at some time or other so there was no need to feel too much sympathy. People did silly things, which often reflected little more than a passing mood. Anyway, the girl's feelings were not her business; she was on to a much more important matter. What was Doug's phrase when he told her of the police tip-off? 'One attempted suicide versus foul torture, rape and murder. Where's the choice, darling? Journalists have a duty to society, and who said it should be pleasant or make them popular?'

'Duty to society,' Sheena repeated the words to herself and conveniently forgot the insulting pat on her bottom that had accompanied them. She walked briskly across the car park and, on the way, crossed with Amy's father.

By the time Sheena had taken the lift to the eighth floor, she had already pictured the headline: 'Victim's Daughter in Suicide Bid.' This was the information she was duty-bound to bring to the world.

Sheena walked through the ward towards the side room where Amy had been taken and where she now sat, clothed and waiting. Behind Sheena came Amy's father, full of caring and purpose.

Amy decided to make a move and, coming out of the room, started between the dozen beds of the ward. The two girls saw each other and stood still. As they stared, Amy's father caught up with the situation, absurd as it was in many ways, with patients on either side, all sorts of equipment attached.

'We're off, then,' said Amy's father, brushing past

Sheena. Amy let him take her arm and they approached the corridor, with Sheena following. They reached the lift doors, all three together, where they waited.

'It's her,' muttered Amy.

Her father caught her meaning at once, and now saw the photograph from that disgusting article brought to life. Blood rushing, heart pounding, a cry of instant rage on his lips, the bull male with his cub, he grabbed Sheena's arm and began to shake her. 'How could you? How could you?'

Amy's father was a big man and Sheena was hard put to stay on her feet, let alone squeeze words like 'duty, public service', from between her clenched teeth.

'Stop it,' said Amy weakly, but action had only enraged her father further, the agony of the night before needing a penalty paid, the sooner the better.

Sheena had stepped right into it indeed. Giving up her high-minded excuses she began to try to free herself, pounding with her free hand and yelling, 'You've no right! No right!'

'No right?' screamed her captor, rattling her harder. 'No right when you nearly killed my daughter?'

'I did not!' shrieked Sheena and, hitting and tugging with extra energy, broke loose. She ran away, through swing doors, watched now by a small group of disapproving but non-interventionist spectators, and found herself at the top of a staircase.

'I won't let you go so easily!' shouted Amy's father, following, while Amy herself leaned weakly against a wall, arms flat to her sides. She would not let her nightmare of yesterday return, and that required concentration.

Sheena teetered at the top of the stairs. Why should she be forced to run down eight flights when she was in the right? Amy's father came to her there, caught her once more so that they pushed and shoved. Swayed.

Sheena fell a dozen or so steps down to a landing. A doctor, passing up, finding her fallen at his feet, sighed and looked at his watch.

'I expect I've broken my leg!' screamed Sheena.

'Oh, I don't think so,' said the doctor.

'And I shall sue!'

Amy's father, shocked looked down. How had this violence come about? He remembered his dead wife's fragile white skin, her long dark hair, their love-making that should never have happened. He remembered the last evening of her life. He sat on the top of the stairs and held his head in his hands, 'I'm sorry. I'm sorry.' He only mumbled but Sheena, being examined for injuries by the tired doctor, had sharp ears.

'Being sorry may not be enough!'

Amy's father looked down, surprised. He had forgotten all about her. 'I'm sorry about you, too,' he said. 'You had it coming to you but I didn't mean you to fall down the stairs.'

'How about getting her a cup of tea?' suggested the doctor. 'Nothing twisted, sprained or broken, I'm glad to report. Come on, heave-ho. Up we come.' He pulled her up and handed over her shoes. 'One casualty, after all. A shoe without a heel.'

How it happened was not altogether clear, but somehow there they were the three of them, Sheena hobbling up and down, heading for the coffee bar at the bottom of this hospital.

They did not stay together long, it was true, and talked of nothing that mattered. They were polite, survivors,

Sheena and Amy's father, apologetically polite, keen to offer packets of sugar and plastic spoons. Secretly, each of the three was amazed at the position in which they found themselves: enemies in an unlooked-for truce. All three wanted to be alone. But, as they parted, after Amy's father had knocked off the other heel to make driving easier, Sheena knew she must speak.

'I promise not to write about you ever again,' she said.

'I appreciate that. And I apologize for my roughness.' He shut her car door, and she drove off.

But as Sheena's journey continued, it crossed her mind that she could not make promises on behalf of the *Daily* — and that Doug was waiting for her report; she would not be the author of any story he cared to write. One must always consider the public interest.

Chapter Twenty-two

Natasha, competently driving her well-serviced car, considered the tall trees that lined the motorway. She had admired them at all times of the year, and now they were shaded in all colours from green to brown to orange to yellow to red, and scarved in misty rain. The sight revived her spirits and reminded her of the kind of happiness that no one could take from her.

Once a month Annabel cleared Walter's office and brought in tables for *The Cucumber*'s famous Trestle Lunch. When he had first become editor, Walter had complained of a day wasted. It was Frank, a shining beacon of such events until his wit was finally overcome by his whisky, who convinced him that these lunch-time excesses were part of an editor's job. 'Word of mouth, old boy. Word of mouth, by mouth, into mouth. See the connection? Spoken word, written word, see the difference? Exchanged word. Intimacy. We all want intimacy, however grand we may be, and if you don't, you may pretend to.'

Walter, who had fled from intimacy all his life, recognized the truth. He saw fierce men soften at the Trestle, dour men sparkle, men previously as tight as oysters pop out their pearls.

On this Friday, the last Friday in the month, Annabel shooed out Walter with particular vigour. She had never accepted that the success of these lunches did not depend on a clean or tidy room or the serving and quality of the food. It was she who imported a shaded lamp and who bought, on office expenses, a king-sized bed-sheet as a tablecloth.

Walter watched her bustle now with resignation. He wanted to say, 'It's only the Home Secretary,' but the words reminded him of Natasha's reproaches so instead he found three of his young men in their office and became engaged in a discussion about whether to abandon the traditional book-review pages for a new formula, half objective summary and half criticism.

'The best film magazines have done it like that for years.'

'It's an excellent discipline for the lazy writer.'

'Readers love it.'

'Think of asking Virginia Woolf or even J. B. Priestley to pot a novel!'

'We don't have a Woolf or a Priestley writing for us, sad to say.'

Soon, on a day like this, it was time for a drink. Walter, invigorated, decided instead on a short autumnal walk. As he walked, he found a rhythm in his head, Lord, have mercy, Lord, have mercy. To his surprise, he found himself picturing Joe Feather's staring-eyed photograph.

The ministerial car drew smoothly up to the kerb and the Home Secretary jumped out. Not quite a year into high office, he still had the will and energy to break the mould. He clapped Walter on the shoulder. 'May I join you? Stretch my legs!' Not waiting for Walter to reply, he called back to his chauffeur, 'Two thirty on the dot, Johnny.'

The car glided away and the two men walked the few yards left to *The Cucumber*. They were the same height and kept stride, although one was red-haired and thin and the other burly and fair.

'Who have we got today, then?' asked the minister.

Walter, flattered by this friendly attention, told him the names of the other guests, adding a little personal history.

'You deal in gossip, of course.' The Home Secretary felt himself on top form. 'Gossip without responsibility. I don't mean you personally,' he added, as Walter looked defensive, 'but that is the essence of newspapers, these days. Filling people's heads with dubious information of dubious importance.'

'Our job is to inform and entertain.'

'Influence? How about influence?'

'Definitely influence.'

They reached *The Cucumber*'s front door, at which stood a hack well known for his virulent attacks on every home secretary for the last decade.

'Aha! Just the man!' Holding out his hand, the Home Secretary bounded up the steps. 'I've been wanting to talk to you about the economics of private police forces. To put it charitably, you've been grossly misinformed.'

'By your department, Home Secretary,' responded the hack, smiling agreeably.

The lunch is off to a good start, thought Walter, leading in the two debating men. Lord, have mercy.

There was no sun that day in the office, only the

glowing lamp and the dull town light, which faded as they sat over their coffee. Walter had not been on top form, although no one had noticed. His conscience, goaded by that refrain, made him become spectator to the working faces, the excited words. Since Frank's advice, he had begun to enjoy the competition, as adjudicator, judge and occasional player, the sense that he was central in the grand design. But today he could hear only the meaning-less chattering of monkeys, the showing-off of clever schoolboys, who flattered each other even as they contra-dicted and insulted. It's all a game, he thought to himself despairingly, no room for reality at all. Yet what did he mean by that? For this lunch was quite as real as anything else, the guests as powerful as any half-dozen men in the country.

It was only when the Home Secretary looked at his watch and saw that it was half an hour later than he had planned to leave that the mask separating Walter from the rest cleared, and he realized that there were no great philosophical questions involved but only a duty to make an enquiry about the legal position of lifers, with particular reference to Joseph Feather's recent experience. A simple question.

'Late. Late. Too much talk. Too many ideas. Always the same at *The Cucumber.*' Pleased with himself, pleased with life, the Home Secretary thrust back his chair – at which everyone did the same in a kind of obeisance – and prepared to dash away.

But was it such a simple question? thought Walter, at his elbow. So precise, so important, not just to Joe. It was for Natasha he should lay it out, set the ball rolling. But that was just the trouble; it was too precise, meant too much; it was, he thought, getting back to that word again, too 'real'. Not at all the way the conversation had rattled back and forth for a couple of hours. He could imagine the surprise in the Home Secretary's eyes, the lowering of spirits, the half-disguised reproach at one who was not quite playing the game.

Yet the question must be asked. Perhaps he could begin with the absurd story in the *Daily* —.

'You're a seductive host, Walter.' They had reached the door now. Soon it would be too late.

'I had meant to raise the subject of the rights of lifers. There's a particular case . . .'

The minister paused at the top of the steps, no surprise in his eyes but a bright, battling look. 'Quite. Frank Halliday's widow's protégé. Saw the *Daily* —, did you?'

'Yes. Ridiculous, of course.'

'Ridiculous, you say.' He took a step down. 'A great lunch, Walter. One of your best.'

'But?'

'Can't comment on the other matter. Joseph Feather was charged this morning. Heard before I left. Over to our legal system. Give my regards to Mrs Halliday. Tell her I still miss dear old Frank.'

Annabel was astonished when Walter left the office. 'It's only four o'clock and it's raining.' Walter left none the less and hardly noticed the rain, sluicing about his head and ears and running down within his coat collar. Despite solicitors' papers having arrived to confirm Natasha's intention of passing over the flat to him, Walter lived there as if it were a hotel and it had quickly become squalid with dirty mugs, plates, books, scattered papers. Perhaps it was a deliberate act of desecration.

Walter made himself a cup of coffee, sat on the sofa and tried to think. After a while, he put away his cup and fell to his knees. Walter's personal prayers, although they had diminished over the last few years, still took the same theme: a plea for simplicity of outlook. 'Make me as a child who sees what is right without the distortion of education and worldly knowledge. Make me pure in thought and deed. Make me unselfish . . .'

But how were any of these things possible in his present position? He had never been further from the simplicity he prayed for, not during the terrible six months of his breakdown when he had confused God with the Devil. At least then he had been deranged, now he had no such excuse.

Clutching his head, Walter fell forward so that his face was buried in the luxurious pile of the carpet. If he could not be a priest and could not be a man, what was there for him? Again he prayed: 'Lord, make me simply good. Lord, hear my prayer. Lord, have mercy.'

And here was that echo again. With horror, he wondered if he was to go mad as he had before, whether that one line would turn into the mocking, challenging voices that had once tortured him. Remembering the number of years that had passed since then calmed him a little. He had proved that he was strong, could command not only himself but others. He was looked up to by other, lesser men. But at what expense to his soul? Walter's spirits sank again. The very word 'soul' infused him with terrible gloom. Back he went to his desperate prayer for simplicity: 'O Lord, take away my vanity, make me as a child . . .'

When Natasha arrived Walter was still on his knees. She entered quietly, letting herself in with her own key, expecting him, as always, to be at *The Cucumber*.

'What's the matter?' she gasped, seeing his prostrate figure.

Walter jumped up, his face red, partly from embarrassment and partly from sustaining a head-bowed position for nearly an hour.

They stared at each other with strangers' eyes, but in that look was desire and desperation. 'Don't despise me,' murmured Walter.

Natasha sat down, suddenly so exhausted that she could have laid her head on the pillow and gone straight to sleep. He was prepared to talk to her. Well! She sat straight, her expression severe.

'What do you want from me? You see, I have left the office. I am not working.'

'What were you doing on the floor?'

'Praying. Trying to pray.'

'Do you often do that?'

'You know I do. You discovered everything about me as Frank lay dying. You wanted another man to be no good.'

'That's not true!' cried Natasha.

'Well, it feels true. And I am no good. Neither fish nor fowl nor . . .' His voice faded. He could not remember the rest of the saying and, anyway, it was only a diversion.

'Of course I don't want you. Want. I've never *wanted* anyone, "want" as in own.'

'It's no wonder you don't want me.'

'I didn't even *want* Naomi. I just wanted her to be alive. For all I care you can carry on the rest of your life without ever seeing me again. You're the one who first talked about love.' She stopped abruptly, offended by her own tone.

'Then why have you come?' asked Walter.

'To find out something, I guess. To find out what I need to find out.' She smiled.

There was a pause while both seemed to examine Natasha's statement. Eventually Walter who, until this moment, had been standing, carpeted as it seemed, sat down beside Natasha. 'I'm glad you came. I needed to talk.'

'Talk to me in particular?' she asked suspiciously.

'You are the only person I ever talk to. Well, there is one other. But I'm not very good at talking to Him at the moment.'

'I suppose you mean God,' said Natasha. 'On the way here I decided I was a pantheist.'

'Perfectly respectable,' murmured Walter. He made another effort. 'I lost the point of things this afternoon. That's why I came here.'

'What do you mean?'

'*The Cucumber*. All that. The Home Secretary.'

'The Home Secretary?' Natasha cried out in surprise. 'Did you talk to him about Joe?'

'Actually, I tried. But Joe's been charged. Did you know that? They must have evidence.'

Natasha shut her eyes and let out her breath slowly. She felt her tired body relax and slip into lethargy. Joe guilty. Was it possible?'

'That doesn't mean he's guilty,' said Walter.

It did. It did. Joe blown away into outer darkness. Joe guilty, beyond the pale. Could she believe that of him, of the man who, in this very flat, had tenderly carried poor drunken Frank to the sofa, who had smiled with such delight at the litter of puppies, who had endured sixteen years of prison without ever striking out, whose most obvious features were gentleness and humility? Could such a man turn into a Frankenstein? He had done so once.

'I'm sorry,' said Walter. 'I expect there's been a mistake.'

'Oh, yes. Everybody looks for the simple answer.' Again that exhaustion. She roused herself. 'I can't believe Joe is guilty. Not with a child. It's out of the question.'

'Yes. I'm sure you're right.'

She looked up and saw that Walter was close to her. He had taken off his jacket and tie and she could feel the warmth from his body. She remembered how they had lain together that night that Joe had been arrested and Sheena had appeared.

Natasha put out her hand and stroked Walter's face. Immediately the same softness came over him that had already come to her. 'Just hold me,' she said gently. Her hand stroked his rough face, went round his neck; her face came closer, the eyes dark and languorous, the skin gleaming pearly pale in the dim light.

'We can't make everything right,' muttered Walter.

'I know. I know. After all.'

They kissed, a sweet kiss. My God, I love her, Walter

said to himself and he knew now they would make love while the autumn mists sealed the windows.

It was the end of season on the caravan site. Each day more people pulled out the little homes that had been so welcoming in the kinder days of summer. Now the field was cut across with muddy tracks, which became deeper each day it rained. A wind came up from the invisible sea; it frilled the edges of bigger puddles and sometimes gusted enough to rock the less stable, almost emptied caravans. It was a desolate scene where few wished to remain and only those with no other home were forced to do so.

Three or four in the morning was the preferred time of departure for those who had to drag their caravan behind an underpowered car or van.

Sam had come to the camp expressly for that purpose. He worked in an electrician's shop and had borrowed their van to do the job. He had left his wife and two small children, driven to the site, spent the afternoon and evening cleaning and clearing, lain down for four or five hours' sleep and was now all ready for the job in hand. Pity about the rain. He had imagined himself rising in starlight, watching them close up shop, one by one, and then, with a bit of luck, just before he entered his dull suburb, there'd be a great big lovely sunrise that would have kept him going through the winter months. Sam was a bit of a romantic, which was why he'd persuaded his wife that they should park their caravan in this remote spot instead of in a more accessible site.

Rain flurried into Sam's face as, torch in hand, he made

his way to the relatively dry path where he'd parked the van. Never mind, he told himself, because the romantic streak in his nature was matched by a practical optimism. There might not be a great big lovely sunrise but there would certainly be a great big lovely breakfast waiting for him when he arrived home.

Cheered by this expectation, Sam put his key into the van's door. When it would not turn he was not at first unduly worried. Other people's locks had their ways. But after he'd jiggled around for quite five minutes and the rain was becoming colder, he began to consider another way of getting in. Round he went to the back of the van where the doors, after more energetic jiggling, finally opened.

Sam shone his torch inside, meaning to climb through to the front. He knew what he'd packed in the back but he could not climb easily with his torch so he left it to the side while he put both hands forward – and heaved himself in.

In all Sam's long and mostly happy life, as he put it later, he never forgot the next five minutes. First his hands felt the girl's cold face – her body was swaddled in sacking – then, just as soon as he realized what he had touched, there was a shouting from the front of the van. A man was there, blundering and swearing.

On his way to catch him, Sam had no doubt about that, and never moved faster. He was out of the back and slipping and sliding back towards his caravan, before his mind told him what to do. In a few seconds he was safely inside, locked in, lights off, fingers on the digits of his mobile phone.

To do them justice, the police were there remarkably quickly. Six of them, too, one armed. However, the owner of the van, or at least the man who lived in it, was drunk, stupid and/or deranged and put up no resistance, except to say that they shouldn't have left the little girl on her own.

Chapter Twenty-three

Joe's solicitor was failing to convince his client of important news. 'You're free,' he reiterated. A small man with a beard, he looked up helplessly as Joe stared somewhere beyond him with an uncomprehending expression. 'Are you listening? Good news,' he began again. 'I'll drive you back to your village, if you like. Or would you rather wait for your probation officer? Do you see?' He was becoming exasperated. 'They've found the murderer. He's the double murderer, not you. The whole thing's nothing whatsoever to do with you. If you hadn't got, well, a record, we'd be suing. I can assure you, they had no grounds for charging you. None at all. They've got the murderer red-handed.'

Now Joe looked at him, a strange questioning. Did this man, this expert, not understand that there was no such thing as 'the' murderer? He had understood that before and he understood it now. Once a murderer, always a murderer. Why should they pretend anything else? At least he wasn't going to play any more games. 'Just leave me to myself.' He had spoken so little in the past few days that his voice was hoarse and soft.

'What?' asked the solicitor.

'I don't need you.'

'Need me? Need me? I'm trying to advise you that the

charge against you has been dropped, that you are free!'
His voice rose.

'No, I'm not.'

The solicitor gave up, chewed at his nails and looked at
his watch. Joe did not even see him go.

The police station had never before tried to release a
suspect who would not leave. When they heard that
another man had been picked up who not only had Karen's
still damp rubber boot in his van but also a second body –
this other crime had been in a different part of the country
– they had felt shocked and oddly cheated. They were
certainly not ashamed of their attitude to Joe. He was a
murderer and best put away where he could do no harm,
that was their view and no one could change it. The pity
was that he hadn't already been transferred to a prison, but
there had been the usual Prison Service excuse of
overcrowding.

So here he still was and suddenly they really wanted
him out. 'We're not a hotel, you know.' It upset them to
see his blank face, to feel the hopeless misery that kept him
obstinately rooted. In the end, they manhandled him into
their car and, in order to let off steam, drove him home at
spee͏d with their lights whirring and siren wailing.

Thu͏s Joe was returned to his village in the same guilty
way as h͏e had been removed from it. Naturally, anyone in
the area h͏eard him coming.

The rai͏n had stopped at last but everything glistened
with water. I͏n the corner of a window a cobweb was
strung with dr͏ops like miniature fairy-lights. The sun was
low and pale a͏nd the air fresh. Joe breathed deeply and
turned to see tha͏t tractor was still in the yard where he
had left it. The rai͏n couldn't have done it much good.

A few hours later, news had reached Mrs Fordyce of Joe's return, his 'innocence', as she termed it to herself with rejoicing. Shutting her own dog into the scullery and putting a lead on the wriggling puppy, she set off into the dusk. As she walked, she recalled the sweltering nights she'd tolerated in the arid places of her husband's postings, and she gave thanks for the gentleness of the English countryside, the sweet drip of the still heavy trees, the rustling of birds in the hedgerows, their whistle and chirrup as they dashed through the pearly sky. How could spite, and worse than spite, fester in such a natural harmony?

'Joe!' She knocked with the door knocker shaped like a cow, tapped on the darkened window, breaking, without being aware, the glistening cobweb.

Joe heard her but he did not move from his place at the kitchen table. The puppy began to whine, scratching at the door, and then bounding away in sudden wild dashes so that Mrs Fordyce was nearly pulled off her feet. Joe lifted his head and then put it back down on the table.

But Mrs Fordyce was not to be put off. She came in, talking. 'If you don't want visitors, you should lock the door. Safely back, then. And here's your puppy too. He's already chewed a rug and one of my husband's slippers. Now, I'll make us both a cup of tea.'

It was not till the following day that all the party who had a particular interest in Joe's fate discovered the charge had been dropped against him and the ... had been released. The news came from Doug at ... Daily — who had paid Sam a sum large enough for ... ry to buy him an up-to-date caravan. Sam's horror ... hands, reaching out in the dark, touched the dead girl's face was particularly well described, or so Doug considered as he read his own words over a third cup of coffee. It was a piece like this, he thought, that made him wonder if he shouldn't turn his talents to movie-writing.

'Doug Spender.' He answered the phone with his finger on the newspaper and a smile of satisfaction on his face.

'Doug. It's me, Sheena. I've just seen today's paper.'

Who was this Sheena? Doug remembered with difficulty, recalling the feel of her plump bottom under his hand before the story with which she'd been involved. The bottom made him friendlier than he might have been otherwise. Young hopefuls with yesterday's story were not his line of business. 'Sheena. How are things?'

'I'm fine. I saw the daughter of Joe's first victim. I mean – but now I see he didn't do it. I mean.' Sheena became confused by Doug's silent lack of interest.

'We must have a drink some time,' said Doug. 'Come round at eight or nine one evening.'

Sheena wanted to accept brightly and ring off like the good girl she was, but her fight with Amy's father and an image of Joe's concentration as he laid his lino or chose his puppy made it impossible for her to behave appropriately. 'I feel terrible about what I wrote,' she blurted out. 'What we wrote,' she corrected herself.

'Look, darling,' Doug had already forgotten her name, 'the man was, as far as I can remember, a murderer. We should have been right but got it wrong. For Chrissakes, the police got it wrong! They charged him, didn't they?'

'After our story. Maybe they were influenced—'

'Balls! Now give yourself a break. We acted in good

faith. That's all you can say, Sheena,' he added, remembering her again, and put down the phone abruptly without repeating his invitation to a drink. A stupid girl like that could spoil his morning.

Sheena sat in her small, ugly, now damp room, in which the rumble and noise of the streets made the walls tremble and seemed to convey some of the trembling to her own youthful frame. She considered the idea of 'good faith', thrown out at her like a bone to a dog. 'Good faith'. She tried the words aloud, as if to see whether they could rise above the lorries and buses and vans and motorcycles and police cars. At just that moment a police car went by, siren screaming. Good faith sounded like the sort of self-indulgent twaddle that well-heeled, well-educated, middle-aged people liked to talk about on Radio Four when she made the mistake of catching it while passing on to something livelier. But it would have to do.

Sheena stood up and looked to see if she had any coffee left. The disagreeable truth was that she had only as much money as she'd earned from her article about Joe – and she hadn't been paid that yet. Journalism was a tough business. She'd take up Doug on that drink and forget all about Joe and his fucking countryside. Swearing, to relieve her feelings, Sheena abandoned the idea of coffee and, finding that a small amount of wine remained at the bottom of an open bottle, swigged it back with gusto.

Walter was the second person to scan the *Daily* —. His heart, so secure, so warm, so well-disposed to the world since his night with Natasha, took a turn for the worse. It had not escaped him that in Natasha's mind Joe's fate had become bound up with his own. It was almost as if the possibility of Joe's guilt had given her a kind of freedom. When Joe had been charged, she had felt free to give herself to Walter.

'Annabel!' shouted Walter, sweat starting on his brow, face tightened into its accustomed lines of harassed severity. But when she arrived, pleased at the renewed tension, which flattered her powers of soothing organization, Walter was standing looking out of the window, disengaged, it seemed, from *The Cucumber*'s needs.

'Thank God it's stopped raining. That drip, drip, drip was getting on my nerves.'

'There're half a dozen calls from last night to return and nearly as many this morning.'

'Yes. Yes.' He did not turn round. 'And if Mrs Halliday should call, tell her . . .'

'What?' enquired Annabel.

'Nothing.'

Natasha had embarked on a thorough cleaning and reorganization of the flat. It was an act of love for Walter, since it now belonged to him in all but the final deeds. As she sprayed and rubbed the spattered windows till they gleamed, and squirted and wiped the kitchen, the bathroom, the lavatory till they, too, gleamed, she was wondering whether she was ready for happiness. This idea, causing her to bustle about energetically for several hours, eventually led her to the little room that had once been Naomi's. She sat on the bed, then lay on it.

The aura of her daughter had long passed from the room. Other eyes had looked through the small window with its view of ornate roofs. The passionate agony of love and despair that Natasha felt after Naomi's dying, when she had willed her own death each night and woken up each morning in anger and disbelief, was nine years out of date. She must start again, and not only in memorial or escape. Walter, although she could not quite imagine this, might wish to become a father.

So far, Natasha composedly imagined, lying, eyes shut, on Naomi's bed. But then, as her mind half drifted into sleep, she began to wonder whether she wanted to give up her exclusive love for Naomi. She might be able to lessen Walter's torments but she was hardly likely to turn him into the kind of family man she was picturing in the optimism of clean surfaces. She might think she loved him but what sort of love would it be? True-life romance or merely wish-fulfilment, a pale shadow of what she had felt for Naomi or even, at the beginning, for Frank?

Amy's father held the car door open for his daughter and then shut it carefully behind her. A week after the event he could scarcely believe that she had tried to kill herself, or in his extraordinary struggle with that girl journalist. It had all been so unexpected, so quickly over, Amy, it seemed, recovered to her usual sensible self. Yet it had left him in that unpleasant state of anxiousness that he remembered from the years following Amy's mother's death.

So he decided to drive her to college and quietly shut the door on her. As the road swept away under his wheels, he took the doctor's advice and asked her if she would like to see a psychiatrist. But Amy refused. 'I'm fine now, Dad.' She stared straight out of the window. 'If you want to know, it had been building up in me ever since that girl started chasing me about. I felt I hadn't done enough mourning for my mother and it all got tangled up with the man – I liked him then, that summer, he was kind to me, showed me his baby calves, that sort of thing. It was obviously a shock about this other murder, of the little girl. I just think I hadn't sorted it out before. I was too young, you see.'

Amy's father sat rigidly, hands clenched on the wheel. He admitted to himself for the first time that the reason he'd avoided this sort of conversation was that he was terrified Amy would blame him for her mother's death. He should not have made love to her that evening. It had been wrong, not wrong enough to cause her murder, although that is what had happened.

'I suppose the ghosts were stirred up and I couldn't face them,' continued Amy, with surprising calm, 'or, if you look at it another way,' she seemed even to smile, 'I wanted to join them, her, that is, my mother. Solidarity, sort of. Stupid. But that's gone now. When I found I was alive, I felt free as air. Well, that's a bit of an exaggeration. But I'd lost the frightening bits, the bits that wanted me to go back to the village.'

'Go back!' exclaimed her father, horrified.

'There's no point now, is there? Now he's shut away again.' She seemed to wait for an answer, which her father was only too keen to provide.

'No, certainly not. Much better not.'

'Just what I think. My mother's dead. And I've got Mum. It's over. Nightmare over. So, you see, I'm just fine and ready for the new term.' She turned to smile at him, her blue eyes keen to convince.

Her father wished to be convinced, too, so he said nothing but gave her what he hoped was a reassuring smile.

In this companionship, they travelled along until the car needed petrol and they pulled in at a service station. Amy's father bent to the pump while his daughter wandered into the shop, casually glancing at sweets and biscuits and papers.

The *Daily* — had used the same photograph of the little girl called Karen that had accompanied the previous piece by Sheena. Her face, the dark fringe, round cheeks, looked out at Amy, who stared and remembered.

Amy's father bought the petrol and Amy bought the paper. As she passed the petrol pumps, she shoved it in a garbage bin, but she had already read enough to know that Joe was not in prison. Not out of her life. Back in the village soon enough.

'You OK?'

'Yes. fine.' She wiped her face before he could catch sight of the light tears trickling.

'Still some fine weather for tennis, with any luck.'

'Let's hope.' She paused. 'Dad?'

The road was steep and narrow, a long curve ahead, cars in front and behind. He had to give it his full attention for a few moments.

'Yes, my dear?'

She looked sideways at his concerned face and looked down again. 'Don't worry about me. I'm strong now.'

*

An autumn wind was blowing round the village, tugging fiercely at anything loose, making the leaves that had already fallen rise up in twirling columns before settling down into a new, restless pattern. The village was restless as if Mrs Wynne's invitation – issued for seven forty-five and delivered to every house – had stirred up layers of sleeping dogs.

In her little house, all was organized hustle and bustle as, with Eileen and another friend, she lined up cups and piled biscuits on plates. 'I never thought I'd be doing such a thing,' she said at intervals, sometimes appearing proud and pleased, at other times quite distressed. Eventually ten guests had arrived and they were all seated in Mrs Wynne's front room.

'Oh dear,' said Mrs Wynne, faced with the enormity of her daring. 'Perhaps, Mr Newton?' And there, like a rabbit out of a hat, was a man to speak for her. 'It comes better from a man,' as she told Eileen later. 'People listen more easily. Especially those who are a little bit hard of hearing.'

So Mr Newton, a puppet chairman, explained, in comfortable tones, that this meeting was a further effort to remove Joseph Feather from their midst. Everybody, except one, thoroughly agreed on this aim and the discussion centred on the means. Perhaps this was the moment to bring in their Member of Parliament.

Mrs Fordyce, the dissenting one, had half expected to be barred from this plotters' meeting. Now she must either make her exit or speak her mind. She pushed her glasses more firmly up her nose. 'May I?'

'Yes, Mrs Fordyce.' Faces turned, angled themselves

more comfortably on their seats. Expectation – but of what? Had she become the enemy? Would they talk of her at their next meeting as they had of Joe at this? All she wanted was a peaceful retirement, books, music.

'What I wanted to say. Two things, actually. Firstly, Joe has been let out of prision because he has paid for his crime and is considered to be no longer dangerous. Secondly, he did not murder that tragic little girl. Which should not be a surprise to those of you who know him like I do. Joe would never hurt anybody. That's all I have to say.' She stopped abruptly, face flushed.

'Thank you,' said Mr Newton. And the meeting carried on as before.

'It was as if I had never spoken at all,' Mrs Fordyce told her husband later. 'Really weird. I felt completely invisible.'

'At least you went and stuck up for Joe,' consoled her husband. 'Unlike the rest of us who would rather just wait and see.'

Mrs Fordyce accepted the praise but that night, with the wind dashing a long trail of wisteria against her window, she could not sleep. The strength of her words, 'Joe would never hurt anybody,' kept returning to her and with them the picture of Joe as she had found him on his return from the police station. Sullen, silent, uncooperative. Not at all like the man she had first met when he had mowed her lawn. It was as if he had shut himself somewhere beyond her reach.

The wisteria clawed and tore at the window-pane, and Mrs Fordyce tossed and turned until she slipped out of bed at dawn to watch shortsightedly as the sun sliced up the clouds. After a cup of tea, she went out with her secateurs and stared up defeatedly at the offending wisteria. She would need a ladder.

Julie also woke up early that morning; she took some pills, drank a glass of water and lugged herself back into bed. She had flu. Her clients would have to look after themselves. The weight of other people's misery and inefficiency and of her own unwieldy body, which she carried daily, lifted. Time for a rest.

Chapter Twenty-four

Sheena inspected the man at her side with disgust: thinning hair, thinning skin, lengthening nose hairs, lengthening nose, skinny in some parts, pouchy in others. Old age was a horrible sentence – which Doug amply diserved. But she did not deserve him. How had it happened that she lay naked with him in this third-class hotel? Drink, ambition, stupidity?

Very carefully, Sheena eased herself out from his hoarily proprietorial arm (how dare he be proprietorial?) and, collecting her clothes and bag from the floor, slipped into the less than salubrious bathroom. For a while she sat on the lavatory, planning how she could escape without exchanging another word, another touch with her shameful lover, before she realized that he would be equally glad if she vanished without trace now that he had got what he wanted. That led to a further lowering of her spirits, which she bravely combated by taking out her makeup from her bag and giving herself a bright new face. Thus armed, she sidled out of the bathroom, past the bed, to whose occupant she directed a look of loathing, and out into the corridor.

As she walked over a green lozenge carpet she would not forget, it struck her that this horrible sexual encounter (the actual sex had been rather frantically enjoyable but that only made it worse) had made it impossible for her to approach Doug again, her very best contact in journalism, which had made her a whore for worse than nothing.

Sheena reached the foyer of the hotel and, keen to avoid the receptionist's curious stare, read the headlines of a magazine on the desk: *Self-respect for Beginners.*

'Smile!' she yelled.

'I gather you were at this famous meeting?' The Reverend Almeric Cooper stood by the fireplace, looking serious.

'And it wasn't at all a pleasant experience.' Mrs Fordyce pulled her cardigan tighter around her.

'Quite. They've convinced themselves he's a monster. Nothing will change them now, I'm afraid. Sad. But there it is. We've all done our best. No one more than you.' He bowed slightly.

Mrs Fordyce showed her surprise at his tone, which might have been termed elegiac. 'Do you mean we've stopped trying?'

'No good pushing against a brick wall. Best he moves. Best for him. Of course, I'll help him find a place.'

'Oh.' Mrs Fordyce turned away so that he should not see her expression: pity, sorrow, relief. Or perhaps she was hiding the last from herself.

'The question is, who persuades him?'

'Not me!' She stopped, ashamed. Why not her?

'Certainly not you. A friend. Someone outside the village.' He took up a posture familiar to Mrs Fordyce from his sermons, fingertips together producing a vault effect, eyes raised just slightly to heaven. 'We have one, I believe.

The farmer who took on poor Joe's farm when he was in prison. Ken's kept away till now but they're old mates, so I'm told, going back to boyhood. He's our man, in my view. What do you say?'

'Good,' was what Mrs Fordyce said and, in order to overwhelm her Judas sense, she repeated it louder, 'Good!'

Sheena telephoned Natasha. She tried her house in the country, picturing as she did so the beautiful pictures and rugs and cushions, and then she rang the flat in London. Here, images of Walter and herself in bed were a deterrent – his bony body mixed through to Doug's as she shimmied down the slippery slope – but she persevered nevertheless. Some things were more important.

'Yes?' Natasha knew it was early, the light had not yet come up behind th red-brick houses beyond the window. But her arm had crossed an empty space in the bed. Walter had left without saying goodbye – which was perfectly acceptable, she told herself, still half asleep; it was his nature. 'Sorry?' It was a woman's voice on the telephone. She woke up further.

'It's Sheena. Please don't be angry. I expect you've heard about Joe. The good news.'

At the name Sheena, Natasha tried to fit the receiver back but it refused to go, sliding down towards the floor and when she grasped it more securely she heard the last words: 'Joe. The good news.'

'I don't want to speak to you,' she said. Why did things shift out of balance all the time? Why could not she and Walter have a few weeks, or even days, to fit quietly together?

'I know. I know. I just feel so bad.' Sheena, sitting cross-legged on her bed, with her mobile tucked under her chin, began to cry. A lorry went by causing her thin curtains to dance on their rails.

'Go away!' yelled Natasha fully awake. 'You're a selfish, stupid, amoral bitch, and we don't want anything to do with you!' Enjoying that 'we', she succeeded in slamming down the receiver so that it remained. 'Aaaah!' screamed Natasha to herself, and rising from the bed, she walked about the flat, reassuring herself with the order and cleanliness that she herself had created the day before. There could be no good news of Joe.

But, relenting eventually, she telephoned Julie. There was no answer.

Ken parked his tractor in Joe's yard. He was nervous, although his weatherbeaten face below its clutch of yellow hair looked impervious to emotion. He had been infected by the fears of others, his wife, his daughters. Even the stalwart vicar, who had come to see him shouting, 'Well done!' had seemed afraid. Joe must have really changed now, he thought. But Ken was a strong man and he crossed the yard with a firm step and knocked on the door with a firm knock. He thought of himself as a bit of a hero.

Joe saw the face of his old friend with great surprise, but any brightening in his face was quickly extinguished as he remembered what had followed Ken's last visit. He had no friends any more. Yet, even as he told himself that, he could not subdue the hope that Ken had come to sympathize with him for being charged with a crime he had not committed. 'Step in,' he said, holding back the puppy who, showing generous lack of discernment, wanted to welcome their visitor with wet enthusiasm.

'I see you've got yourself a dog.' Ken took a pace forward awkwardly; he held a bag half behind his back.

'Not much of one.' Joe smoothed down Charlie's ears. 'A sheep-dog doesn't know what he's about till he's seen a sheep. Leastways, a cow will do.'

This sounded like a challenge to Ken and set him to his business. 'You're still fixed on farming, then.'

'It's my life, isn't it?'

They were still standing near the door, the bulky man and the tall one, just at arm's length. 'You're asking me in then?' Ken tried a smile, although he felt it come out false. He reminded himself that he was acting in Joe's own best interests.

Joe showed him the way to the kitchen table without speaking.

'You've got it cleaned up nice,' said Ken. They sat facing each other. 'So what are you doing with all that money I gave you?' He tried a jovial tone.

'That's not for spending, that's for the animals, like I said.'

Ken didn't think he'd said that but let it pass. 'I'll tell you what, how about a cup of tea?'

Joe made the tea. He put down a bowl of milk for the puppy and his lapping was the noisiest sound in the room.

'You could be even richer,' began Ken.

'I'm not rich,' said Joe. 'It's all spoken for.'

Ken gulped his tea, burning his mouth. He thought Joe looked at his discomfiture with pleasure and was given a puff of daring. 'You can't stay here, you know, Joe. I told you right from the beginning the villagers won't have it.

They'll get you out one way or another – back to prison, if they could. You should never have come back. People have long memories and—'

Joe stood up, too agitated to speak. The puppy bounded about his feet, barking. He put a hand down to soothe him. 'This is my home, my farm, my land.' He kept his hand on the dog's soft coat. 'It's all I have.'

'That's not true.' Ken had to have his say. It was now or never. 'You've got a hell of a lot of money, and if I buy the farm from you, you'd have a hell of a lot more. You could go right away. Australia, New Zealand. Start again, like you did before. Build yourself up. You're a young man still. Strong. Healthy. I know you're not too good with reading or writing . . . but there're lots of people like that out there. I've thought it all through, you see. You can get special teachers – and who knows? Out there, where nobody knows you, you might even get yourself a wife.'

Joe listened to Ken, at first with disbelief and then with contempt. Ken was a farmer too. He knew about land, what it meant to a man. It was not something you could swap for money, like a television or a piece of furniture. This land was not just his, it was *him*. Ken knew this as well as he did, which meant that there was only one explanation to his offer: greed. He wanted the land for himself, to add to his farm. At least he could have come out and said so, instead of pretending it was an act of friendship. Contempt made it easier to stay quiet but as Ken moved on to his 'reading and writing', Joe's mood changed – no one had the right to talk about that – and, as the word 'wife' was produced, he took a step forward, raised his arm in anger.

'No, Joe.' Ken bent placatingly, picked up his bag. 'I brought you a present. We're old mates, aren't we?' He took a bottle of whisky and held it up, as a white man dangles beads to a native.

Choked with hatred and misery, Joe snatched the bottle. Did Ken not remember what had happened before? Or was it a deliberate insult? He took a step forward.

'I'm going. I'm going!' cried Ken, nervously backing to the door.

Joe threw the bottle as Ken reached the door. It missed him by a whisker, crashing against the door jamb and shattering in glittering shards to the floor. A vast smell of whisky rose up into the little room. The puppy cringed, cowered into a corner, and Ken ran out, raced away towards his car.

Joe stood at the door, shouting, 'And don't come back! And don't come back! And don't you ever dare come back!'

Natasha walked slowly along the street in which *The Cucumber* had its offices. When Frank had worked for it she had made a point of never visiting, except for the summer party. He had put it out of bounds, a man's place where only the bravest ventured. She had been young at the start of their marriage, and believed him. But now, trying to capture her wifely dreams of the night before, she walked carefully along the pavement, examining the stones beneath her feet, the neat but dingy façades on either side, the sickly grey sky above her head, as if she was estimating the cleaning products that would be needed to bring them up to standard. This time she would not allow herself to be overawed and banished.

'Mrs Halliday has come to see you,' warned Annabel,

entering Walter's office with Natasha so close behind that it can only have been illusions of power that made her pronounce the line.

Walter stood, either defensive or welcoming; each woman hoped differently.

'I thought we might have lunch together,' said Natasha. She had dressed carefully for this man's world, in trousers, flat shoes and a jacket. Annabel, in her blouse and skirt and earrings and nicely set hair, was a surprise to her, as were the amount of very youthful faces in the room beside the front door.

'Walter never takes lunch.' Annabel smirked.

'Don't exaggerate.' Walter came to life. He took Natasha's arm, kissed her cheek.

'Who is that woman?' They walked together along the street and Natasha did no examinations.

'No one. She's very useful.'

Walter put his hands in his pockets with the cheerful look of a schoolboy who has passed a test. Natasha thought how extraordinary it was that men paid so little attention to those who were prepared to wait on them and wondered if she should regret cleaning the flat. But that, of course, had been done for herself.

They ate in a small restaurant, quickly, after Walter had explained that he must go to a meeting in less than an hour. Natasha asked, 'Have you always been so busy. All your life?'

'Yes. At school, I worked very hard. At home, I read. When I tried to become a priest I worked and read and thought. Now I work and read, although seldom books, and listen and talk.'

'You don't think any more, then?'

'Certainly not!' He smiled facetiously. 'I try to see life as a crossword puzzle. That's a trick my shrink gave me. When I fear my madness might come back, I put everything into little square boxes, then paste them down on a sheet of newspaper and hold them at arm's length. Not literally.' He was so good-humoured.

'What sort of things do you put in boxes?' asked Natasha, warily.

'People, ideas, events, problems.'

'I don't know how you can have any ideas without thinking.'

'Ideas. Disconnected from me. Don't be cross. I'd never put you in a box.'

'Never?'

Still smiling, Walter leaned closer to Natasha, looked into her black eyes so she could see the flecks of gold in his. 'Would you rather I put you into a box or went mad?'

'I don't know why you're so happy about it.'

'Because I'm with you.'

'But what about me?'

At last his smile faded. 'I hoped you liked being with me too.'

It would have been easier to take pity. 'You make yourself sound like a hamster, running round and round on a wheel.'

'Ah, I see.' Walter looked down. Had she brought him here to mock? 'People get very fond of ginger rodents.' Natasha is not perfect, he thought fleetingly. Doubtless it was a lesson worth learning, however painful. He glanced at his watch.

I have expressed my disapproval, thought Natasha, of his life, his office, his Annabel, now we can be loving to each other again. But instead she heard her voice announce, 'Sheena rang earlier this morning and told me there was good news on Joe.'

Walter half stood and then sat down again. 'Joe. Can anything good happen to Joe?'

Natasha was not mollified by recognizing her own thought earlier in the day. 'Perhaps your prayers have been answered.'

'Joe has been released, it's true. I read it earlier today.' He studied the door to the restaurant. 'I should have told you.'

'I expect you were busy,' commented Natasha, and it came out more sharply than she had intended. Could he not see that she had come to celebrate their night together, her attack only a pathetic form of defence? But perhaps this meeting that kept his eye on the clock was more important. Besides, now there was Joe between them again.

'I'm sorry.' Walter thought of taking her hand. It lay on the table, a small, white, elegant hand, but her expression was hardly encouraging and he would soon be keeping waiting six very busy people.

'Go. Please. Go.' Natasha sat back in her chair and waved her hand at the door. 'I can't bear men who sit on the edge of their seats.'

Mind already on his agenda, Walter did not answer but, with an apologetic peck on her cheek, hurried from the restaurant. As he dashed along the street, he regretted for a moment not having suggested they met that evening but it was too late to return, nor was he certain that she would welcome the invitation.

*

Sheena tried to remember what autumn had been like when she was a child. In the outer ring of London, where her family had had a terraced house, there had been trees and even a small field where two skinny horses searched restlessly for new blades of grass. The trees were far taller than the houses, far older, and in the summer they took away all the light. But in the autumn they showered the road and pavement with many-coloured leaves, which the wind blew into unstable mountains. When she was very small, she had not connected these bright wild leaves with the heavy trunks, which seemed as dead as poles to her. She had thought the leaves came down from the skies like rain or snow.

Sheena stumbled on an uneven pavement slab and, reaching out automatically, found her hand taken by a large, hairy man with a dog at his side. 'You shouldn't wear stupid shoes like that,' he said, mockingly.

She snatched her hand away. 'I always do and always will. I wear them in town and I wear them in the country. You shouldn't hang around street corners.'

'I'm selling.'

She knew him well enough; one of the crowd who hung around the entrance to the Underground. Usually his Alsatian lay collapsed on a bit of sacking instead of sniffing her up. 'You should keep your dog under control.'

'He likes you.'

Sheena stared at the man, at his greasy hair, his grey stubbly face, his reddened eyes, his sagging cheeks, his bent, defeated back. He was probably still in his twenties but he looked an old man. 'Here.' She found a pound and gave it to him.

'Don't forget your change and the paper,' he called out, as Sheena began to push between the crowds.

'I'll come back for them.'

The point is, thought Sheena, encouraging herself, as she hurried to see what petrol there was in her car, you have to do what seems right at the time.

Ken had work to do that couldn't wait. At least, that's what he told himself. There was his biggest field to be ploughed before the earth got too heavy; there were fences to be raised against a group of marauding deer – not that anything kept them away except a bullet in their guts but you had to try. There was a problem with his new milking equipment, and one of the tractor's tyres was playing up. He hardly had time to stop for lunch, but time enough for his wife to ask the question, 'Did you see him, dear?'

'Not yet,' he lied. It was just a temporary lie for he knew that as soon as he explained what had happened – Joe's rage, the bottle used as a missile, missing him by a hair's breadth, the yelled threats – he knew that his wife would say that a man like that, with his record, wasn't safe to be out of prison for one more minute. And, of course, she was right, and he would inform the police as soon as he had a minute. But, all the same, there was something about his part in it that he didn't quite like. He didn't want to be the one who put Joe in prison, not directly, like; they went back a long way, after all. He wanted to be the one to help him, which was why he had suggested New Zealand.

So Ken did not tell his wife or go to the police, but

stayed out on the land till it was so dusky dark that he couldn't see the post he was trying to knock in, and then he had to rush along for the milking without even stopping for a cup of tea.

Sheena ran out of petrol just before she reached the village. She was amazed to have got so far and began to sing, 'Don't cry for me, Argentina!' Her voice was sweet and innocent and quite unlike her speaking voice. It was cool outside the car so she walked quickly, pointing her toes and now and again raising her eyes to the sky, which seemed to be circling downwards as it grew darker.

She was glad to be in the country, she thought, whatever welcome Joe gave her.

Joe came in from outside and, shutting the door on the whisky-smelling kitchen, went upstairs to his bedroom. Although it was nearly dark, he did not put on a light but lay on the bed in the same attitude in which Natasha had once seen him and admired: stretched out on his back one arm behind his head. He was waiting for the police to come and take him away.

Sheena knocked on the door. Since the curtains were not drawn downstairs, she could see there was no one in the front room, so she went to the back.

Joe, aroused from his strange immobility, came down the stairs, a big man, even without his shoes, stooping to avoid the ceiling. He unlocked the front door and opened it. He smelt the damp sweetness of the evening air, of falling leaves, wood-burning fires, distant manure, of fields and woodlands and, for a second, he stood, bathed in nostalgia, forgetting to wonder why the police were not there. Besides, there were no cars.

'Joe. It's me! Please don't be cross.' Sheena came running from the back of the house.

Joe stared at her as if at an apparition. She did not figure in his life: just one of those women who had tried to help and failed.

'I'm sorry about the article. I really am. I've been in such a state. Can I come in, please? Congratulations, incidentally. I'm so glad you're out. That's what's so dreadful, I knew you were innocent. Can you ever forgive me?'

Sheena passed by him into the house and Joe, after looking up and down the road, followed her. He put on the light. The naked bulb glared in the small room.

What's the smell?' asked Sheena, nervously.

'Whisky.' Joe turned as he drew shut the curtains given him by the vicar. They must have been from a child's bedroom and were decorated with toy soldiers. He remembered the article now. At least, he remembered the picture of Sheena, her breasts pouting out. 'It's all right,' he said, seeing her expression. 'I didn't drink the bottle. I broke her. In the kitchen.'

Sheena sat down, knees pressed close together with unusual attention. She was suddenly frightened. Joe seemed different today. Some of Mrs Wynne's words came back to her: 'He was a nice little boy but always strange. Something not quite right about him, if you know what I mean.'

'I'll not stay long. I just came to apologize, see if you were managing.' But how was she to leave with no petrol

271

in her car and, with renewed agitation, she realized she had left her mobile in the glove compartment. Journalistic headlines ran in her mind: 'Alone and Trapped With a Killer.' But this was real.

'Would you like a cup of tea?'

Sheena subdued her racing imagination and forced herself to look at Joe. She saw the abstraction. She tried to feel reassured, but instead the blankness in his eyes made him seem inhuman, 'not quite right'. Why was he so little interested in her? Before, they had got on well. And where, she thought, looking around, was the puppy?

'I haven't long,' she said.

'I've run out of milk.' Joe went to the kitchen door. He spoke away from her. 'No cows, see. We always had milk. I brought it fresh to my mother.'

Sheena immediately felt cheered by this overture. Contact, that's all she ever wanted. A bit more conversation and the old Joe would be back and she wouldn't feel threatened at all. She followed him into the kitchen. 'Phew! What a stink.'

'I should have cleared it.' Joe stared down helplessly.

'Forget the tea and we'll do it together. You'd better put on some shoes or you'll get cut feet.'

Obediently, Joe went to find his shoes. He still expected the police to arrive at any minute, but meanwhile this interlude had been thrust upon him. It brought back memories of the happier times, working in the yard, refurbishing the house, collecting the puppy – Joe stopped thinking and hurried back to the kitchen.

Now Sheena could see beyond abstraction to the pain in his face. She touched his arm and began a new apology. This time he seemed to listen. 'I'm truly sorry about that rubbish I wrote and truly happy you're out.' They worked together, sweeping and swabbing round the door, although neither had their mind fully on the job and a large piece of jagged-ended glass remained under the table while the smell hardly seemed to have diminished. They took their tea to the other room. Sheena wanted to ask how the bottle had got broken but didn't find the nerve.

'Ken came,' said Joe suddenly. 'He told me to go away. To leave my own land. Then he gave me the whisky so I threw it at him. So they'll come and get me. The police. There's no way out. So I've put everything, everything, in order and now I'm waiting. That's what I was doing when you knocked. Waiting. It's all over now.'

'Oh, I'm sure not,' said Sheena, without understanding but glad he had decided to talk. 'I'm afraid I've run out of petrol. I don't suppose you've got any?'

'Wait here.' Joe went outside to his yard. He was away for some time. He poked among the things in his shed, which he had never expected to see again. He found a partly filled can. He shook it and, taking off the cap, sniffed it.

'Any luck?' asked Sheena, when he returned.

'It's outside.'

Sheena looked at his face. Something terrible had happened. Something more than his arrest or the broken bottle. His eyes were full of suffering. She couldn't bear the knowledge that at least some of it must be due to her. She stood up and went over to him. She put out her hand and stroked his damp cheeks, moved her fingers up a little so that she touched his black curls. She thought of all the men she had touched and kissed and made love to, and none of them had moved her like this. She had lost all her fear and was filled with the same longing that had set her off on this journey.

'Joe?'

He looked down at her pretty face, the long, dark hair, the soft skin. He touched her cheek. It was much too late. He felt strangely sorry for her. She was so young, had so much more living to get through. He couldn't envy her that.

'Just come.' Sheena led him upstairs and, as he stood beside the bed, gently undressed him. He waited on the bed, watching her. She took off her own clothes and got in beside him. How many men had she done this for? Why was this the only way she knew? She stroked Joe, felt his desire, the beauty of his body.

'Touch me,' she said.

It was dark and cool in the room; very quiet. A dream-like silence had come over the countryside all around. They lay down. Joe thought of that other woman he'd loved so long ago. He stroked Sheena's shoulders and back and ran his hands down the length of her body, learning her shape through his fingers. She was not like that other, slimmer-waisted, her breasts heavier, pressing into his chest. He remembered the feeling of loving, the joy of losing himself. He felt the pain of those years of suffering, his loneliness and the knowledge that he had killed the person he loved most in the world. He grasped Sheena's body and, as they joined, an unexpected happiness came over them both, which was almost like love.

A brief coupling in the darkness. A cry. The sound of weeping. They held each other kindly and fell asleep.

Chapter Twenty-five

When Ken finally arrived home the lamp was switched on over his front door. Usually he enjoyed the way it silhouetted his spear-like cypress tree but tonight he heeled off his boots without looking up. As he was expecting, the moment he was inside the kitchen, his wife cross-questioned him about his meeting with Joe. Now he had to describe it all, his kindly meant efforts, Joe's rage, the bottle thrown at him.

'That's assault!' cried his wife, as he'd known she would because she was absolutely right. 'You must get on to the police at once. Heaven knows what he might do with that broken bottle, the mood he's in!'

So Ken rang the police.

Natasha drove out of London. It seemed the best she could do, go back to her studio, her lovely house and garden and think things through. But, as she drove between those tall trees again, she became impatient with the thought of the silent and empty order and changed her mind.

It was completely dark by the time Natasha arrived outside Joe's cottage. She felt very tired and sat for a while in her car. Light came through the thin curtains across the front room, spattering the straggly front garden, the narrow path, disorderly with fallen leaves and gritty dirt. By the door stood a large can. Why had she been so keen to see Joe? Reluctant now – but she could hardly be fool enough to drive all this way and not go in – Natasha got out and went through the wooden gate, carefully closing it behind her. She stood by the door and, still playing for time, she bent to the can. It smelt strongly of petrol.

How strange, thought Natasha, when Joe has no car, and trying to imagine why it should be there, she felt her sluggish heart begin to pump again. Could it be preparation for some further village iniquity? Last time it had been manure shoved in through the kitchen door, perhaps this time it was petrol through the letter-box, a lighted match. Not stopping to question why, if that were the intention, the can had been left in full view of any passer-by, Natasha knocked urgently on the door.

Joe, who had been expectant even in his sleep, put Sheena gently aside. He could not understand why she had come to him but hoped that he would be able to disappear into the night without disturbing her. He dressed quietly and went downstairs. Sheena, worn out by the emotions of the last few days, did not wake but slept the calm sleep of the shriven.

Natasha and Joe blinked at each other in the bright light.

'There's a can out here,' began Natasha. 'A petrol can. I don't know what—'

'Oh, yes,' Joe interrupted her and, with an expression she had never seen before, murmured, 'That's mine.'

Natasha gazed in bewilderment. He did not ask her in. Indeed, he stood as if barring her way. His hair was tousled and his cheeks rather flushed. Behind him the stairs ran up, dark. She found herself picturing him lying naked, as she had seen him, on his bed. 'Joe. I came because . . .' Smiling, she took a step towards him. She put out her hand.

'Sorry. I'm busy.' He stepped backwards abruptly.

What had he seen in her face? Natasha felt a hot blush rising. 'Can I come in for a moment?' She tried to speak briskly, although the blush remained.

'I had an accident,' said Joe. He must protect the girl from this woman's prying. Why had she come so late? Although it wasn't really late, only dark. It was because the girl slept upstairs that it felt like the middle of the night. If only it was the middle of the night, he thought, then nothing could happen till morning. 'I'm fine!' he said, growing more agitated.

'What are you hiding, Joe?' asked Natasha, becoming agitated herself. 'You know I want to help you with any accident. Do you remember how I cleared up after that manure?'

'No. No.' Joe's voice had become louder.

'What's wrong?' cried Natasha, frightened that he had done something terrible, she didn't know what. He seemed so determined that she wouldn't enter the house. 'It's my duty to help you!' she cried wildly.

'No! Leave me alone. I don't want your help.'

'But, Joe, don't you see? I need you! I want you to help me!' Hardly knowing what she was doing, she tried to put her arms round him.

As she did so, a figure draped in white appeared behind him at the top of the stairs. In the dimness, Natasha could only see the outline but she had no doubt it was a woman.

Aghast, she dropped her hands and took a step backwards. 'I see,' she muttered. 'I see now.'

Joe turned round. 'No, you don't. No, you don't.' It was a despairing cry.

Natasha, her own ridiculous, pathetic, crazy, shameful words ringing in her head, was about to leave, would have done so in a second, when Sheena called down the stairs, although the distance was hardly great enough to need a call, 'Fuck off, you perverted old maid! Can't you see when you're not wanted? Mind your own constipated business. Mind your own Walter! Leave Joe alone, like he says.'

Natasha lost her temper. When she heard Sheena's voice and, as she descended the stairs, saw her naked body, rising plump and youthful from the thin coverlet, all the misery and frustrations of the past years rushed into a mindless rage. As Sheena reached the little hallway, Natasha brushed past Joe and smacked her face. The contact, hard and direct, made a loud noise in the confined space.

'That's what I think of you!' screamed Natasha. 'You're a slag! You're a thief! You're a slut!' She scrabbled to hit her again as Sheena, one hand to her face, the other clasping the coverlet across her bosom, stood still, too shocked to move.

But Joe was between them, pinching Natasha's arms between his big fingers. Nevertheless she escaped, sideways into the living room. 'I don't regret it because you're a slut, a fucking whore! Is there one man in the world you haven't had sex with?' She stood defiantly in the glaring little room. As she expected, Joe and Sheena both followed her.

'You mustn't call her names!' Joe held her arms again as she wrestled and stamped.

Sheena watched. She knew this was all wrong and terribly wrong for Joe. 'Don't touch her!' she commanded. 'Whatever you do, don't hurt her. She's flipped. She doesn't know what she's saying. Let go of her!'

Joe let her go, but the moment Natasha was free, she ran at Sheena again, trying to pull at her hair, scratch her arms, even tug down her coverlet, as if exposing her naked body would turn her into the whore of her accusation. 'Whore!' she shouted. 'Lying, thieving whore. How could you not see that, Joe, after what she wrote about you? She's corrupt, don't you see?'

But Joe had Natasha in his grasp again so that she had only briefly felt the silkiness of Sheena's hair, the elasticity of her skin. She could feel Joe's strong hands trying to pinion her without pressing too hard. At first she had not understood Sheena's command to him not to hurt her but now she understood. 'I'll have bruises already, Joe. Bruises enough to put you inside for the rest of your life. You should have thought before you went with a dirty slut like that!' Now she could hear her own voice, the madness in it, but she still didn't care. The pleasure in letting go was too great and not to be contained too quickly.

'If I were you,' Sheena advised Joe, 'I'd put her outside the door and lock it. Let her cool off. Let the village hear her ranting and raging. At least someone might have an idea who started it. She's probably hit menopause, I shouldn't be surprised!'

In her struggling, Natasha and Joe had reached the door from living room to kitchen so it was easy enough for Joe to turn the handle and push Natasha through.

Sheena turned away. 'I'm going to dress. It's the old story, Joe, a woman scorned. You should be flattered.'

The noise from within the cottage, the shouting, the tussling, a chair falling, carried to the lane outside. The cool, still air, without a breath of wind, was filled with the ugliness of rage and despair. A young moon had risen just high enough to top the chestnut trees the other side of the lane.

Three cars pulled up quickly and their occupants, jumping out, paused to listen.

As soon as he saw the policemen Joe let go of Natasha but it was too late. He ran backwards into the living room.

'Are you badly hurt?' one of the policemen shouted at Natasha. They had heard her shrieks and were prepared for murder or worse.

Icy pale, Natasha gasped for breath. In a nightmare she saw one of the policemen swoop up a large piece of glass lying under the table while two more swept past her after Joe.

'I'm not going to press charges!' she screamed. Whisky fumes swirled about her head.

'Who's talking about charges?' A confident voice came from somewhere. 'He's a lifer, isn't he?'

At the same moment, Sheena, catching her foot in the trailing coverlet as she tried to escape upstairs, pulled the covering half-way down her body. 'Fuck!'

'Look, sir!' exclaimed the first policeman to burst in at

the front door, 'He's got another woman in here, a fucking naked woman!'

Joe, receding from the kitchen door, arrived close enough to the hallway to hear this. With a suicidal display of manhood, he hit the speaker with his bunched fist. The policeman, holding his nose, fell sideways.

'Oh, shit! Oh, shit.' Sheena collapsed into a sitting position on the stairs.

'Got you now and for ever, matey.' Five large policemen converged on Joe. One of them was the officer who had once driven him home. Exhilarated and relieved by their success – this was a killer they had been hunting down who might have been armed – they uttered whoops and grunts of triumph as they kicked and punched.

One on the stairs and one in the kitchen, the two women slumped in similar abjection.

Walter was still in his office when Natasha telephoned him. He had taken out his manuscript of the life of Jesus again, and had been reading it through and making notes for several hours. He was only vaguely aware that it was the middle of the night, but when he heard Natasha's voice he immediately assumed a reproach and began to apologize for not having returned to the flat. 'Old habits . . .'

'I've done something terrible,' interrupted Natasha, her voice thick with tears. She sat in her car outside the police station, crouched over her mobile. She had tried to explain to the police and had failed or, at least, had been made to feel unnecessary. Joe had smashed a bottle over a man's head, he had attacked a policeman. If she decided not to press charges, that was her business but it would make no difference to Joe's fate. They had enough to put him away for years, probably for ever. They were conquering heroes, and one of them had a broken nose.

She had tried to reach Julie, but her voice was so faint as to be unintelligible except for the one word 'pneumonia'. Natasha was desperate. This was not something terrible that had happened to her, as her father's disloyalty, Naomi's death, Frank's removal of himself into drunkenness, but something terrible she had done herself.

Walter tried to concentrate. He pushed away the manuscript. Was Natasha having a nightmare?

Natasha tried to explain. 'Joe's in prison, for good this time, and it's all my fault!' She tried not to sound hysterical.

Of course, it would be Joe. Discounting the last part of the sentence as unbelievable, Walter prepared to be sympathetic. He saw Joe as Natasha's weakness. 'Where are you?' he asked, meaning to come to her and hold her in his arms the way he had learned. The thought gave him pleasure; that he could be the protective male was more than he'd ever hoped.

'Outside the police station. In my car.'

'I see.' The image of comforter disappeared.

'Joe hit a policeman because – because . . .' Natasha's voice faltered and stopped. It was not true to say that Joe's punch had been due to her; he had hit out because of what the policeman had said about Sheena. He had been defending Sheena's good name. She gave something between a sob and a laugh. She realized it was impossible to try to describe what had happened over a mobile phone in the middle of the night. 'I'm driving back home. Can you get here tomorrow?'

'Tomorrow. Wednesday.' Walter was shocked. Surely she knew Wednesday was press day, not a moment free. 'I'll come later on,' he prevaricated.

Natasha leaned her head on the wheel as, with one hand, she switched off the mobile. No help there. Not that she deserved any. 'While temporarily of unsound mind', that was the best she could do in mitigation of her behaviour.

Three police cars had come to capture Joe and one had stayed behind. The two occupants completed their duty by searching the house and adjoining land. They had left their blue light whirling on the top of the car, like a lighthouse beacon in the dark countryside. Gradually, despite the lateness of the hour and the dark cold, a group of villagers gathered to watch. A little ashamed of their curiosity and excitement, of their secret wish that something cruel and violent had happened in their peaceful corner of the world, they hung back as if behind an invisible cordon. With their anoraks and scraves, gloves and torches, they might have been spectators on Guy Fawkes' night, the revolving light an exotic blue catherine wheel. Among them stood Mrs Fordyce's husband, who had been out walking their dog.

A young father had taken the trouble to wrest his two sons from the television and bring them out to appreciate live action; their eyes gleamed bright and pleased. They were the same boys who had enjoyed taunting Joe from their bicycles. No one had approached near enough to either of the policemen to discover what had actually happened, although the rumour had already circulated that

Joe Feather had been arrested yet again and that at least one woman had been involved, perhaps more.

In the yard, one of the policemen, holding in front of him a powerful flashlight like a weapon, went into the shed. After a few minutes he came out holding a spade and called over his colleague. The group of spectators drew closer until they could see the silver gleam of the blade as the policeman ran his fingers down it. They had found fresh earth, proof that it had been used recently. Taking the spade with them, they disappeared round the back of the cottage.

'They're looking for a grave,' said one of the little boys knowingly. But to his disappointment he could see nothing further for nearly fifteen minutes. Some of the spectators had even drifted away before the policemen re-emerged, one holding something in his arms.

'I told you so. He's got a body!' One brother gave the other a shove.

'Don't be silly. It's much too small.'

The policeman came closer.

'I know what it is. It's a dog. He's gone and killed that puppy!' As far as the boys were concerned, television would have to prove itself after a night like this.

'He strangled his first victim in our house,' said their father generally. 'My wife's pregnant again, you know.' And those around him, most of whom owned at least one dog, felt that, really, they had got more than they had bargained for.

'Killed his puppy, did he?' Mr Fordyce raised his voice.

'Only weeks old, I'd say,' answered the youngest

policeman, looking near tears. 'Strangle an innocent little puppy. What sort of man would do a thing like that?'

Sheena was taken to the police station, questioned and released.

'I'm not going anywhere!' She plonked herself down on a bench in the reception area.

'Suit yourself.' At first no one bothered her, and then an older policeman came on duty. 'You can't sit there all night,' he said, in fatherly tones.

'If you're concerned for my comfort,' replied Sheena tartly, 'please don't worry. I should tell you I'm a journalist and I'm on a job. I'm working, just as much as you.'

The elderly policeman had been joined by another and he began to smile broadly. 'So that's what you were doing with him, then? A bit of investigative journalism. Isn't that what you call it?'

'No,' glowered Sheena, furious with herself, the policeman, everyone. 'I want to know what will happen to Mr Feather. What he'll be charged with.'

'He doesn't have to be charged with anything. Just as I don't have to tell you anything,' said the younger man.

'Why don't you go home, Miss?'

'I can't!' Sheena tried to sound defiant, but the genuine concern in the man's face made her feel like crying.

'Can't doesn't make any sense.'

'I can't because my car's at the village, or near the village, and anyway it's run out of petrol.'

'Not a very wise virgin,' said the younger policeman, in

a loud undertone. But the older one came over to Sheena and put his hand on her shoulder.

'Come on, Miss. I'll find you a can of petrol and someone to give you a lift.'

Sheena gave in. But she was far too tired to drive back to London. After the policeman had filled her car, she pretended to drive away and, as soon as he had gone, pulled over on to a verge. After carefully swallowing two sleeping pills from her handbag, she climbed into the back seat.

At three or four in the morning, the night that had been silent, with hardly wind enough to rustle the dying leaves, began to change its nature. A great depression out in the Atlantic, which had already caused a turmoil of waves and gale warnings all along the cost, roared and blew itself across the south-west.

Sheena woke blearily with the sensation that the car was rocking. Opening her eyes she saw up to the sky through the opposite side window, and it seemed to be filled with flocks of flying missiles, lit up in flashes by the light of moon and stars that went on and off crazily. Not realizing that the clouds tearing across the sky were causing this strange sporadic illumination and that the missiles were only leaves snatched off the trees and shot into the night by the violence of the wind, she felt as if she were watching an invasion from outer space. After the events of the night before, nothing seemed impossible. Hardly awake enough to think clearly, soon, and despite the buffeting of the car, she closed her eyes and did not open them again, even when a rumbling noise further down the road indicated that the wind had taken a victim.

Mrs Fordyce heard the rumbling, too. She had been lying awake, listening to the rise of the storm, to the frantic whipping of the still unshorn wisteria against her window. She was thinking of Joe and the horrible thing he had done. However hard she tried, she could not imagine how anyone in his right mind could commit such an act of pointless, wanton cruelty. She pictured the puppy, his trusting eyes and wobbly legs. Restlessly, Mrs Fordyce turned in her bed, which seemed too warm, too comfortable with her husband snoring beside her, for the thoughts she was trying to confront.

If Joe were mad, which indeed was the most charitable conclusion, then she had been wrong about him all along. It struck her with a deepening unhappiness that Joe had loved the puppy and, by all accounts, he had loved the woman he had also murdered. If Joe were insane – and now Mrs Fordyce began to feel convinced of it – then it was better he was put inside for the rest of his life before he did more damage.

The storm rose. The giant sycamore toppled over and Mrs Fordyce cried a tear or two for Joe and Joe's dog while her husband and her dog (snoring too, but in the kitchen) slept contentedly.

Natasha, who, like Mrs Fordyce, did not believe in pills to change the nature of reality, lay in bed. In her well-ordered garden, nothing was loose to batter or bang. Even the trees were properly lopped and trimmed so that the wind could not get a hold and topple them, like a ship under sail. Natasha's garden, even by this early point in the autumn, was reefed and made secure. Yet she, too, lay awake.

Walter stayed most of the night in his office and, although the wind had not altogether blown itself out by the time it reached London, he was unaware of any dramatic weather conditions. He had been disturbed, however, by Natasha's untypical telephone call and found himself unable to concentrate on a chapter from St Thomas Aquinas, 'The Nature of Love', from which he had planned to take notes.

Between five and six he decided to walk back to the flat for a couple of hours' sleep and found himself following a miniature garbage truck mounted on the pavement. Progressing slowly and noisily, it cleaned and gobbled up paper, racing evasively, and rolling cans. It left a glutinous wake behind, as a snail or slug leaves a shiny trail. Walter wondered if he should not be examining the nature of beauty rather than the nature of love, and he pictured the scene in Natasha's garden when he had declared his love for her. He remembered her white dress against the dark trunks of the tree and the sunlight dappling through on to the pale grass. There, it had been impossible to separate love from beauty or beauty from love.

The storm was at its strongest on the part of the southern coast where Amy's university was situated and where she lay, sleepless, in her narrow bed. Her room was in a modern building near the sea-front and the wind seemed to blast through the insubstantial walls in waves of noise, receding only to attack even more fiercely. Amy imagined the watery waves tossing up above the sea wall, and did not even attempt to sleep. Besides, she was reminded of another evening when she had heard the wind gusting round thin walls.

Bravely, Amy allowed herself to recall the sound of wind in trees, funnelling down narrow lanes, flinging about anything loose or light. When her father had come to the door, it had swung wide, making her laugh excitedly; she could remember the exact tone of that laugh. Then he had gone upstairs with her mother while she sat cross-legged in front of the television, and above and around the wind clattered and banged. Or had that part been inside her head?

Joe had been her friend; that was the point. That was the truth. She had liked, perhaps even loved him. It was much more than the odd visit to his calves. He took her for rides on his tractor, he allowed her to run with his dog and jump off his bales of straw. He showed her the foxes' den and where the first cowslips grew, and where the mushrooms were big enough to make tables for her dolls. He showed her all this, taught her how to love the countryside, gave her confidence and independence – and then he murdered her mother. How could he have done that to her? Amy cried, sobbing out loud into the noise of the storm.

After a while she quietened again and made herself picture the village, not just their little house but Joe's too and his yard where he had milked his cows and tinkered with his beloved tractor. She understood now that the reason why they had got on so well together was that, in some ways, he had been like a child, with a child's eagerness and innocence. And then he had murdered her mother.

There is no way I can really put it all together, thought Amy, but for my own sake, now he is back there in the village and not shut away, out of sight out of mind, I must try. Then she told herself – as bold and resolute in life as she was on the tennis court (her sweeping forehand famous) – that the only way to deal with the dark fears of childhood was to confront them in the bright light of maturity. So she told herself, and so she determined to pay a visit to the village and to Joe, as soon as was practicable.

The wind was followed by rain, which swept cleanly over countryside and town. The hole from which the police had removed the puppy filled with water to the brim, and Walter's snail's trail was washed right away. Towards dawn the fierce clouds thinned until they were only black stripes against an orange dawn. Then the earliest risers – farmers hurrying to see what damage had been caused by the storm, the sleepless, wan-faced at their windows – looked up in awe and saw a tiger sky.

Joe, locked back into the same police cell he had inhabited before, was aware of neither wind nor rain nor sky. He lay on his bunk and tried to remember those few hours of happiness with Sheena, but already their memory was fading and, quite soon, he began to wonder if she had only come to him as a set-up for the police. His mother had always warned him about girls who took advantage. But then he remembered again the softness of her skin, and those moments when, together, they'd left the world behind.

Chapter Twenty-six

Winter came early that year, as if the storm, inaccurately called by some newspapers a hurricane, had swept away autumn. Weeks of cold rain were followed by frosts that hardened the ground to several feet down and turned plants into icy fossils.

Amy walked through this bleak land like a perfect stranger. She had never read about Joe's reincarceration, and had been planning every day to visit the village. But it was only in December that she borrowed a car and set off under a white sky. The journey had taken her less long than she expected – a few hours to cover a lifetime – but now she walked and waited for recognition. One of the problems was the frozen aspect of the countryside, for she and her mother had arrived in April and their story had been over before the leaves were off the trees. She had parked the car at the centre of the village where she had felt certain there had once been a vast old tree but now there was a trio of small, obviously newly planted saplings in a circle of paved ground with a bench. It was all rather suburban, she decided.

Their cottage had been down a lane beyond this green, at the opposite end of the village from Joe's farm. It seemed, after all, easiest to go there first; nevertheless, she half expected to hear a tractor behind her and turn to see Joe's face behind the glass. Already the dead-eyed convict of his photograph in the paper was changing to an image of a young, cheerful man, about the age she was now. But no one was outside on this freezing morning and Amy heard her own footsteps and watched her white breath floating ahead of her as she walked bravely down the lane.

The cottage was both smaller and bigger than she remembered. An extension had been added to one side from which there was a loud sound of hammering, but the original building seemed as small as a doll's house and was almost overwhelmed by a prickly creeper covered with bright red berries. As she approached, a large bird flew past her with an offended squawk and a berry fell at her feet. It was hard not to see it as a drop of blood. Amy rang the front-door bell but the hammering continued undisturbed. She peered through the window and was shocked to see a television in exactly the same place as it had been all those years ago. The room was empty.

She went to the window of the extension and saw a young man bent over a worktable. She knocked on the glass, and he looked up.

'So you used to live here, then?' He had asked her in at once, relieved, it seemed, to be released from whatever piece of wood he was torturing, explaining that his wife and kids were at the doctor's. They sat in the kitchen in the company of a large bear watching from a high chair. Amy did not remember the room.

'I was just passing through,' she said evasively, although accepting a cup of coffee with gratitude. Her hands were shaking with the cold.

'In this very house, was it?'

'I'm not quite sure. It was so long ago. Tell me, did there used to be a big old tree in the middle of the village?'

'Absolutely right there was. If you'd come a month or two earlier you'd have seen it still. But the night of the storm – you remember that storm? – it blew clean over, terrible sight, roots waving in the air like arms. They even tried to get it back up again but it wouldn't go. It left a pit twenty feet deep, as deep as this house is high . . .'

He was voluble. Amy didn't like his volubility or the look of his unshaven, not unhandsome face. There was an eagerness in his regret for the passing of the tree; she thought he was the sort of man who enjoyed disasters, as mitigation for the lack of good news in his own life. She knew he would tell her everything about the man she had come to visit and she didn't want to hear it from such a person.

'That was quite a night altogether. You might have read about it. The *Daily* — did three pages. They interviewed me, you know. The money came in handy, I can tell you.' He laughed.

'What happened?'

'That murderer, Joseph Feather. He did it again. Ran berserk. Drunk as a stoat. Waving a broken bottle.'

Amy, knees trembling, hands clutched round her empty cup, listened to the story of that night, told in the most lurid detail that its teller could remember or imagine. By the time he paused for breath, she was hardly clear whether one or three people had been killed.

'I never read about it,' she murmured. 'And so many dead.'

'Well, only the poor little puppy actually died. My boys had nightmares for weeks afterwards. I told my wife she

294

should take them for counselling but then she got a part-time job in a bakery. So I got them a puppy instead . . .'

He was talking again, the details of his family life mixing with further stories of Joe's iniquity and madness. 'Even Mrs Fordyce who came to our protest meeting – we tried to get rid of him, you know – admitted after that night he was mentally round the bend. Mrs Wynne, who'd known him since he was born, had always said the same.'

'I remember Mrs Wynne.'

'Well, she's still here, although her rheumatism . . .'

He was off again.

'So Joseph Feather went to prison?'

'You're telling me. They say his cottage and land will be up for sale and there's talk of council housing on his old yard. Good idea, I say, although it will make him a rich man, and what use all that money will be where he is . . . If you ask me, they should take it and distribute . . .'

He talked, and when she could bear it not more, Amy left. She walked back down the narrow lane with its steep, enclosing banks and was surprised to see a pale sun rising out of the blank sky. Perhaps she would go in and see Mrs Wynne. Sometimes she had been allowed to take down from the mantelpiece a china lady dressed in layers of china skirts. The kindly Mrs Wynne might have been a better choice of informant than the voluble young man. But, in the end, she got into her car and drove away without speaking to anyone else. If she hurried, she could get back while the sun still shone.

It seemed to Amy, on that hurried backward journey, more like a flight, that if her object in this visit had been to match the man she remembered with the man who had murdered her mother, then the news she had been told had made that quite impossible. The whole expedition had been utterly pointless – except that now she knew Joe was back in prison, perhaps for ever. That should be a comfort.

The bitter winter was a comfort to Natasha; it suited her mood. She bought an ornate iron stove with a funnel for her studio into which she pushed branches from a neighbour's tree, fallen in the storm. She worked there all day, seeing no one except Paula, and by Christmas she had so much material that she decided to visit New York with some samples.

In the first days Walter had telephoned, leaving enquiring and occasionally witty messages on her answer-machine. She listened to them, but could hear nothing in his voice to show he really cared. The Saturday after the storm she looked through her studio window and saw him walk nervously through the cool rigidity of the garden. She had hung several roundels of coloured glass against the window and, as she moved along to watch Walter's progress, he became changed, by turns, with crimson, emerald, topaz, cerulean. In all these guises, he was a stranger.

Natasha slipped out of her studio and fled across the frozen fields. In the middle of one there was a small, steep valley in which an old brick-built shed, with tiles barely supported by tottering pillars, had been left alone to rot. She sheltered there shivering, hardly thinking at all, until she looked up and saw that a herd of small black bullocks were slowly surrounding her, curiously lowering their heads, daring each other to come closer. She waved her arm and they pranced backwards, snorting white breath through their nostrils.

After an hour or so, she went back to the house and Walter had gone. He had not waited long, she thought.

In New York, she stayed with Felicia, for the first time frightened of being alone it that tireless city. It was Christmas, and, coming directly from her bleak country-side, the bravura lights and decorations she had known all her life seemed more beautiful, more startling.

'Your stained glass is just as beautiful, just as extra-ordinary,' protested Felicia, when Natasha asked her view on why people wanted to create this glittering, unreal paradise.

Was her laboured work as tawdry as Christmas decora-tions? It was popular, at least. And, if she had any need of money, she would, she supposed, rejoice in her orders. But when she was offered a show to herself by Gino, she told him she was not ready and hastened back to England.

Felicia had, of course, questioned Natasha on her love life. Several conversations began and ended in confusion.

'It was never a love affair.'

'But I understood . . .'

'We thought we loved each other. We were wrong. We did not understand anything.'

'How did he fuck?'

'Oh, Felicia.' She could not make herself say the truth: It is not a good fuck I want but a good lover. Besides, Felicia knew it anyway.

Another evening Felicia found a copy of *The Cucumber*, which, in a weak moment, Natasha had bought at the airport. She read the editorial closely.

'Your Walter's a clever man, I'd say.'

'He's one of the stupidest men I've ever met. He hasn't a clue.'

'The trouble is, you've been on your own too long. Are you sure he's not gay?'

One morning over coffee, Felicia decided to link Natasha's perverse attitude to Naomi, or failing that, Frank. 'You have to admit Naomi was always the love of your life.'

'She was my only child.' Natasha did not say, I gave her up for Walter, but that, too, was at least part of the truth.

'You shouldn't let her stand in your way.'

'And I admit to loving Frank, too. See how strong I am.'

'I recommend a shrink. Perhaps two.'

'I had a shrink. I had three shrinks.'

Finally, over lunch in the restaurant that had once been a bed of flowers but had now been transformed into a winter wonderland of twinkling, frosted branches, Felicia raised the subject she understood least. 'You never talk about your murderer.'

'He's nothing to do with anything,' replied Natasha quickly. She could not bring herself to tell Felicia about the guilt and humiliation of that wild night.

Nevertheless, on the aeroplane back to England, Natasha determined to write a letter to Joe. Julie had sent the address of the prison where he was being held. She had also volunteered the information that the prison was in the far east of the country in the middle of a reclaimed marsh and, since it would involve four train journeys for her to visit and a very large bill for the tax-payers, she was handing over the case to another probation officer nearer the area. 'It used to be the dumping ground for old rolling-stock,' Julie had written, untypically caustic. 'I suppose they hoped the carriages would sink in the mud and now they hope the same for the prisoners.'

The letter also informed Natasha that, at some point or another, Joe would have to come to trial for assaulting a police officer, 'but I understand you know more about that than I do'.

Sensitive to reproach, Natasha read the letter again, she had it now on the aeroplane, smoothed out on her table. But all she could see was that the good Julie had moved off the case and left it behind. A postscript in her own childish handwriting added, 'My bronchitis turned to pneumonia and put me in hospital. I came out a stone lighter and have lost another since. Silver-lining time!' Natasha remembered having assumed that Julie was content with her weight and felt ashamed. Always shame.

'Dear Joe, I don't know how much you remember about that night. In many ways it was more like a nightmare.' Natasha put down her pen and ordered wine from the attendant. Joe had made love to Sheena that night. She must not forget that. Perhaps that was the one thing he remembered. What did she know about anyone?

'Dear Joe, I have been meaning to write for weeks but only just found out where you are. I am still so ashamed about my behaviour.' But why should he care about her feelings? He probably hadn't even noticed her rage or had certainly forgotten it by now.

'Dear Joe, At last I have your address. Would you like a visit? I hesitate to say, as I did before . . .' Hesitate is right. Natasha crumpled up her piece of paper and finished her glass of wine. What was the point? She did not want to see him unless she could say the things that must remain unspoken. And he almost certainly – certainly did not want to see her. Yet she wrote one more letter: 'Dear Joe, If you would like a visit, let me know. I am so sorry.'

This she put in an envelope and addressed and propped it on her dinner tray. Outside the port-hole window, she watched the blue sunlit sky turn prematurely golden and orange and red until the sunset was overtaken by the vast unbroken darkness of night.

Natasha stamped and posted the letter at Heathrow airport, but over the long bitter weeks of January and February she received no reply.

Joe had been in this prison before. It was fairly new, new red-brick and new high wire fences, but his cell was like all the others: small, cramped, airless. All the same, he spent his free time there even when he could have been unlocked for 'association'. He did not want to associate. He was back to the bottom of the prison cycle but this time round he had neither the expectation nor the desire to work his way through the system and out the other side. He had a job, fitting together bits of plastic, and that was enough for him. He soon gained a reputation as a hard man who was best left alone, and that was exactly what he wanted.

One or two people attempted to break through this self-imposed isolation. His new probation officer popped in to introduce herself, but it needed only a few minutes to establish a tacit agreement that there was very little she could do for him.

The chaplain was more persevering. 'Third time lucky,' he announced, when Joe opened his cell door to him. 'I was beginning to think you were like Mouldy Warp, hibernating for the winter.' Reluctantly, Joe let him in.

'I hear you're a bit of a loner,' said the chaplain. He was a small, thin, talkative man with anxious big eyes, and for some reason Joe did not shut his mind against him. Perhaps it was just chance that he had come at a time when Joe had something to say. 'And never any visitors, I'm told,' continued the Reverend Allen. 'Nor letters. It doesn't do to get too cut off, you know.'

They sat, in the confined space, very close together, and the chaplain noted the cell's extreme tidiness, and saw nothing personal that gave any clue to its inhabitant's personality.

'I keep myself to myself because I like it that way,' said Joe mildly.

'I wondered, just wondered, if you might like to come to a service one day. It covers more or less every belief, although the Muslims are being a bit difficult. You're not a Muslim, I presume? No. I knew a countryman like you who was, though. He'd inherited it from his father who'd inherited it from his father who'd inherited it from his father, who'd gone east as a servant a hundred years before and when his master converted he followed suit. Funny, though, hearing a man with a real Sussex accent declaring he was a Muslim. Knew chunks of the Koran. Word-perfect. Not that I've anything against Muslims, you understand.'

'My mother and I didn't hold with church-going.'

'In a village, was it?'

Joe nodded. 'She fell out with the vicar when I was a child.' He paused, giving the impression that he had more to say.

'But perhaps you still believed in God?' It was a much practised and hopeful question mark, and since it produced no response, he added, 'His mercy.'

'No. I can't say as I do – believe in His mercy, that is. Not for a man as has done what I did. It wouldn't be fair or right when you consider how some people live all their lives doing nothing but good. I reckon I deserve damnation, and the sooner it comes the better.'

The two stared at each other, both more or less aghast, Joe because he had spoken to this stranger of things he hardly knew he felt, and the priest because this was the sort of challenge for which he had joined the Prison Service and for which, over the years, he had felt himself becoming more and more inadequate. He found himself having to stifle a longing to look at his watch. It was very hot in the cell. Bravely, however, he launched on a lesson in the Christian message of repentance and forgiveness. From Joe's face he could not tell whether he was listening or merely keeping silent out of politeness.

There came into the Reverend Allen's mind a line from the Apocalypse which he had read in his Bible that morning. He could not remember it exactly but he managed a paraphrase: 'To him that overcomes suffering I will give a white pebble and on that pebble will be inscribed a name which is his alone and that no one else will know.' He looked at Joe awkwardly, himself moved at the words. 'So you mustn't just write yourself off,' he said. 'God knows the name of each one of us, even though we may feel like just one of a million pebbles on the beach.'

'I like that.' Joe seemed to be making a pebble shape with his fingers. 'I'll think of that.'

The chaplain rose. He was sweating but his heart was

light. This is what true inspiration is, he thought, inspiration to say the right thing. How often he had prayed for it, and how often failed. 'I'll come again some time.'

'I don't mind if you do,' said Joe.

Amy knew nothing about prisons, except the few ideas she'd picked up from the popular press. But now, wherever she turned, it seemed to be the principal subject of discussion. Every time she heard the word she was reminded of Joe, until she found herself trying to guess at different times of day what he would be doing just then.

Naturally she did not share these thoughts with anyone for she thought them unwholesome and neurotic. Instead, she took up squash and trained so hard that she was on the verge of being chosen for the college team seconds. In order to avoid this, she went home for the weekend. It was the middle of March and already the garden was filled with primroses, and the daffodils were beginning to cast off their sheaths. Amy walked between them with her father.

'Well, now you know he's inside – for good, I hope. There you are. All over.' He hesitated. Amy saw her step-brother and -sister at the end of the garden, petting a large lop-eared rabbit. 'Yes. Yes. I had a letter from that journalist.' He looked at Amy's face, which was impassive. ' "Confined", that's what she wrote, quite unreachable in a prison for the worst sort of murderers. Child abusers. IRA bombers, that sort of thing. So we can all get on with our lives. That journalist girl, too. She's working in a shop now.' He tried to see his daughter's face, but she had bent to study an emerging daffodil. 'Would you like the letter?'

Amy took it, sliding it quickly into her jeans pocket.

Then she went to admire the rabbit, which was new and a birthday present.

It was true that Sheena was working in a shop, living at home and setting off each morning with her father to the suburban shopping centre that gave them both employment. She did not think of it as her future, of course, but it would do for now. Until she felt less exhausted. More in control. She, too, wrote to Joe and received no answer.

Chapter Twenty-seven

Amy could not keep her father's words out of her mind: 'There you are. All over.' The more she heard them, the less they seemed to be true. On a Saturday, when an early spring astounded everyone, the air so mild that it soothed the skin, the ground soft and springy underfoot, Amy set out for the prison at the address described in Sheena's letter.

She travelled by train and, as Julie had informed Natasha would be the case, it was necessary to change often. After the first few hours, she began to have the inappropriate feeling that she was on holiday, heading out for a remote destination where the sun would be hot and her heart light.

Amy looked out of the train windows and stood on empty station platforms and began to count the number of church spires that filled her view, each more magnificent than the last. She felt she was behaving like a tourist but could not dim her rising sense of hope.

Her final station was at a red-brick town where no spire was visible. It was a town, judging by the solidity of its buildings, although it seemed only the size of a village. The land had been absolutely flat for some time and it continued so ahead. All around the sunlit sky spread in unbroken blue. She waited outside the station, leaning against the warm wall, and after a while a taxi appeared. 'Yes?' A middle-aged man put his elbow and face out of the window.

She told him her destination, unable to stop a self-conscious blush.

'On a Saturday?' was all he said, before setting off at dashing speed through a prairie of green wheatfields. The high barbed-wire fence and walls, stretching round a solid encampment of brick and concrete varied only by towers at regular intervals, arose out of this verdant scene.

They drove down a driveway, through a car park and reached a reception area in the outer rim of defences. Amy told herself that the actual entrance, if she ignored so many walls and fences, looked no different from the building where her father worked. She paid the driver without looking at his face, and went inside.

'Yes, Miss?' Despite coming from behind a very thick piece of glass, the voice was unmistakably aggressive. Surprised, Amy made out a man in a uniform white shirt, leaning not forward to make communication easier but back, almost lounging back, she thought, and saw a cup of tea in his hand.

'I'm looking for someone.' Now she could make out a second white-shirted man, although his voice, too, was turned away. She got out her letter and, ignoring the lack of interest beyond the glass, began to read out her information. 'It's from a friend. Last year . . .'

'Before you go any further, Miss, that is, if you're planning to visit, there are no visits today and, moreover, where's your VO?'

'VO. I don't know. What's that?'

The first officer began to laugh. 'You don't know what's a VO. A VO is a Visitor's Order, sent to you by the prisoner, and if you haven't got one of those then you can't get in, whether it's Saturday or Monday or Wednesday.'

Amy could only hear half of this but enough to make her realize that she would not get to see Joe and her journey was wasted. She stood still, staring blindly at the two or three layers of heavy bars and sheet glass in front of her. The brilliant sunshine of the afternoon hung like a curtain behind her. To her mortification, she burst into tears and stood weeping copiously in the middle of the hall.

The second officer appeared a little softened by this feminine lack of control, or perhaps he merely wanted to get rid of her. He leaned forward and lifted up a glass lid. 'He's your boyfriend, is he?'

Amy shook her head.

'Brother, then?'

Amy turned from his questioning and hurried out into the sunshine. His voice, quite kindly now that it was too late, followed her, 'Next time, tell him to send you a VO, and make sure he's still in this prison. Last year's a long time to be in the same place.'

Amy walked more slowly now, through the car park and out on to the same long, straight road that the taxi had followed. She had no way of reaching the station except on foot but the walking gradually lessened her unhappy frustration. Whoever said that her search would be easy? It had taken over sixteen years to reach this point; a few more months hardly made any difference.

After she had walked for ten minutes or more and the prison had disappeared over the skyline behind her, she became aware of a high-pitched trilling that seemed to be keeping pace with her. At first she could see nothing, just the empty sky and the endless lightly swaying green of the unripe corn, but then she felt rather than saw a flutter at the edge of the field and, just for a moment, she caught the flash of a tiny bird. A skylark. Her own skylark, weaving in and out of the stalks and now, suddenly, as if realizing his cover was blown, he left the earth altogether and soared directly upwards while song poured out in thrilling arpeggios. Delighted, Amy watched until he was only a black speck in the sky.

The chaplain read Amy's letter to Joe. He had tried to persuade Joe on to a literacy course but Joe had refused. The letter made the chaplain very nervous, although he supposed a confrontation between murderer and victim or, at least, victim once removed, should be just the thing for a man in the service of Christ to encourage. The murderer confronts his crime and the victim (or victim representative) forgives. Wasn't that how it went? Yet he feared for Joe, whose fragility he had begun to recognize. And he worried that the girl, who, admittedly, seemed normal enough and educated, was asking for the meeting out of some unhealthy form of curiosity. The letter was so short as to be almost peremptory, and reminded Joe that, if he should allow her to visit, he must not forget to send her a Visitor's Order.

The chaplain put down the letter and looked at Joe. He had invited him into his office so the space was less confined than their cell interviews but, even so, he felt rising the same sense of claustrophobia that he always suffered in Joe's presence. It was as if Joe was beyond some civilizing process that distances one man from another and makes each other's personality less oppressive. Joe, although he never raised his voice and moved gently and politely, had a forcefulness that weighed on the chaplain. Joe never spoke unless he had something to say. Now he was staring down at his fingers, which were formed in the habitual pebble shape.

'You don't have to hurry with an answer,' said the chaplain. 'No one says you have to see her or even answer her.'

'That's right.' Joe stood and held out his hand for the letter.

The arrival of the Visitor's Order threw Amy into confusion, partly because there was no covering note and partly because it was for a specific period of time, which turned out to be either the following week or the week after. Since she had posted her letter to Joe on her return from the prison, she had hardly thought about him at all. The tennis season had opened with the fine weather and she was playing every day so her body felt taut and healthy, strong enough to repel unhealthy obsessions.

She looked at the Visitor's Order with dismay.

'What's that?' asked her friend, Jemima, also picking up her mail.

'Nothing. Nothing interesting.' Amy hid away the envelope and was aware, as she did so, of the secret compulsion starting up inside her head again. She knew she would have to draw to its conclusion that first long journey.

Joe sat in his cell waiting to be called to the visiting room. He wore the regulation prison clothing of blue and white striped shirt and blue trousers. His hair was cut short, a black rim round his face, which had regained its prison pallor. He looked unnaturally clean, like a child whose mother had scrubbed him and told him to sit still and keep out of mischief till she's ready for him. He had been ready for an hour before the visiting hour and this was the fourth day he had waited. Since Amy had not responded to the VO, it was possible she had decided not to come, after all, but he had to be prepared. So he sat still with a hand on either knee.

His memories of Amy as a little girl were not very clear. He knew she had been physically unlike her mother, which had made their connection seem less strong and therefore the child less important. The emotion of those summer months had been so heightened that he had hardly seen anyone or anything clearly. He was aware only of a dazzling kaleidoscope of scenes with the woman, which had spun into their blurred and desperate end. Somewhere among those scenes was a chubby fair girl, who was startled by the countryside and pleased when he took her with him up the hill or in his tractor. These expeditions had left little impression on him because he had only done them for her mother, and her shadow made everybody and everything else vague.

On the sixth day of Joe's vigil, a Friday at about two o'clock, a prison officer came to collect him.

'You're in luck. A pretty young girl prepared to spoil her day!'

Amy's journey had been very different from the last occasion, so much so that she hardly felt as if she were entering the same land. The weather was hazy from the start, and when she entered the region of churches their towers or spires were hardly visible, bound in misty stoles. By the time her last train reached the flatlands and the red-brick town, the mist had dissolved into a fine rain that hung in the air with hardly enough weight to fall.

There were to be no holiday feelings on this day, no skylarks. Amy realized that there had been an unreality about her last attempted visit which had protected her. Today, although the contours of the land might be disguised, the cornfields on either side of her taxi hazy (the same taxi, she thought), she was proceeding inexorably to a conclusion.

This conviction was confirmed by the long and dreary process of entering the prison in the company of a handful of other visitors, who all wore the same look of refugees who cannot quite believe where they find themselves. One or two, certainly, knew the ropes. A large middle-aged woman took the trouble to notice Amy's extra-bewildered air.

'First time, is it, love?' She tried to explain the system, although it was never the same one month to the next, she assured Amy, with a mixture of pride and resignation. 'I've been visiting courtesy of HMP for twelve years and you wouldn't believe the things they think up. Last time it was shaking out my handkerchief – for cocaine, they said, as if they didn't know my husband's a Christian Scientist and won't even take an aspirin.'

Under this lady's guidance, Amy learned that when her name was called she would be shown into a hall where she could choose a table and wait for her inmate to be brought to her. 'You can have a cup of tea ready for him,' she advised. 'It breaks the ice, if you know what I mean. Got no children, then?'

The assumption behind her question silenced Amy.

'Don't mind me. For all I know he's your father. The worst thing is they've just banned smoking.'

'Yes,' agreed Amy, impartially.

The hall was large and, with its rows of tables, reminded Amy of the college hall where she had sat for examinations the year before. However, it was only sparsely occupied so she was able to choose a table not too overlooked. Settled there, she found herself unable to summon up the will to buy tea, as recommended, from the counter ahead of her. Her head had begun to throb and she had a dangerous pit of sickness in her stomach. What if she vomited, fainted or ran from the room? She looked at the prison officers, like exam adjudicators gathered at the end of the room, and decided they would have dealt with worse. In fact, probably everyone here had dealt with worse.

Joe entered the room from behind the prison officers and had his visitor pointed out to him. He was relieved to note she had her head in her hands so that she wouldn't watch him make the long walk towards her.

Amy looked up only as he stood awkwardly above her. Immediately she was amazed by his youth as if a time warp had left him unchanged during those intervening years. Although in another second she compared him with that past man and realized that this one, despite his apparent youthfulness, was altogether different from that other. It was as if he'd been skinned, she thought, taking off the tough farmer's burnishing of wind and weather to reveal the man inside. A torture victim. She dismissed that thought quickly.

'Hello.' She stood up, half held out a hand.

Joe did not dare touch her. Worse still, he was afraid he felt tears at the back of his eyes. He had not expected her to be the same age as her mother had been. The tears receded but sweat prickled his skin.

Amy's stomach stopped heaving quite so badly. 'Shall we sit?' Her voice was composed.

Joe sat. He wanted to stare at her, but instead he looked over her head, his blue eyes straining as if trying to make out something in the distance.

'Do you get many visitors?'

'No. No visitors.' Joe set his hands on the table, and began to make a circular shape with his fingers.

The horrible thought struck Amy that it was these hands that had strangled her mother. She remembered a phrase in Sheena's article, 'strong hands of a killer'. A painful flush spread over her whole face and neck.

Joe saw her eyes fixed on his hands and removed them hastily to his lap.

'Would you like tea?' asked Amy.

'No.' He saw her desperation. 'Yes. If you like.'

Amy got the tea, which neither of them wanted, and now it was Joe's turn to watch her fingers, like butterfly's wings, he thought, as she poured tea and milk and stirred both cups with her spoon.

'Thank you for seeing me,' began Amy.

Joe stared. He tried to find the words. 'You have the right.' But he could not say them. The silence became acute. Suddenly his expression seemed to change. The most extraordinary idea had just struck him. Why he had never thought of it before he could not imagine or perhaps it had been at the back of his mind, the reason he had wanted her to come.

Amy noticed the change of his expression with alarm, even though it was more a lightening than anything else. She could see he had found something he wanted to say and that was enough to frighten her. She began to talk: 'After that horrible article, I knew you were out of prison and I had to think of you in the world. I pretended it meant nothing to me but inside I was scared stiff. Not of you, exactly, although that was a part of it, but of what had happened to me all those years ago. I didn't know the details, you know, for years – perhaps I didn't ever really take them in until that article. I'm quite a placid person normally. I play games a lot, work, enjoy a beer in the pub. I thought I was all sorted, that's what I'm trying to say.'

Sustained by the knowledge of what he would soon be allowed to say, Joe managed to listen fairly calmly. 'Please,' he tried to interrupt once, when the words had to be said, but she wouldn't let him talk yet. It seemed as if, contrary to what might have been expected, it was she who had come to confess to him. She told him about her childish feelings of hatred – not just for him but for her mother also – of her problems with boyfriends, of her happy memories of that summer when he had been kind to her, of how much she had liked him, almost had a little girl's crush on him, of her guilt, her isolation, her friendships, her successes, her failures, the out-of-nowhere, terrifying despair that had led to her attempted suicide.

Joe twisted his fingers. Now he must speak. He must

speak, for the words were beginning to feel inadequate for all she was saying, for a whole life altered and dislocated by his act of madness. 'I'm sorry!' he whispered. Halted in her flow, Amy stared at him with a look of surprise, almost as if he were a stranger and had nothing to do with her.

Miserably, Joe repeated the words. 'I'm sorry.'

Amy picked up a teaspoon and focused her gaze on it with blind intensity. 'Yes. Yes,' she said eventually. 'Yes. I expect you are. I see you are. You didn't need to say it, you know. Not for me. I mean, I didn't come to hear you say that. I didn't come to forgive you either. I just wanted to see you again. Bring myself up to date. Fit you in.'

Gradually, Joe's brightness lessened. It was true, what she had said, he understood it now. His words meant nothing to her. She had her work cut out sorting her own life without worrying about his feelings. For her, he would be what he always had been, her mother's murderer. She did not want to hate him, she just wanted to get over him, like a boulder in her path. That was her right, at the very least.

As Amy continued to talk, growing in confidence, Joe bitterly and humbly bowed his head. It had been stupid to think anything could be changed with a few words. Words had never helped him with anything. He used to know about simple things: earth, crops, trees, cows, rabbits, deer, rain, night, moon.

At the end of the room, the prison officers began to check their watches and take more notice of what was going on in the hall. It was nearly the end of visiting time.

'Do you remember,' said Amy, 'that day when you took me to pick cowslips for my mother's birthday? There were nettles and cowpats and then, under the lee of a bank, half hidden in the grass, these little yellow bell-like flowers. You picked them for me and put them in my hand. You told me to give them to my mother. I can remember handing them over to her, the stalks warm from the palm of my hand. She put them in a jar by the sink and I was a bit sad because their heads drooped. We hadn't been in the village long. We didn't know about the country but she was pleased. My birthday present to her. So I was pleased, too. Later, there were the badgers' holes and their own private road across the field and, I think, once you showed me a fox with its cubs. Although that might have been in a book. Memory's a strange thing.'

'That's right. It is,' said Joe. He had his eyes on the officers as they had their eyes on him. It was time for her to go, to stop talking like this. He couldn't bear much more.

'Well, I'll be off,' said Amy, her face glowing. 'Thank you for letting me come. I won't come back. I have to get on with things.'

'Yes,' said Joe. He had to walk away first, those were the rules, so he couldn't watch her leave, see how she walked, how tall she was.

There were other things I could have said, thought Joe, as he was escorted away down a corridor, about loving. But not to her. He remembered picking the cowslips, all right, because about a week later *she* had come by and asked him where he'd picked them. Her daughter was with her father, that's what she'd said. So he'd showed her where. They went together and when they came back she helped him bring in the cows and then she'd wanted to try the fresh milk, straight from the udders. How she'd laughed at him! That was the day it started. He would have liked to have talked about loving to someone. But not to this girl. Her daughter. That other would have understood, the one who came into his bed.

Joe, for no particular reason, was strip-searched before he was allowed back into his cell but he was used to that and carried on thinking, naked, bent double. He thought about his land, the good soil clogged with ragwort and thistles, the tumbledown shed with the rusted milking-machine, the tractor tied together with bits of wire, his house furnished by charity. He could never get any of it back to what it had been. Even if he was let out in five or ten years. It was too late. The way he felt now it had been too late from the beginning.

Amy, sitting once more on a train, passing through mist and rain, closed her eyes and leaned back against the seat. Outwardly passive, her mind was still racing with all the things she had thought and said.

It was only as she made her second change of train and stood for twenty minutes on an empty platform that she began to reflect a little on Joe. Perhaps it was the reappearance of one of those spires, silver grey and sharply pointed, in a sky that was now revealing a pink lining. Staring at the spire abstractedly, she heard again her own words, 'I didn't come to forgive you . . .' What had that been in response to? His words. Yes. Now she saw his face as he whispered, 'I'm sorry.' And she had not listened.

Amy watched the train come into the station and wondered whether this visit had not been only about closing doors as she had expected. 'He killed my mother,' she said, mouthing the words as if to make them more real.

But instead of that simplifying matters it merely brought the image of his strangely youthful face in front of her again as he repeated hesitantly, 'I'm sorry.'

She had not been generous. And yet, why should she be?

Joe pulled on his clothes and went back to his cell without exchanging a word with anyone. He sat on his bed and considered his visitor, Maria's daughter. He allowed the name into his brain because she was there now anyway, picking cowslips, laughing, leading him up to her bedroom. He started as someone hammered on his door. Time to collect his supper. Get that over and done with and then it's lock up for the night. Time to really think.

Joe lay on his bed. The best thing I can do for Maria's daughter, he thought, whispering the name, is to remove myself altogether. I was on the right track all those months ago when I strangled that puppy. No one will miss me, and the chaplain can tell his white-pebble story to someone else.

Amy woke her father, who had fallen asleep in front of the television.

'I wish you hadn't come that evening. I wish you hadn't taken her upstairs. I wish she hadn't gone. I wish I hadn't been sitting watching television.'

'What? Sorry.' He was only half awake.

'Of course I don't blame you. Or her. It's just a tragedy, I suppose.' She stared at her father, tousled,

318

blinking, pretending to be less aware than he was. 'Bad timing. Bad luck. Bad conjunction of the stars.'

Now he roused himself. 'Don't talk rubbish! Murder isn't a matter of bad luck.'

'I'm exhausted.' She turned away and then back again. 'You told me it's all over. But it never can be, never.'

Joe's meetings with the chaplain were fairly well known throughout the prison so, even without his professional interest, he would have been called to the cell as soon as possible. They had only just found the body, although he should have been checked first thing in the morning when his cell was unlocked. 'Just one of those bad-luck blips,' as the governor would console the wing officer later. Not that being found earlier would have made any difference to Joe. Being a countryman and handy with knots, he had made a thorough, no mistake, job.

The chaplain looked at Joe's body, which they had laid out on his bed while a bag was found. The officers withdrew as the chaplain knelt at his side. This was, he recognized, his failure. It had happened before, but that didn't make it any easier. He prayed for hope.

'There's a note for you, sir.'

The chaplain walked through high fencing into the prison garden, where the earthy beds were planted with stumps decorated with pictures of roses. Gravel, newly laid, spread from the paths to the earth and above his head the sky was low and grey. He held the scrap of paper in his hand. Joe, always so reluctant to pick up a pen, had written a will in laborious, illiterate capitals. He had even managed to sign and date it, and have it witnessed by another prisoner.

Well, at least I can still cry, thought the chaplain, bending his head; at his feet the gravel swam mistily. After a few minutes, he crouched down and picked up a handful of the stones. They were yellow and orange, misshapen, angular, ugly, he thought. Yet he selected one paler than the others and, standing again, put it in his pocket. It could stay there, he decided, and as his fingers played with it over the years, the sharp edges would gradually become smooth.

Chapter Twenty-eight

The creepers on the front of Joe's cottage had started to grow again, tangling over the doorway, reaching pointed fingers across the dusty window-panes.

Sheena pushed open the door, her face discoloured and swollen despite heavy applications of makeup. She had already stumbled through the field at the back, paced up and down the yard and hidden her tears behind the tractor in the shed. But she had been aware all the time of cars arriving and knew the moment must be faced. The little room was full with black, standing figures. Sheena shuddered nervously. She was wearing a bright blue padded jacket, which made her legs, perched on their usual high heels, look as dainty as a child's. Natasha came to greet her and, without speaking, they clasped hands. Over her shoulder, Sheena saw Mrs Fordyce and Joe's probation officer, now, it seemed, half her previous size. Sheena thought she looked as slack as a pricked balloon and, twitching at her own padding, repressed a hysterical giggle.

'We were waiting for you,' said Natasha.

'Sorry.'

'I didn't mean that. I meant we were glad you were coming.'

'The vicar's already in the church,' announced Mrs
Fordyce.

And Joe, thought Sheena. Joe's body waiting in its
coffin. Dimly, she recalled her last meeting with Natasha,
her extraordinary, hysterical rage. But none of that mattered any more. There were others in the room she didn't
know, a couple of men, but not, she noted, Walter. What a
mess!

They walked in a procession down the hill; opposite
the three slender trees, which were covered with small pale
leaves, Mrs Wynne came to join them. She wore a battered
black straw hat and one of her neatly ironed frocks, but her
face expressed none of its usual confidence.

'Oh, Ken!' She grabbed the arm of the burly farmer.
'Old family friends. We must trust in prayer!' Ken said
nothing and they did not meet each other's eyes.

Mrs Fordyce had decorated the church with wild
flowers, cow parsley and ragged robin, daisies and butter-
cups. It was she who had arranged that Joe's funeral should
take place there. The Reverend Almeric Cooper, after
reminding her, first, that suicide was a sin and second, as
far as he knew, that Joe had never been baptised, became
equally enthusiastic. 'Reconciliation' was repeated several
times, gaining in volume, and Mrs Fordyce guessed that he
had found the makings of a funeral address.

'Well done,' he said now, in welcoming position at the
church's porch. Funerals are rum things, he was thinking.
You never could tell whether there'd be one or two in the
front, quavering out 'The Lord Is My Shepherd' or a
rousing full house. He had assumed that at this morning's
service, for a man without a family or friends – a pariah,
you might say without exaggeration, an outcast and a

murderer – he had assumed there would be a handful of the curious at the church and no one but him at the crematorium. But already there were half a dozen in the pews and now here was quite a crowd threading their way through the gravestones. 'Well done!' he repeated, raising his head to see the sun turning the corner of the church tower and slanting down on to the path.

'Good morning, Mrs Wynne, and Mr Dibble, isn't it?' Reconciliation, he reminded himself, but because he was an honest man, another less savoury word stumbled along at the back of his mind.

Those of the congregation who had never visited the little church, tucked in neatly behind the manor, were taken aback by the beauty of the old stone and the arched windows. Natasha watched the sun making prisms of light through the small clear glass panes and wondered if staining them crimson or cerulean could make a more perfect effect. As an unseen person began to play on an organ, she glanced round the church. What did it all mean? she wondered hopelessly. How could she put it together? New York, her father's betrayal, her mother's death, England, Frank, Naomi, Walter, Joe. Their ghosts gathered round her in this place where believers – she presumed they were believers – had worshipped for more than five centuries. They were singing, 'The Lord Is My Shepherd' round her now, even Sheena, in a husky voice. But she could not sing. She remembered her irritation with Joe's obstinacy, worse than the red glass, the hardest colour to work with. He had never let her anywhere near him, that was what it was. She could not understand him at all. All those years she had visited him, she had never come near him or he her.

All those hours spent together, and Joe had never talked about his crime and she had never told him about hers – a child dying alone, a guilty mother, body still warm from a lover who meant nothing, hurrying too late down the street. She would see that accusing red sun for ever. She would feel for ever the silent softness of her child's body, without a heartbeat to match her own. Blaming Frank had scarcely eased the pain. She had been an alien before Naomi's death but afterwards she was an outcast to herself. That was her curse. Joe's too. Perhaps Walter's as well.

How desperately she had grabbed for Walter! How foolishly she had hoped for reparation and love! And, worse still, that terrible night when she had tried to snatch Joe, as if his innocence could give life to her cold sadness. Innocence! That was an odd word to use. And now Joe and Walter had both gone. Aliens all.

Natasha looked at the coffin, decorated with a bunch of white tulips she had brought from her garden. The hymn finished and the priest began to read the prayers.

Funerals bring the worms out of the woodwork, thought Mrs Fordyce. There was that disloyal farmer friend and, beside him, stupid, sad old Mrs Wynne. Yet it was a consolation to her that Mrs Wynne had been so unexpectedly and deeply upset by Joe's suicide; it was as if she had never realized that her vicious actions might lead to a further level of tragedy. There was Joe's sister, too. Her appearance at this late stage was a real cause for indignation, Mrs Fordyce told herself. Let's hope she received a nasty shock when she heard who gets all Joe's money.

The sister, together with her family, filled a pew. She was tired and plump and grey-haired, and had brought with her an uneasy-looking husband in an anorak and a son, with his wife and child. The child was fair and pink-cheeked and ate sweets silently and contentedly, even when the vicar, perhaps inspired by his unexpectedly large congregation, embarked on a lengthy address.

'There are many mansions in our Father's house . . . Joseph Feather was born and bred in the village, a countryman . . . as many of you here today . . . questions without answers . . . deeds that have no explanation . . . tragedy that increases and spreads . . .'

But where is 'reconciliation'? thought Mrs Fordyce. What is all this doubt and darkness? This is not at all Almeric's usual style.

The vicar thought the same, peering down at his notes, which were sliced across by a thin sunbeam. Where was reconciliation? He began again.

'Jesus came for everybody but especially for the sinners, for the poor, for the outcast . . . the Church has room for each one of us that repents . . . We cannot know . . . this earth, all is darkness and confusion . . . pain, lies, despair . . .' He hesitated. The door at the back of the church had opened and a man, bent respectfully, hastened into a pew.

The Reverend Almeric Cooper drew a breath. If he did not take heart, what hope was there for anybody? In his view, cheerfulness was the gift the Lord had given to him so that he might pass it on to his parishioners. Cheerfulness and comfort in the righteousness of the Lord.

'There is cheerfulness and comfort in the righteousness of the Lord . . .' he declaimed, not quite liking the sound of the word and then he was again distracted for the door had been opened with more confidence and another man, remarkable for one detail that he wore a dog collar, had taken his place at the back.

The vicar remembered advice from his uncle, also a vicar: 'When in difficulties, end quickly and with a flourish.' He tried to do so but the proper flourish evaded him. Quotations buzzed about his head: 'Abomination of desolation . . . The tree is known by his fruit . . . And some there be that have no memorial . . .'

None of them seemed quite to fit the bill. Instead, as he floundered on, he was overwhelmed with the ghastly truth that he, as much as anyone, must be held guilty for Joe's failure to readjust after his release from prison, which had led inexorably to his final downfall. Guilt was not a cheerful word. He fell silent, eyes downcast. The sunbeam had passed on from his notes and rested instead on the ornate clasp of the Bible behind. The brass decoration danced in front of his eyes:

'Lord, have mercy!' he bellowed. 'Lord, have mercy!'

'Lord, have mercy!' repeated a voice at the back, although most people assumed it to be an echo.

The sweet-eating child stopped sucking for a moment, pulled at her mother, and both let out high-pitched giggles. Across the pew, Sheena sobbed.

The vicar, astounded, mesmerized by the Bible clasp, head ringing with his own words, stood transfixed. A wheezing and clanking indicated that the organist, an elegant lady in a hat, had decided to fill in the gap.

I am slightly less unhappy, thought Natasha, as the congregation stood for a final hymn and the vicar returned to the world with a bewildered smile. Those wild words were said for all of us and that is what a priest is for. Lord, have mercy on our sins. Now perhaps I can sing too.

Walter, who had been one of the late arrivals, waited for Natasha outside the church. It struck him as strange that, in their short friendship, this was the second funeral they had attended together. He had seen that Sheena was also in the congregation so, ever the coward, as the church emptied he had slipped quickly through the porch where the mourners gathered and mounted the tufted grass. There he attempted to merge with a tall, cross-shaped gravestone.

He found himself, however, near a group who had also detached themselves from the rest. Two of the women were sniffing. 'He was such a merry little baby!' sobbed Mrs Wynne, holding to her face an embroidered handkerchief that smelt of lavender.

'A lovely boy!' agreed Joe's sister, through her tears.

'You'd never have guessed!'

'It would have killed Mum to see the change!'

'Your mother was my dearest friend. She gave him everything. Nothing was too much trouble.'

The men in the group shifted uncomfortably as the two women continued in unison, softly bewailing the loss of that lovely merry little boy.

'And to think of him strangling a dumb animal. A puppy!'

'The Joe I knew *loved* animals. I can picture him now running through the fields with his dog bounding beside him.'

Walter began to get the hang of the relationships involved and soon grasped the theory behind the women's mourning. They believed that, first of all, there had been a lovely boy, and second, quite separate, a murdering monster (although, in deference to the occasion, they refrained from such distasteful words). Such a notion clearly contributed to their peace of mind since the contract of family relationship or friendship could be considered null and void when faced with such a total *volte-face* amounting, as it might seem, to a change of identity.

Reflecting on this, Walter took his attention from the church porch and found the last of the mourners had passed and were now standing in the lane to watch the hearse with coffin and vicar disappearing off to the crematorium. No one accompanied them. Nor had anything been arranged for after the funeral since Mr Fordyce had advised his wife that there should be limits to her involvement and she had agreed.

Mrs Wynne, still mopping her eyes, led off her group to tea in the cottage on the green. Her grief was genuine enough. She was old and looked back to more cheerful days when she and Joe's mother had met every morning for coffee and the handsome little boy had collected eggs from her chicken house and arranged them according to size and colour. In those far-off days she had always preferred him to his sister. So had his mother. If only she hadn't died, Mrs Wynne thought, and that woman hadn't turned up so soon after. A good-looking boy like Joe was always going to be a target for women. Just look at the church – full of them, even now.

'The best thing for Joe would have been if they'd never let him out of prison,' Mrs Wynne said, over her shoulder, as she opened her cottage door. 'It would have saved so much pain . . . all this. He would still be alive.' Hand to heart, she hurried to the kitchen where, without strength to put the kettle on the hob, she sat down heavily in her chair.

Joe's sister, who had been longing to enquire about

the other mourners, particularly the women, moved sympathetically to her side.

Outside, the sun still shone. Walter was about to leave the churchyard and approach Natasha, who still stood in the lane and obviously hadn't noticed his presence, when a hand touched his shoulder. He jumped round nervously.

'Sorry. Sorry.' It was the second priest. The two men, not unlike, thin, anxious, stared at each other. 'I'm desperate for a coffee. You're not a local, are you?'

'No.' Walter saw Natasha begin to move off. 'No. I . . .' He took three steps forward. 'Natasha!' he shouted. Natasha turned. She appeared amazed. Sheena turned, too, and looked away again.

The prison chaplain, who had been driving since dawn, was resigned. He started to walk away. 'Wait.' Walter waved at him.

Natasha came to Walter. She seemed to be trying not to smile. 'But it's Wednesday,' she said and, thinking again, added, 'So it was you who shouted, "Lord, have mercy."'

'One of my habits at the moment,' agreed Walter, 'probably a bad habit. I never thought to hear an Anglican vicar at it.' Seeing Natasha there, so close to him after so many months, made his head spin and his legs weaken. He sat down abruptly on a tombstone.

Now Natasha seemed to be trying not to laugh. 'However did you get here?' she said. 'Whatever did Annabel think?'

The prison chaplain watched them. He had seen such meetings at funerals before. Heightened emotion, he thought, a little jealously, and then remembered he got far too much of that sort of thing in the prison. He felt the warmth of the sun on his face and shoulders, and he, too, sat on a tombstone. So this was Joe's village, where he should have lived out a quiet, countryman's life. The chaplain had read too many files of men convicted of the most horrific crimes to be surprised by circumstances. Yet the particular charm of the valley, the hillside above, like a backcloth hanging against the sky, the bright trees and cluster of old houses, saddened him. There was no logical reason for this, he told himself: Joe had merely been luckier than a man born on a Glasgow slum estate. On the other hand, it would account for Joe's defencelessness and that was why he could not get his face out of his mind. Perhaps Joe had been not so lucky, after all.

Sheena walked slowly with Julie back up the hill to Joe's cottage. Julie needed to confess to someone that her illness at first and subsequently her concentration on the demands of her diet had caused her to abandon her client. But she was so unused to considering her own feelings – even when they were feelings of self-reproach – that she could not speak.

'I need a drink,' said Sheena, in a bright voice, as soon as they reached the cottage. 'And luckily I brought one!' She pulled out a bottle of whisky from her bag. Was it her imagination or did the kitchen still have a faint smell of that whisky bottle smashed by the door?

'Do you think you should?' asked Julie. Sheena filled two mugs and drank several large gulps out of hers before answering.

'You mean because I'm pregnant?' She tipped her mug again.

'Yes, I do.'

'No one else noticed. No one else cares.' Sheena lit a cigarette. Julie stared and thought, a little sadly, that nothing really surprised her. 'Whose is it?' She was, after all, trained to ask personal questions.

'Father unknown!' Sheena drank again. 'At least one of two, or maybe three. It's a gamble. Roulette.'

Sheena took off her padded jacket and Julie saw that she was much more pregnant than she had realized. She sipped at her own whisky but it was against the rules of her diet and, besides, she didn't really like the taste.

'At least I'm rich enough now. What do you think? Should I have an abortion? Should I? Shouldn't I?' Sheena poured more whisky into her mug. 'We should have had a fire, you know. A fire in the grate would have been more cheerful.'

'You've left it far too late for an abortion.' Julie wanted to leave. Suddenly, she realized she couldn't go on being a probation officer, not for another day, not for another minute.

'You're quite right! Far too late now! Actually, I was only joking. About the abortion, I mean. Funny, isn't it? You thin and me fat whereas before it was kind of vice versa. Who knows? I might strike lucky. Come up with the right father, I mean. Got to take your chances in this life.' Sheena picked up the empty bottle and waved it above her head like a flag of victory. She seemed to have become very drunk very quickly. 'Do you think I'd be happy living in this village?'

'No,' said Julie, standing. Even under the circumstances she was proud that she could stand straight, with no bulging fat.

'It's so pretty. I always thought so, right from the beginning. I was really happy here. I didn't admit it then, of course. How could I? I helped him, you know, round the farm, getting things going, not just . . .' Her bravura performance slackened for a moment before being jerked back into place. 'You think you're right again, don't you? I should sell, take the money. You do know about my inheritance, I assume?'

'I'm happy for you. But I've got to go.'

'Yes, you have. And to think that not one of us followed him to the crematorium! Why was that? Fingers pointing, in my case. Cowardice. Don't go.' Sheena tried to grab at Julie's clothing and missed. She was ungainly and there was not so much of Julie to get hold of now. 'I want you to be the first to congratulate me. My very first guest in my new home!'

Julie hurried to open the door and stopped for a moment as she smelt the sweetness of fresh-cut grass. Somebody was mowing their lawn.

'I'm going to have Joe's baby!' cried Sheena, following after her. 'Can't you see I'm five months pregnant already?' Her voice lowered to a mutter. 'At least, I hope it's Joe's because if it's that swine Doug's I'll kill myself . . . or, better still, him . . . Oh, fucking stupid Joe. If you'd waited a little longer I might even have told you. On the other hand, I might not have. I'm such a fool . . .' She went back to the table, sat down and laid her cheek sideways against the worn wood.

The door closed behind Julie and, after a few minutes, Sheena lifted her head again and, picking up the whisky bottle, flung it as hard as she could at the kitchen door. She stood up, delighted at the sound of crashing and breaking. 'That's one for you, Joe,' she yelled. 'Solidarity! Liberty! Freedom! And I'll tell you what, I've always been determined to live here from the first moment they told me it was mine. I had a good time here, Joe. We had a good time together. Stuff them all! Why shouldn't I? And, if the baby turns out to look like bloody Doug, then I'll not be bothered. I'll just call him Joe and carry on.' Sheena grabbed the back of the chair and began to giggle weakly. 'And if it's a girl, I'll call her Josephine. Josephine Feather.'

She giggled some more and, crunching over the broken glass, went out through the back door. To her left, a blackbird in a whiskery lime tree started an energetic peeping. 'And that's another thing,' she said, suddenly quiet. 'First thing I can, I'll plough up that field of yours and plant it with something that isn't weeds. Maybe,' Sheena swayed at the doorway, 'I'll plant it with grass, bright green fresh grass. Yes, that's what I'll do. I'll plant it with grass and trees and cows and sheep.' She stopped, sat down on the doorstep and whispered to herself, 'And moon and sun and wind and rain.'

Natasha drove Walter to her house with Joe's prison chaplain, as he had introduced himself, following behind in his car.

'I had forgotten you lived so close.' Walter kept his eyes on the road ahead.

'Chance.' She glanced at him.

In the house, Natasha opened a very expensive bottle of wine and they all three took their glasses to sit on the lawn under the tree where Walter had declared his love for Natasha. Then she had been dressed in white; now she wore black.

The chaplain began to talk, about Joe's life in prison,

his solitude, their talks, his hopelessness, his determination to see the daughter of the woman he had killed. 'I do believe he felt his guilt all the time. I mean all the time. Every second in every minute. It was "against nature", that was how he put it to me. He always thought he deserved the punishment – not just imprisonment, although, of course, he accepted that too – but the everlasting guilt. Nevertheless he dared to hope it could be lifted just a little if he could work on the land he loved. His land. That's all he asked for. He never expected to be happy.'

'And then he saw the daughter,' said Natasha.

'And then he came back to prison and the daughter turned up. I advised him against it. She was too much for him to bear.'

'She had a right to see him,' said Walter. 'It was brave of her, too. He might have ruined her life. In fact, didn't I hear she tried to commit suicide?'

'Of course, she's not to blame.' The chaplain looked at Walter wonderingly. 'Definitely more sinned against.'

'There would be an argument,' persisted Walter, 'for saying this story has an appropriate ending.'

'Judgement Day on earth. Is that what you're after? When I arrived at the village, I asked the way to the church and a boy pointed it out to me, and then added, 'I know, you're going to the funeral of the man who killed the puppy.' That's Joe's worst sin, as far as his neighbours are concerned.'

'Yes. Odd, that. Appalling, really. Or perhaps it's what's called ordinary humanity.'

'I suppose people feel there are no extenuating circumstances for killing an animal, just as there are not for killing a child. They are both entrusted to our care.'

'What about a rabid dog?' said Walter, standing.

'Walter . . .' Natasha put out her hand appealingly.

'I'm not going away.' He brought out his mobile. 'I need to call my office.'

'And I must be starting my drive back.' The two men shook hands, but then the chaplain sat down again. 'Do you know him well?'

Before Natasha answered, she listened to Walter's voice coming across the lawn. He was not, she knew now, what she had thought she wanted, but these things didn't seem to be a matter for sensible choice. 'No. Not well.'

'Surely it was him who cried out, "Lord have mercy," at the funeral?'

'He's better on theory than practice, if that's what you mean. Or to put it another way, he finds ordinary human beings very difficult to reconcile with his desire for perfection. And that includes himself.'

'You seem to know him extremely well.'

'I might be wrong. I hope I'm wrong. Yes, once I thought we were close.'

'So. We must all do the best we can.'

When Walter returned, invigorated and hardly bothering to be shamefaced, the chaplain was on his way to his car. 'At least the funeral made me realize that Joe had not been always alone,' he said.

After opening another bottle of wine, Natasha and Walter went back to the dappling tree. 'I feel light-headed already,' said Walter.

'Everything all right at *The Cucumber*?'

Walter was as pleased by the question as she'd intended. 'Yes. Yes. A few things I had to check.'

'Don't apologize to me. Once I asked you whether you

had always been so busy. Tell me now, have you always been so ambitious?'

He seemed surprised but eager enough to answer. 'Passionately. Since I was a child!'

'I don't quite understand. When you wanted to be a priest?'

'But that was ambition. I wanted to be best at everything. Best at worshipping God. I wanted to be top of His form. I couldn't though. That was the problem.'

'I thought Christianity was about humility, self-sacrifice. A daily examination of your conscience.'

'It is. It is.'

'Then how could you have ever thought of becoming a priest as an ambition?'

'My ambition was to be the best at humility, self-sacrifice.' He began to laugh. 'Your face, my darling.'

He had called her darling, but she would not give up. 'You mean you couldn't achieve your ambition to be best at being good so you decided to be best at being bad.'

'No.' He became serious. 'Not bad. A journalist. I'm still a Christian.'

'But you're not! You're not!' They stared at each other, both equally surprised at her vehemence. But it was too late for her to stop. 'You've closed your heart.'

'That's not true.' Walter was pale, his eyes half shut. 'You're wrong to say that. Quite wrong. *The Cucumber* is a fine, honest weekly. I'm proud of *The Cucumber*.'

'I'm not talking about *The Cucumber*!' Natasha shouted. 'I'm talking about you. You!'

'But I express myself through *The Cucumber*. I . . .'

Natasha tipped back her chair, looked at the complicated pattern of branches and leaves above her head and took a long breath. 'What did Joe mean to you?'

Walter did not answer for a long time. Then he sighed. 'Nothing. Why should he? Just another victim. The world is full of victims. There was nothing special about Joe. Except that he had done something terrible. He deserved at least some of what came to him. I could never be fond of such a man.'

'And what do I mean to you?'

Again Walter was a long time answering. He looked at his thin fingers clasped round his knees. 'I don't know. I want to love you. I want to love you very much. More than anything, I think.'

'You're not sure?'

'I do love you.'

'If you could love anyone, you mean. You could love me more easily than Joe, for example?' She hardly bothered to wait for an answer. 'You know something odd? Nobody ever asks why he killed her. It's enough that he did it.'

'Why did he kill her?'

'You don't believe I can tell you, do you?'

'Tell me.'

'I'm not sure you'll like it. Let me ask you first. Would you kill for me?'

Walter forced a laugh. 'Of course I would.'

'I'm serious.'

'I don't believe in murder.'

'There you are. I told you you wouldn't like it.'

'What do you mean?'

'Joe loved so much, he murdered.'

Walter thought of all the things he could say, about the

civilizing process, about the ignoble savage. About Joe being no Othello, but then who was he to judge? Really, he understood what Natasha was saying and she was right. 'I can't compete with Joe, in that area,' he said. He desperately wanted to touch Natasha but it felt impossible. Instead he implored her, 'Why are you doing this? Why?'

'Because I want to know what sort of man I love.'

He paused to look at her, but only for a moment. 'Then why make Joe part of our love?'

'Because he is. Because even Frank would have understood about Joe, although the knowledge made him drink so that he could forget and that meant I couldn't live with him. Because I don't want you to be like Frank. Because.' But now Natasha could not go on.

They sat silently until the sun went in and the brightness all around became dim.

Natasha stood up and stretched. 'You came here, that's the most important thing. On a Wednesday.' She smiled at him. 'If I hadn't drunk all that wine, I shouldn't have asked for anything more.'

They walked together across the grass. It had not been cut with Natasha's usual efficiency and white daisies, shut tight now that the sun had gone in, bounced up from under their feet. 'I'm sorry,' said Walter.

'I'm sorry too.' Now she must say a little. 'You know, I'm quite as bad as you. Worse, perhaps. I had more of an idea what I was up to. I needed Joe more than he needed me, although I wouldn't admit it. I never really loved him as myself. In fact, I shall never forgive myself for what I did.' Natasha stopped and looked at Walter's intent face.

He gripped her arm. 'Tell me about Naomi.'

'What do you mean?' She was shocked, even affronted.

'Tell me why you carried your love for her about like a burden. Why you made Frank suffer for it. Why you made me feel as if I'm killing her by loving you.'

'No. That's not right . . .' Natasha tried to escape but he held her tight.

'It is, isn't it? You won't share your love for her, will you? You punished Frank with it and then you were preparing to punish me. You took on Joe as a penance but then he turned into a punishment for anyone you might love. Shall I tell you something, Natasha, which may seem unbelievable? If you let me, I can share your love for Naomi. I can be part of your happiness. While we've been apart I've been thinking—'

'But I haven't been thinking of her!' Natasha interrupted him. 'Joe's nothing to do with her.'

'Every second of every minute. Every minute of every hour. From the moment she dies. Tell me what happened, Natasha.'

'No. No!' Now she broke away from him, poised herself, hand protectively at her face, a few feet away. 'She had a heart defect. A congenital heart defect. She was always going to die. I was only a few minutes late.'

'But you blamed yourself.'

'No!'

'As much as Joe blamed himself.'

'Of course not. Of course not. It's utterly different. He murdered someone. You're being ridiculous.'

'Naomi died.'

'Oh, yes.' Natasha covered her eyes with her hands. 'She was dead when I got there. I thought if I held her close enough, I could give her a second chance. Make her be born again. I thought if I had been there instead of that teacher – horrid, ugly woman. If I had been there, she might have lived.'

'Where were you?'

Natasha uncovered her eyes to look at Walter. 'Nowhere very much. With a man. He was nothing very much. Strangely, when I took Joe to *The Cucumber*'s party, I saw him again for the first time. We were involved, selfishly involved. It wasn't love. Although he said it was. Perhaps he was right. I hope so. The moment Naomi died it became nothing. I never even told him what happened. I was only such a few minutes late.'

'Bad luck.'

'Very bad luck.'

'Natasha. Don't cry.'

'Why not? It's not too late, is it? Have I changed so much that I cannot even cry?'

They still stood back from each other. Natasha cried, found a tissue, cried more, blew her nose, cried more.

'So you were making love when your daughter died?'

'I was hurrying down the street. The sun was a red eye. I can never forgive myself.'

'No.' Walter took a step towards her. 'But I forgive you.'

Natasha sighed and looked vaguely at the big tulip tree. 'Oh, you. You can't do that.'

'But I want to be your lover. And I wouldn't come between you and Naomi.'

'But there's Frank!'

'Frank died. As you've often said, he set himself on that road long before you met him.'

They were both shivering, the grass damp under their feet, their faces icy white, their eyes dark. 'I wasn't looking for absolution,' said Natasha, because that was what he was giving her.

'We have a chance,' he said. 'Although I don't know why. And if my phone rings, I might easily answer it. But I think we understand . . .'

They were still some distance apart and Natasha suddenly looked frantic, words unbearable for even another moment. She found herself picturing Sheena, sorrowing face, swollen stomach. 'I'd like to show you some of my work!' she cried.

Walter had forgotten all about her work, her stained glass, but he followed her obediently to the corner of the house.

The studio still retained the warmth of the sun and, as they brushed against a plant standing in a pot by the door, the air became filled with the sweet smell of rose geranium. But the dull late-afternoon sky persisted as if it would drift into evening without ever revealing the sun again. The glasses, pendant along a westerly window, were as grey and colourless as death. A rose, a speckled fern, a spider's web, cornstalks, a sickle moon, two kingcups, a pale leaf dangling, all merely dull imitations of nature. Walter started to make polite sounds but Natasha cut him short despairingly. 'Stupid of me. I wanted to give you something. I hadn't realized the sun had gone in.'

'Oh, ages ago. They're very pretty all the same. Tremendous workmanship.' He stepped closer to examine a small roundel, which had a red hart bounding at its centre. As he bent, the clouds, as if forced open by a greater power, lifted above the horizon in a straight line, leaving a gap through which golden light streamed in a burst of glory.

At once all the glasses came to life: the rose was radiant, the moon glittered, the kingcups glowed and the leaf flickered with an iridescent green.

Walter turned to congratulate Natasha and saw that she was transfigured, her black outline dancing with colours that shimmered and merged. She was remembering how he had passed by outside when she had most needed him, and he had seemed so far out of reach, out of touch that she had not been able to call for him. But he was watching the colours, which in front of his horrified gaze were turning into leaping flames ready to engulf her thin body and white face. He leaped across to gather her in his arms before she burned up and disappeared. He held her, crushed her, kissed her, and the dazzle was shut off as abruptly as it had been switched on, leaving them in greater darkness than before, but hugged tight in each other's arms.